soul
searching

soul
searching

Thirteen Stories About
FAITH AND BELIEF

edited by
LISA ROWE
FRAUSTINO

SIMON & SCHUSTER
BOOKS FOR YOUNG READERS
New York / London / Toronto
Sydney / Singapore

SIMON & SCHUSTER BOOKS FOR YOUNG READERS
An imprint of Simon & Schuster Children's Publishing Division
1230 Avenue of the Americas, New York, New York 10020

Library of Congress Cataloging-in-Publication Data
Soul searching / [edited by] Lisa Rowe Fraustino.
v. cm.
Contents: The shunning of Sadie B. Zook / Linda Oatman High—The funeral / William Sleator—The olive grove / Elsa Marston—A daughter of Abraham / Dianne Hess— Words of faith / David Lubar—The evil eye / Dian Curtis Regan—The see-far glasses / Minfong Ho—Going to Kashi / Uma Krishnaswami—Dust to dust / Nancy Flynn—The Moth of God / Jennifer Armstrong—Star vision / Shonto Begay—Elvis lives / John Slayton—The tin man / Lisa Rowe Fraustino.
ISBN 0-689-83484-5
1. Religions—Juvenile fiction. 2. Spirituality—Juvenile fiction. [1. Religions—Fiction. 2. Spirituality—Fiction. 3. Short stories.] I. Fraustino, Lisa Rowe.
PZ5 .S6989 2002
[Fic]—dc21   2002070571

FIRST EDITION

For Barbara Evangaline Ladd Reardon—
I love you, Grammy
—Lisa

CONTENTS

INTRODUCTION

The wondrous Tao consists in carrying water and chopping wood.

—Zen saying

I don't know what to write.

The blank screen often flummoxes me when I have to say something important, but, like the protagonist in David Lubar's "Words of Faith," who undertakes the writing of his own short-story collection for extra credit, I trust that the right words will come. Today I am not so sure of that. On this day in history, a week after terrorists attacked the World Trade Center, what are the right words to introduce an anthology on the theme of soul searching, containing stories from the world's religions?

I had intended to write something about how interesting it is that so many contributors sent me stories about death and grandmothers. It intrigued me that so many people from so many cultures associate religion with those two themes. Isn't religion supposed to be about how to live as much as—or even more than—how to cope with death? But now I will leave the analysis to you.

I had planned to write an introduction about the role of

religion, about balance. But now the balance of an anthology seems of little importance when the world itself is off balance.

I don't know what to write to introduce an anthology of stories about world religions when the world is at the verge of what some call a holy war.

My original plan was to talk about the amazing role religion has played in improving mankind by teaching the highest civilizing principles (and who teaches more than grandmothers?). The power of religion can be truly miraculous, as in Jennifer Armstrong's "The Moth of God." But just to talk about the positive influence of religion would be to ignore the fact that, when taken to misguided extremes, religion can also lead humanity backward to our lowest, basest animal instincts. That's what happens in "The Evil Eye," a story by Dian Curtis Regan about a cult in Venezuela.

It was not so very long ago that a self-righteous fanatical leader misused his power to attempt the annihilation of the Jewish people. The Holocaust left ripples in family dynamics that are felt by the younger generation in "A Daughter of Abraham" by Dianne Hess.

And today the world fears a holy war instigated by terrorists in the name of Islam. Do the terrorists truly speak for the Muslim religion? No. They do not. A different aspect of religious motivation is shown in "The Olive Grove," Elsa Marston's gripping story of a Palestinian boy caught in the struggle.

Though I was raised Baptist in a strong Christian family and was "saved" one summer at Bible camp, I have always felt nervous in church, uncomfortable with the insistence that belief in Jesus is the only way to God. To me this seems an illogical and arrogant belief, given that the majority of the world practices other religions that lay equal claim to the truth. Isn't God supposed to be a lot smarter and nicer than that? What kind of God would create amazingly wonderful diversity throughout the world and then set up a picky maze to get to heaven along one narrow path?

When we get too caught up in the words of our great books and in worship of our great religious figures, we return to our clannish instincts. We forget the underlying principle of virtually all religions, expressed this way by the ancient Chinese *Tao:*

> *There was something complete and nebulous*
> *Which existed before the Heaven and Earth,*
> *Silent, invisible,*
> *Unchanging, standing as One,*
> *Unceasing, ever-revolving,*
> *Able to be the Mother of the World.*
> *I do not know its name and call it Tao.* [1]

Tao means "The Way" or "The Teaching." Doesn't this concept sound familiar, whatever your religion? I believe all honest religions have the same source and lead to the same place—back to the source. They just take different paths in different cultures. And this means that by hurting one another, by hurting the world in war, we hurt ourselves—for we are all connected to the Eternal.

The main reason that I don't know what I should write in

---

[1] The translation of Chang Chung-yuan (1963)

this introduction is that I don't know what is going to happen in the name of religion between now and next year, when this anthology comes out. I don't even know what is going to happen between today and tomorrow. But one thing I know I can say, because this truth won't change no matter what happens, war or no war: in times of peace as well as times of stress, we all need stories such as those found in these pages. Not only are they soul searching, they're soul food.

When our fears lead us to anger and violence, we ought to remember that peaceful feeling of the unwed Amish mother in Linda Oatman High's "The Shunning of Sadie B. Zook," a feeling that no words can describe at the birth of her baby, "sacred and holy: straight from another place. A place of no divisions or religions." We are all the same at that moment.

We ought to remember the feelings of William Sleator's Thai monk Lep in "The Funeral" at the death of a pregnant woman killed stepping on a land mine from an old war. All religions have prayers to protect the spirit from dangers, to help us find our way through this life into the next one, whatever that may be. We are all the same at that moment.

With Mallika celebrating Hindu traditions in "Going to Kashi," by Uma Krishnaswami, we must fight the tendency to reduce the world's cultures to sound bites and remember that all religions in all countries are composed of real people, individuals such as Vidya who all need the same basic things: food, shelter, friends.

In our moments of difference over big abstractions such as religion and politics, we can't afford to forget the sameness we share in the concrete details of life. We all gaze at the same sky as Shonto Begay in "Star Vision," looking for answers to life's mysteries. In our nostalgic minds we all wear "The See-Far Glasses" in Minfong Ho's story. Ling's grandmother, though blind, can see across the world and back in time to tender moments shared with her family, cooking crabs caught on the beach.

Like the agnostic Irene in Nancy Flynn's "Dust to Dust," who loses all of her possessions in a massive flood and questions the unquestioned Christian faith of her family, we can learn the importance of finding a calm place to contemplate and accept what cannot be changed. Everyone is looking for answers. If we don't find them in established traditions, we'll find new cultural icons to symbolize what we seek, as in John Slayton's "Elvis Lives."

It's difficult to war against people when we envision their faces kissing babies, falling in love, feeding the homeless, sifting through ruins for heirlooms, rescuing others from death, crying at funerals, defending ancestral olive groves, gazing at stars. These are the visions sent out into the world with this book.

These stories will unplug your emotions. You will laugh, you may cry; some characters you will love, some you may hate. A few plots may be perceived as controversial. We in the United States are blessed with the right to express opinion and personal experience in our literature, and for that I feel deeply grateful.

Lisa Rowe Fraustino
September 18, 2001
Forty Fort, Pennsylvania

soul
searching

THE SHUNNING OF SADIE B. ZOOK

BY LINDA OATMAN HIGH

Sadie B. Zook is dead at seventeen. Even though her heart beats and Sadie breathes, she's gone. There's no hope for her soul. Sadie B. Zook is shunned.

It's suppertime. Sadie's six sisters and five brothers are gathered in their usual places on the benches around the big kitchen table. Sadie's father folds his work-weathered hands upon the tattered family Bible, saying grace for the meal to come. Sadie, perched nervously on a squeaky oak rocking chair in a far corner of the room, is not allowed to pray with the others. Whispering her own blessing, she carefully balances her plate, which has been filled directly from the steaming pots on the stove so that Sadie doesn't touch the serving bowls of her family.

She takes a deep breath.

Yes, Sadie still breathes. Her heart still beats. Nobody notices. She's invisible. She's wicked. Her flesh is evil. The baby rolls in the ocean of Sadie's swollen belly. Sadie feels it physically but has no emotions except for fear and disbelief. It could just as easily be a fish swimming in the bowl of her insides.

The kitchen is warm and cozy with flickering golden lantern light and sugar-cookie smells. It's January, and the coal stove glows. It's snowing. Sadie's brothers and sisters chatter about sledding. Sadie has never felt so cold or alone. She knows that her parents care for her, but they're not allowed to show it. The rules of the Amish church matter above all things. Sadie accepts this.

Be ye not conformed to this world. Sadie's whole life has turned in a circle around those words, taken straight from the Holy Bible. Sadie is Amish, and this religion is all Sadie has ever known. It's like a straight pin holding her to the fabric of her life. If that pin was to be taken away, Sadie would fall and fall, lost. It would be like dropping off the end of the earth.

Born and grown in this same home, an old white farmhouse in Blue Moon, Pennsylvania, Sadie has tried so hard to be obedient. No devil's music. No electricity. No worldly books or garments or photographs or automobiles. No sneaking peeks at TV programs as she cleans the homes of worldly neighbors.

Sadie's mistake was lust. Not love, which comes from above, but lust, which comes from below. Sadie's flesh betrayed her soul, and soon that flesh will bring a baby into this strange world.

Tomorrow morning, Sadie must take the train into the city of Philadelphia. She'll stay in the home for unwed mothers, surely the only Amish girl among the others. A stranger in the world.

The church has made this decision, and Sadie's parents are abiding by the wishes of the bishop. Sadie has never been so scared in her entire life. The baby is pushing hard against her heart. Sadie forces chicken potpie noodles from her plate and into her mouth. She chews. Nothing tastes good. Minutes feel like hours. It's her last night at home, and a tear trickles down Sadie's cheek.

Nobody notices.

Sadie is lugging an old black suitcase from the attic, which is dark as the inside of Sadie's heart. The cumbersome trunk bumps awkwardly against each step, banging hard, and Sadie swipes spiderwebs from her face. The grandfather clock chimes nine times. It's the saddest sound Sadie has ever heard. She drags the suitcase to the bedroom she shares with three of her sisters. The suitcase smells like mold and must, and it's coated with dust. Nobody has ever used this suitcase, as far as Sadie can remember. Nobody goes away from home.

"When will you come back?" whispers Lydia, who is Sadie's littlest sister. Her eyes are wide and her chin trembles. Sadie's heart clenches. She'll miss Lydia most of all.

Sadie puts a finger to her lips. She doesn't want Lydia to be punished for speaking to her.

"Soon," Sadie whispers. She gives Lydia a quick hug. It's just the two of them in the room. Rachel and Sarah are sledding in the meadow.

Sadie folds long black dresses and woolen stockings, placing them in the suitcase. She packs only black, which suits her mood, leaving purple and green and blue. Black is a mourning color, and Sadie is in mourning. She's mourning the girl she used to be.

Sadie packs a burlap bag of sewing materials: needle and thread and patches of fabric. She packs her Bible. That's all that

Sadie will take . . . all that she needs. Her sewing and the word of God. She pulls up the dark green window shade and stares out at the night. A blanket of soft white covers the earth, and the moon is full. Sadie can see the black silhouettes of her brothers and sisters, sledding, whizzing fast down the hill. They're laughing, and the sound of their happiness carries far through the darkness.

Sadie sighs. She'll never laugh again.

Sadie's father is driving the buggy, taking her to the Blue Moon train station. It's early morning, and the sky is gray as stone. Sadie glances at her father's grim profile. He gazes straight ahead, not speaking. Cold puffs of air make gloomy clouds before his face.

The horse *clip-clops* solemnly along the road, cars whizzing past and rocking the buggy with their fast wind. The steel wheels clatter. It'll take the better part of an hour to get to the station. Sadie wishes that there was something to say. She wishes that her father would look at her. His eyes are dull beneath the black brim of his hat. Sadie wonders if he feels as dead as he looks. She knows that he is deeply shamed, and so is her mother.

Mother baked a shoofly pie this morning, which filled the kitchen with the smell of molasses. Sadie's favorite pie is shoofly, and she knows that this is her mother's way of saying a kind good-bye without out-and-out breaking the rules of shunning. Sadie licks her lips, and she can still taste the brown sugar. It's the sweet taste of Mother's love.

Finally, Sadie and her father arrive at the train station. Sadie reaches back into the buggy and yanks the trunk into her lap. It smells like trains and good-byes. Father doesn't speak. He doesn't look at her or offer to help. He makes no move to walk into the station with Sadie. She can see the rise and fall of his chest beneath his black jacket. He's breathing hard; his eyes are narrowed. He places a map of Philadelphia on the seat between them.

Sadie doesn't know what to say. She doesn't know what to do. There are no rules for those being shunned.

"I'm sorry," she whispers. She picks up the map, clutching it tight.

Father doesn't reply, but Sadie sees his lip twitching above the beard. His cheeks are flushed from winter wind, his nose is red, his eyes water. He sniffles, and the horse snorts, stomping its hooves against the cold macadam parking lot of the train station. Rain is smattering the top of the buggy.

Sadie trudges away, lugging the trunk, but she looks back. Tears stream down her father's cheeks.

The sky is crying, too, when Sadie arrives in Philadelphia. Ice sleets sharp against her face, glazing the city streets. Sadie makes her way, slowly and carefully, head bowed down low. She pulls her shawl close against her chest. Bitter wind creeps inside her wool bonnet, stinging Sadie's ears. She almost falls.

Sadie studied the map in the train, ignoring the stares of the other passengers. She knows which direction she needs to go. It seems impossibly far. Street signs are coated in ice. The frigid air squeezes Sadie's lungs.

Sadie walks and walks, slipping and sliding. She feels lost. People gawk. Sadie is ashamed. She just wants to sit down, but there's nowhere to rest. Her belly is so heavy. So is her heart. Breathing hurts.

Finally, Sadie arrives at a cobblestoned street. Just a few more steps, a few more breaths, and she'll be there. The home for unwed mothers looms ahead, rising high into the gray sky. Sadie stumbles through the door and into the warm. The world spins, then goes black.

"Take a deep breath." Smelling salts burn Sadie's nose. "Everything will be okay. You fainted."

Sadie blinks hard. She's flat on her back, cold and wet. Her cheeks burn. Girls are gathered around her in a circle, gazing down silently. All of their bellies bulge. A lady leans over Sadie.

"She's the Amish girl," someone whispers.

Sadie shivers. She closes her eyes. She sees stars. She opens her eyes. She sees staring girls. She closes her eyes again, and keeps them closed.

"What is this: the circus?" A voice squawks like a duck. "Come on, everybody. Give her room to move."

Sadie opens her eyes and sees a freckled girl with short hair that grows out in spikes, three shades of burnt orange. She's got a ring in her nose and another in her eyebrow.

"Hey," the girl says. "My name's Amber. I'm your room-mate." The girl is barefoot, and Sadie sees a showy yellow rose branded on her knobby ankle.

The other girls begin to move away. They whisper and shrug. Some giggle.

Amber grasps Sadie's hand and pulls her up.

"Welcome," she says.

Sadie says nothing.

Sadie follows Amber through bright hallways, lined with pho-tographs of plump babies. This is like no place that Sadie has ever seen. The walls are painted in rainbow colors, and there is a television in every bedroom. In one room a row of washing machines swish with laundry. There are telephones, too, and electric lights and heat. There are noisy handheld dryers for wet hair, and Sadie sees girls using irons to make straight hair curly or curly hair straight. There are mirrors. This place is full of the world.

Sadie stops at a mirror and gazes, dumbstruck, at her reflection. She's never really seen her face, except in a spoon or reflected in the water of the pond at home. This is like looking at someone she might see in church: just another brown-eyed, dark-haired Amish girl.

"Take a picture. It'll last longer," says Amber.

"Photographs aren't allowed in my religion." Sadie can't stop staring. She's never seen herself talk. Her lips move funny.

"Amish, right? I've seen a few in movies, but I never met a real one in person. Until now."

"It's strange to see how I look from the outside in," Sadie says. She gawks at her face, pale as fresh milk in the glaring electric light. Her eyes are the color of homemade root beer, and sad. So sad.

"You don't have mirrors at home?"

"No."

"Ooo-kay." Amber crosses her arms. She shakes her head. "Wacky religion, if you ask me," she says. "So how'd you get pregnant, anyway?"

Sadie flushes. Her face is red as beets. She feels the blood pumping to her neck.

"I don't mean how," Amber says. "I mean who. Who to? An Amish dude?"

Sadie nods. She can't look at Amber.

"Do you love him?"

Sadie shakes her head. No.

"Does he love you?"

Sadie shrugs. Her shoulders slump. Eli Stoltzfus's blue starburst eyes flash in her mind. The eyes are looking down at Sadie, as she gives in to sin in the dimness of the Stoltzfus barn. Sadie again feels the prick of straw on her back. She bites her lip.

"I haven't spoken to him. We are both too ashamed."

"Does everybody know that he's the father?"

"It's not spoken of," Sadie says.

"Well, didn't the dude offer to marry you or something?"

Sadie shakes her head.

"Hope you get him for child support," Amber says.

Sadie doesn't answer. She doesn't understand exactly what "child support" means. She assumes it has something to do with money.

"So is your family mad? Did they, like, kick you out?"

"Yes," Sadie says. "I'm shunned. It's as if I don't exist."

"Just like in the movies, huh? Cool. Is he shunned, too?"

Sadie shakes her head.

"Boys will be boys, says the bishop."

"Well, that's stupid."

Amber turns into a bedroom. There's a television and a telephone and a stereo. It's worldly. Ungodly.

"This is it," Amber says. "Home, sweet home."

Amber has more curiosity than winter has snow. Sadie is dizzy from the questions, which fall fast as a blizzard from

Amber's lips. They've only known each other for an hour, but a lifetime of questions have come.

"So," Amber says, "not all Amish kids are goody-two-shoes?"

"Of course not," Sadie responds. "We're human, just like you."

"Did any of your friends get shunned?"

Sadie's heart skips a beat.

"No."

"So they're perfect."

"Far from perfect," Sadie says. "They're sowing their wild oats, just like every other teenager. The Pennsylvania Dutch word for it is *rumspring*."

"So what do they do? When they're *rump-spring*?"

Sadie can't help herself. She smiles at Amber's mispronunciation of the word, just for a second.

"Run around. Go crazy," Sadie says. "The girls change into worldly clothing in the restrooms of gas stations. They wear makeup and let down their hair."

"Are you serious?"

Sadie nods. "They just shove their religion into brown paper bags. Some drink. Some smoke. Some experiment with drugs."

Amber's jaw has fallen. She rakes a hand through her spiky hair.

"Some of the boys park secret cars in barns. They have parties, with electric guitars plugged into generators. People dance."

Amber squawks. "No shit."

Sadie catches her breath. Her mind flashes back to the barn party that changed her life. Drunken boys walk barefoot across barn beams and breathless girls watch wide-eyed from below. The quiver of light from gas lanterns flickers across faces. Beer bottles glow like the fires of hell in boys' hands. It's late. Eli is on his eighth beer. His friends are attempting to play rock 'n' roll music they've heard on the radio. The sound is too loud in Sadie's ears. Her heart pounds to the beat of the drums. Eli's breath is strong with alcohol. He presses his lips, hard, against Sadie's. Sadie has always liked Eli's eyes. She kisses him back.

Sadie blinks. She wants to forget, not remember.

"I'm too tired to talk anymore," she says. "It's time for bed."

A week later Sadie is still not accustomed to the sight of her own reflection. She can't get over how her corn-silk hair shines smooth from shampoo. At home Sadie used lumpy lard soap to wash her hair in the tin tub on Saturday nights. Here, it's common as breathing to shower and shampoo each morning. The hot water comes so easy from gleaming silver faucets, and soap is purchased from the grocery store. Sadie's skin has never been so clean; if only she could soap her soul. She imagines a pink soul-foam, lathering away the black soot of the world, leaving Sadie's insides as sweet and clean as her flesh. Her sinful, wicked flesh.

"So why don't you have mirrors at home?" Amber asks. She's painting her toenails in slow careful strokes, and the purple strong-odored paint is the same color as Sadie's best church dress.

"We're not supposed to be proud or vain," Sadie explains. She lowers her eyes, guilty, from the mirror's reflection.

"That is, like, so bizarre." Amber blows toward her toes, the bulge of her belly keeping her from going too low. She flops back on the bed and waves her feet in the air. She's wearing a silver ring on one of her toes.

"Amish people have so many stupid rules," Amber says. "Like maybe they think they can obey more because they're better than everybody else."

"We're not better, just different."

Amber is watching something called MTV, where people are indecently dressed and devil's music plays. Sadie can't help but look, and listen. *Satan is taking control of my soul,* she thinks. But she doesn't turn away. The television screen flickers wickedly, and Sadie blinks, hard. This world of the home is the strangest world Sadie has ever seen, and it feels like a bad dream. Sadie just wishes that she could wake up, and everything would be back to normal.

Sadie is in Baby Care class, which takes place each morning at ten o'clock. A stern lady named Mrs. Smith teaches the girls how to bathe and hold a baby. She makes them practice changing diapers on a doll. Sadie feels silly. She's changed thousands of diapers in her life. She's bathed babies on Saturday nights. She's fed them and burped them and dressed them and loved them.

"Sadie," barks Mrs. Smith. "Come up front."

Sadie blushes. She shuffles to the front of the classroom, feeling as if everyone is staring at her clothing.

"Everybody watch Sadie change the baby," says Mrs. Smith. "She's a natural."

Hot and shaking and hating to be the center of attention, Sadie takes the plastic doll baby from Mrs. Smith. Someone has chopped off most of the doll's hair. It has a hole where one eye should be. It smells like a garbage can.

"Notice how she supports the neck," says Mrs. Smith. "This is a girl who knows how to hold a baby."

Sadie places the baby on the changing table. She peels off the tape and lifts the disposable diaper from the doll's bottom. Mrs. Smith has squirted chocolate syrup into the diaper. Some drips onto Sadie's hand. Amber honks and Mrs. Smith glares at her.

"This is not a laughing matter," she says. "Raising a living human being is not funny business."

Sadie takes a wet wipe from the box. She cleans the doll baby's bottom. She sprinkles powder, carefully. She places a new diaper beneath the baby, and expertly fastens it in one smooth movement. These diapers are so easy. At home they use cloth diapers. Pins. Plastic pants. The wash lines flap daily with diapers, bleached clean.

"Sadie is one of twelve children," Mrs. Smith announces. Somebody whistles.

"Sadie Zook," pronounces Mrs. Smith, "is a girl who knows what she's doing."

"So what are you going to do, Amber?" Katherine asks. Katherine is a Catholic girl with a delicate silver cross hanging on a chain around her neck. She sometimes wears a dark blue sweater with the embroidered words of her school: "St. Mary's of Providence." Her mother kicked her out, and so Katherine has only a few outfits, all of them from her Catholic school. Sadie and Amber are visiting in Katherine's room, which has a little statue of Mary. Jesus's mother. Someone has painted the statue's toenails red.

"What am I going to do about what?" Amber asks.

"About your baby. Keep it?" Katherine lifts her cross to her lips. Her belly is big beneath the sweater. She wears a plaid skirt and white socks that go to her knees.

"I can't decide. One minute I think yes. Next minute I think no."

"What about you, Sadie?"

Sadie flushes. She lowers her eyes. She shrugs. She doesn't want to believe a real baby will come soon. Sadie tries not to think about it. She pretends that this is a game. It's not a real baby. It's a watermelon. A cantaloupe. Something good, from God. Something that grows in a garden, not in a girl. Something that doesn't need to be changed or bathed or fed or loved. Something different.

Anything but a baby.

Sadie is sewing. She sews a lot. It calms her nerves. It stills her mind and helps her to think. Her heart beats slower and Sadie breathes without gasps. She's at peace with the smooth movements of the silver needle. The weight of the fabric in Sadie's lap comforts her. The strength of the thread holding materials together makes her feel strong. When Sadie sews, she knows her soul. It's there, still inside of her. She's Sadie B. Zook. She's still herself. The sin didn't erase her.

Sadie is sewing a quilt. A little quilt, made from patches of outgrown clothing from her brothers and sisters. There is the bright purple of her brothers' shirts and the green of baby clothes. Sadie started it at home and now it's almost finished.

Sadie doesn't know what she'll do with the quilt, but the sewing has been good. Sadie has been sewing for almost as long as she's been walking. Mother taught her. Sadie taught her little sisters.

Sadie is still Sadie, when she sews.

It's another Sunday suppertime—the tenth—and Sadie is silently praying, saying grace for the food she's about to eat.

When she opens her eyes, Amber is digging into her mashed potatoes, spooning a hole for gravy in the middle of the pile.

"You're really into praying," she comments.

Sadie blushes. No one else here bows their head before meals. Not even Katherine. "It's good to give thanks." She picks up her fork, and a pain stabs her stomach. It moves to her back.

"Oh," Sadie says. She drops her fork.

"What's wrong?"

"A pain. Right here."

"Labor pain?"

"I don't know."

Amber spoons a huge mound of mashed potatoes into her mouth.

"It's about time, huh?" she says, chewing. "Pop that baby out."

"Oh. Another. Oh." Sadie touches her stomach. She doubles over in her chair. This is the worst pain she's ever felt. She deserves it. Punishment.

"Owww." Sadie moans. This is her sin, piercing through her middle. It radiates to her back. The pain is awful. Sadie was so bad. So wicked. Eli was, too, but he doesn't feel anything. Sadie is so angry at Eli that she could spit in his face.

"Aaarrggggg," screams Sadie. Her face twists in agony.

"I think," Amber says, "it's time to get help."

Sadie holds her brand-new baby in her arms, next to her heart.

The baby is wet from birth. Sadie is soaked in sweat. Her hair is down. The hospital is filled with activity, but all that matters is in this room.

The baby's skin is red. She's wrinkly, and she has wispy black hair. She cries. She opens her eyes. Her arms move. There are no words in the English or Dutch languages to describe the feelings flooding through Sadie. No one could have told her this, for there are no words.

"A baby," Sadie whispers. "My baby." She's finally decided on a name: Rachel, from the Bible. Sadie hasn't slept for twenty-eight hours straight, but she's never been more awake in her life. It's like floating. The hospital walls blur from the tears in Sadie's eyes. The baby smells sacred and holy: straight from another place. A place of no divisions or religions or shunning.

A place of nothing but love.

Sadie is nursing her baby. It's three days after the birth. Sadie and Rachel are back in the house of rainbow walls, recovering from the birth. Amber's baby still lives unseen inside of her. Katherine is still big beneath her blue sweater. The days before the baby's birth seem like another lifetime to Sadie. It's as if Rachel has always been here with Sadie. She doesn't know what she'd do without her. She doesn't even want to imagine it. Suddenly, the world seems like such a dangerous place. There are fires and falls and bad people taking babies. There are earthquakes and train accidents and heavy bureaus that fall on children. There are cliffs and rocks and knives and guns. There is hate. Life is unfair. Sadie wants to wrap this baby in a bubble wrap of love and never let her out.

"So you decided to keep her?" Amber asks.

"Yes." Sadie brushes the tip of her index finger across her daughter's flower-petal cheek. "I'll keep her for always. No matter what."

Sadie wishes that she could gently pierce her overflowing heart with a tiny pinprick, draining the emotions so that she doesn't burst or explode. Now she knows the meaning of the saying, "My cup runneth over." Sadie's cup is spilled all over this city . . . all over the world.

Poor Eli, for he feels none of this. Sadie's anger is gone. Now, she just feels pity for Eli.

Amber sighs. She presses both hands against her huge belly.

"I still can't decide. How'd you make up your mind?"

"You need to search your soul," Sadie says. "Get real quiet and alone, and look deep inside of yourself where nobody else can see. Find something that takes away the noise of the world. For me, it's sewing."

Amber runs a hand through her spiky hair.

"I hate to sew," she says.

"Maybe painting your toenails." Sadie smiles, and so does Amber.

"So, are you going home?" Amber asks.

Sadie nods. The baby's mouth opens like the beak of a tiny bird.

"At least for now," Sadie says. "It's all I've known."

Amber's jaw drops and Sadie shrugs.

"The tradition and religion hold us tight, in the Amish culture," Sadie says. It's hard to explain to someone like Amber, who's been part of the world since she was born.

"Will they shun Rachel, too?"

Sadie strokes the downy fuzz of her child's head. There's still a soft spot beneath the fluff, and Sadie knows that she must be so careful. This is like trying to walk across the earth with an egg in the palm of your hand. Very scary.

"She will be shunned," Sadie whispers. She pictures how it will be: Sadie's parents will lower their eyes, not showing their love to the baby. They won't hold her. Rachel will never feel their hearts beat against her skin. Still, they will love her. They will. Sadie knows this, and that's why she'll return.

"Will it be awful for her?"

"It won't be easy," Sadie says. "But whose life is?"

Amber is quiet for a few minutes, as Sadie stares at the infant, memorizing every inch of her. She knows this baby by heart. This must be how God feels about each human being He creates. Sadie now knows without a doubt that she's been forgiven for her sins. God loves Sadie; Sadie loves her baby. God loves the baby, too. Sadie is content with this.

"Can I hold her?" Amber asks. Sadie smiles.

"Of course."

Amber reaches out and slowly takes the baby from Sadie's arms. She lifts Rachel to her shoulder, awkward and careful.

"You know this part right here?" she asks, tracing the baby's shoulder blade. "Do you know that there is no human purpose for shoulder blades? I think it's where the angel wings were attached."

Sadie catches her breath, looking at this worldly girl with the golden earring in her nose and the yellow rose on her ankle. Yellow: the color of hope. She hopes for all things good for Amber and her baby, no matter what decision Amber makes.

"When I first met you," Amber says, placing the baby back in Sadie's arms, "I thought that you were really weird. Some kind of alien or something."

"And I," says Sadie, "thought the same of you."

Both girls laugh. The baby gurgles. Her breath is warm against Sadie's neck, like puffs of love from heaven.

"But beneath the clothes and the hair and the things of the world," Sadie says, "we're both the same."

"Have you thought really hard about leaving the Amish?" Amber asks. "You could just become, like, a regular person."

"I've thought of it," Sadie says. "I'm still thinking. Trying to decide. I need to go deep inside and find out what's right for me. And for her. It might take some time to decide."

"Even if you leave," Amber says, "you'd still be you. Just in different clothes. And you could paint your toes and wear rings in your nose."

Sadie laughs, which hurts. She feels fragile these days, as if she might break into a thousand pieces. Still, she's never been happier.

Amber leans over and pulls Sadie and her baby into a hug, with her own unborn child kicking in between.

"Sadie B. Zook," she says, "you're a pretty cool chick."

It's time for Sadie to go home. It's odd, but the electric-light house with the rainbow walls and a television in every room has become home. Sadie feels safe and protected here, in this city place of new babies and big-bellied worldly girls. It's a good place, a haven of acceptance, and Sadie is no longer a stranger. The people here never even heard of shunning, until Sadie told them about it. These are people who have hope for Sadie's soul. And so do I, Sadie realizes. She feels set free and light, like she could fly.

"When I came here, everything was hard," Sadie says to Amber. She's packing her battered black suitcase for the train trip. "The whole world seemed dark. I felt invisible."

"You were too big to be invisible," Amber says. "And look at you now."

"Yes. Look at me now." Sadie gazes into the mirror, comfortable with the person looking back at her. Her hair shines smooth and silky from shampoo and it's neatly rolled beneath the prayer covering. She lifts her baby from the cradle, holding the little rosebud face next to her own. The baby wears a yellow sleeper, the color of butter and sun and honey all melted into one.

"Look at us now," she says.

"If you decide to leave the Amish," Amber says, "come back to see me. I'll take you to the piercing place."

Sadie laughs. The baby's blue eyes open wide, like tiny pieces of summer sky.

"I've had holes in my soul," Sadie says. "I don't need them in my flesh."

"It was that bad? Holes in your soul?"

"It was that bad," Sadie says softly. "But I've learned things here. Everybody makes mistakes. People can change. No sin is too awful for forgiveness. And everything will be okay."

"Everything," Amber repeats, "will be okay. Keep telling me that."

"Keep telling me that," Sadie says. She hands the baby to Amber.

"Hold her while I finish packing?"

Amber nods, singing an off-key lullaby to the infant in her duck-squawk voice. Sadie folds long black dresses, heavy wool stockings, and terry-cloth sleepers in pastel shades of yellow and pink and green. This child has added so much color to Sadie's life. Sadie takes the miniature quilt from her sewing bag. She places it on the bed, for the next girl.

"I have a little gift for you," Amber says as Sadie closes the clasps on the antique suitcase.

"Just knowing you," Sadie says, "has been a gift."

"No, seriously. I made something."

Amber opens a bureau drawer and reaches in, rummaging.

"Ta-da!" she says, holding up a delicate creation of gossamer white. It's a tiny angel, made of gauze and cotton and lace. The baby coos.

"To remember me," Amber says. She flies the angel through the air, placing it on Sadie's shoulder.

"How could I ever forget you?"

"You know what they say," Amber whispers, handing the baby back to her mother. "Hope is the thing with wings."

"Hope," Sadie repeats, brushing the angel against the baby's cheek, "is the thing with wings. I like that."

Amber lifts the suitcase, waddling through the door and into the hallway.

"Walk you to the train station," she says.

Sadie follows, and they walk through the halls of the home for unwed mothers. Sadie looks around, memorizing this place by heart. They step outside, into winter sunshine so bright that it hurts Sadie's eyes.

"Get ready, baby," Amber says. "You're going to have to get used to the cold."

"But springtime's coming. It always does," Sadie says, taking a deep breath of the city air, which smells of soft pretzels and trains. Her skin tingles, and Sadie's insides lift like a kite. Her heart beats, she breathes, she's here. And so is the baby, Rachel.

Sadie B. Zook has never felt so alive in her life.

LINDA OATMAN HIGH

My husband's grandmother, Nellie Zook, was adopted by an Amish family when her parents died of yellow fever. Nellie was raised Amish, but she made a mistake at the age of seventeen. To the great shame of her parents and the Amish community, Nellie became pregnant. Her parents sent her to the city of Philadelphia, where Nellie lived in what was then called a Home for Unwed Mothers. She gave birth to a baby boy and returned home to her community, where the baby was raised by Nellie's parents. Nellie was shunned and eventually excommunicated, which basically means that she was kicked out of the Amish church. However, she continued to dress in the Amish tradition and practiced some of the cultural rules. In her heart, Nellie Zook was Amish until the day she died, at the age of ninety-five.

"The Shunning of Sadie B. Zook" is based on Nellie's story. It's about hope and forgiveness and the unconditional love of a higher power. It's also about the ability of human beings to heal, and to move on. We all need to heal. We all need hope. We all need forgiveness. We all need love. No matter what religion we practice, we share these needs. Every religion believes that their way is the right way. It's when they believe that their way is the only way that intolerance darkens days. At the end of the story, Sadie steps from the Home for Unwed Mothers, into bright sunshine. She moves forward. Her soul is lighter and so is her heart.

We, too, can move forward. We can step out of any situation, with the will to change things. We can have faith. Like Sadie B. Zook, our hearts beat, we breathe, we're here. We're alive, and souls never die.

Linda Oatman High is the author of many picture books, novels, stories, and poems for young readers. Several have Amish themes, including *Maizie* and *A Stone's Throw from Paradise*. She lives in Narvon, Pennsylvania, with her family and a golden retriever named Angel.

THE FUNERAL

BY WILLIAM SLEATOR

So you want a live hand grenade, Lep?" Nga said. "Well, just happens I've got a nice new one. Found it yesterday." Nga reached into the pocket of his clean shorts—school uniform shorts, which Lep didn't have—and pulled out the round gray metal object.

Lep's heart jumped at the sight of it—he hadn't expected Nga to come up with one so immediately. The grenade was from the war in Cambodia across the border, only a few kilometers from their village in Thailand. They weren't easy to find in the jungle. Nga had an eye for spotting them, but he rarely shared. The grenade would help Lep out a lot. He eagerly reached for it.

Nga whipped it behind his back. "Hey, not so fast," he said, and pushed Lep away with his other hand—he was a lot bigger than Lep. "You think I'm going to give it to you for *free*?"

Lep wasn't surprised. Nga was good at spotting hand grenades and land mines, but he wasn't good in school. And Lep was the best student in their third-grade class. They were both eight. "What do you want for it?" Lep asked him.

"Write out the answers to the homework questions for me. Then I'll copy them over in my own writing. The teacher will never know."

Lep sighed. This was a special homework assignment, very important for passing this semester of third grade. Lep didn't like doing this for Nga, not because he thought it was wrong, but because he didn't want Nga to get the idea he could do it very often. He didn't have time—he had too much farmwork to do, as well as his own schoolwork.

But he really wanted that grenade.

"Okay, but just this one time," he said. "I can't do it every day."

"And I'm not going to offer you a grenade every day, either," Nga said.

They were a good distance from the school yard now. They stepped off the path into the jungle—Nga keeping his eyes on the ground for mines—and Lep knelt down beside a flat rock and quickly wrote out the answers in Nga's notebook.

"You sure they're the right answers?" Nga said when Lep handed the notebook back. "It didn't take you very long."

"They're right. You'll see," Lep said. He held his hand out. "The grenade, please."

Nga pulled it out of his pocket. "This is the pin. It'll go off about ten seconds after you pull it out. Throw it as far as you can. Then lie down, put your hands over your head, and look the other way."

"Got it," Lep said. His fingers closed around the grenade, his fingers nearly shaking with the thrill of holding something so powerful. He slipped it carefully into the pocket of his old dirty cutoffs, getting too small for him now, his only pair of pants. His sister could not afford to buy him a real school uniform.

Lep's mother had died when he was three, and soon after that his father married another woman who did not want Lep around. So he had to go and live with his sister, who was many years older than he was. She already had two babies then, and now she had two more. She really didn't want another child to feed, but she had to take Lep out of family obligation. That meant he had to work harder than her own children.

It also meant his sister didn't want him in school—she believed school was a waste of time for poor farmers like they were. The law said all children had to finish fourth grade. Lep knew after that she wanted to pull him out so he could work all the time.

But he loved school so much! He had learned to read and write faster than anyone else. The teacher said he was special. And maybe, with the grenade, he could show his sister that he could help the family even while he was going to school.

And have some fun, too.

Other boys did different things with grenades, and sometimes they got hurt. But Lep had been planning this for a long time. He left Nga and hurried down to the river. First he checked carefully to make sure no one else was around. Then he stepped back as far away from the water as he felt he could throw. His heart lifted as he touched the pin.

He pulled it out with a whoop and hurled the grenade into the water. He ran back as far as he could in a few seconds, fell to the ground, looked away, and covered his head.

There was a satisfying rumble and then a huge splash, like all the kids jumping into the water at once. Lep felt water raining down on him. He also felt what he had hoped to feel: the cool slimy pelting of fish.

He jumped up. There were more fish than he had dared to hope, bigger ones than he could catch with a hook. And this was so much faster! He pulled off his shirt and ran around gathering up the fish from the riverbank, using his shirt as a bag to carry them. He also stuffed more into all his pants pockets.

Laughing, he ran home to the one-room shack—with big gaps between the boards that let the mosquitoes in—where he lived with his sister and her husband and their four children.

His sister, small and gaunt, was just starting to cook the rice over the charcoal brazier outside, holding a screaming baby on one hip. All they ever ate was plain rice with chili peppers—it was all they could afford. Lep was so excited about the fish!

"You're late," his sister said, barely looking up at him. "You're late bringing the buffalo home. Adoon's with them now over in—"

"Look! Look what I brought. *This* is why I'm late!" He held open the bag of his shirt, displaying the fish. There were so many, and so many big ones, that some of them slipped out onto the dirt.

His sister's mouth dropped open. "Did you steal them?" she said instantly.

"No, no, I caught them myself, I promise!"

Then she looked right at him and actually smiled—she hardly *ever* smiled at him. "We can grill some for tonight," she said, "and I can make soup for the next few days, and the rest we can dry in the sun. This will feed everybody well for a long time. Good for you, Lep. You finally did something right."

"I got those fish because I'm good at *school,*" he said, trying not to sound like he was begging. "If I wasn't going to school, we wouldn't have that food."

Her smile disappeared instantly. "Go to work. Get the buffalo." And that was the end of the thanks he got from his sister.

Later that year Lep was selected as the one student from his school to compete in the provincial singing contest—usually they picked someone older than a third-grader. Lep and the teacher and a lot of other students who came along for the fun walked ten kilometers to the big school where the contest took place. They camped out on the school grounds with students from twenty other schools and had a barbecue the night before—it was better food than Lep had ever had in his life.

Before he performed, the teacher lent him a school uniform, so he wouldn't embarrass the school with his normal clothes. He was a little nervous when he went out on stage in front of all those people and the ten judges. But he was more excited than scared—he knew how good his singing was. He sang without accompaniment, a very difficult song called "Tayo Ja," about a woman pretending to be a man, so it had many high notes—higher than the other boys could sing.

And he won first prize, out of twenty schools. They presented him with a book, a pen, and one hundred *baht.* His sister took the money but did not congratulate him. She did not congratulate him when he won the contest again the next year, in fourth grade.

And when school was over, she took him out and wouldn't

let him go back. He worked in the sweltering rice fields for a few *baht* a day, and he took care of the buffalo, a small boy for his age leading four big animals. He hated leaving school, but he did love the animals, and took good care of them, and kept them clean and better fed than he was.

Sometimes he took them to the pond to cool off, and when they came out of the water they would have leeches on them. He hated the leeches for feeding on his animals, and would carefully pull them all off.

Once there was a particularly big and tough leech on his favorite buffalo, Bom-bom. The leech was hard to pry off, fat with his animal's blood, and he did it more carefully than usual. He was angry at the leech, and he came up with a plan.

He found an old nail and stuck the nail through the part of the leech that was not full of blood, and nailed the leech right on top of a red ant colony. The ants went nuts feeding on it, and the leech writhed in agony and Lep watched, feeling satisfied. And then the ants gnawed through the blood bladder. A torrent of blood came bursting out, and many of the ants drowned.

Lep was always hungry and rarely had time for such games. But sometimes he did run off with the other kids. They swung from ropes tied to trees into the cool brown river, so refreshing in the constant heat. They stole fruit from farmers' fields, running and giggling before they got caught.

Once Lep *did* get caught, and the farmer came and told his sister. Wordlessly, she took Lep by the hand and pulled him to the center of the village, where everyone could see—she was small, but very strong. She tied his hands to a tree branch and whipped him with a stick of bamboo, everywhere but his face. He couldn't help crying in front of them all—it was the humiliation as much as the pain. The other kids laughed at him for days, in their uniforms on their way to school. After that, he didn't steal so much.

And he still longed to study. He would walk past the school with his buffalo and look inside at the other kids who weren't too poor to go to fifth and sixth grade, and even higher.

And that was what made him start thinking about becoming an apprentice monk. In Thailand, you didn't have to be a monk for life, though some men did. But it was also the custom for boys to spend several months or years living as monks at the temple, to make merit for their parents and families.

While they were at the temple they had to follow many rules. If you were a monk for life, which made the most merit, there were 226 things you couldn't do. If Lep became an apprentice, there would only be five: He could not kill animals; he could not lie; he could not be impure; he could not drink alcohol; and he could not steal. Some of these restrictions would be no problem for him; others would not be so easy to stick to.

At the temple they would study Pali, an ancient language like Sanskrit, and learn how to sing the prayers in that language. Lep loved to learn. And his sister could hardly object to Lep being an apprentice monk and making merit for her and her husband—it would mean they would be better off in their next life, maybe not so poor.

Practical things they taught at school, like mathematics and agricultural studies that would help him in this life, were not important enough to take him away from his farm chores. But making merit was.

Lep also loved to play, and he knew that a monk's life was very hard. He was well aware that he wanted to do it for the wrong reason—not really to make merit or to be spiritual but just so that he could *study* something. The other monks might be able to tell. The Lord Buddha might know! Would he be able to get away with this pretense? Being caught misbehaving at the temple would be much, much worse than being caught stealing fruit.

He thought about it a long, long time. And he decided that he wanted to learn, more than anything else in the world.

And so when Lep was thirteen one of the old monks shaved Lep's head and eyebrows, and he went to live at the village temple and wear the monk's saffron robes.

They had to get up at four every morning and pray for an hour, kneeling on the temple floor in front of the statues of the Lord Buddha, Lep's stomach aching with hunger. Then Lep had to work hard cleaning and cooking the sparse food. No monks could ever eat anything from twelve noon until after prayers the next morning. He was so hungry by then, and, like at home, all there was to eat was a small portion of rice and some chilis. At the temple there was no playing games with leeches and grenades, and no swimming. It was a hard life.

But he could study and learn.

And he was just as good at learning how to read and write Pali as he was learning how to read and write Thai. He also had to memorize the words and music to different prayers for different occasions. There were prayers for funerals, prayers for weddings, prayers for blessing new houses, prayers for festivals such as the feeding of the hungry spirits. Many of the monks just memorized the sounds of the prayers, without knowing the meaning. But Lep, even though he was only an apprentice, learned the meaning of the words, too, so that when he sang the prayers, he knew what he was saying. He would open his mouth wide and breathe deeply and lose himself in the words and music. He would *become* the prayer, and when he was singing there was nothing else in the world.

It was the joy of singing that made it possible for him to endure the difficult life at the temple. And the more he sang, the more he began to feel that he really *meant* the prayers he was singing.

One day when Lep had been at the temple for five months, they were singing one of Lep's favorite prayers, and he was especially carried away by the music, so that he almost felt like crying. There was a silence when they finished the prayer.

And then Pra Ong said, "I couldn't hear anyone else but Lep in his screaming voice." He did not dignify him with the monk's title, "Pra." "I think he should be told to sing more quietly, and not be so full of pride. He sings like he is the star and everyone else is the chorus."

Several of the other monks nodded. Pra Ong was important. He was twenty-five and had been at the temple for ten years, not just an apprentice like Lep. He was always sent to funerals and weddings and house blessings, where they fed the monks better and more food than they ever got at the temple, so he got a lot more to eat than Lep did, and was thick and strong. Lep was skinnier than anyone.

Lep looked down. It was not his place to say anything or to defend himself. He felt very embarrassed. Had he been making a fool of himself?

"Lep's voice is a rare gift," said Pra San, who was sixty-five and had been at the temple for fifty years. Lep shared a room with Pra San, and cleaned it. "And he can understand what he is singing—you can tell it by the way he phrases the words," Pra San continued. "The way Lep sings is a greater tribute to the Lord Buddha than the singing of some of the monks older than he is."

Pra Ong didn't know where to look. It didn't make Lep feel any better that Pra San had defended him. Now Pra Ong would resent Lep even more, for being rebuked in front of everyone.

The next day when Lep was walking through the blazing temple grounds, he passed Pra Ong and some of the monks in his coterie. Pra Surin said to Lep, "What are you doing in those robes, skinny little boy?" Lep tried to keep his steps slow as he walked past them without speaking.

And during the next month, Lep was aware of Pra Ong's eyes on him. Pra Ong and his friends would always whisper now when Lep walked past them. At school he had been looked down upon in one way because he was the poorest, but in another way the other students respected him because he was such a good student.

But now at the temple it was worse than it had been before. Pra Ong and his friends—all of the young monks—stopped talking to Lep, except to make fun of how skinny and weak he was, when the older monks were not around. Pra Ong's friends took a lot more rice at breakfast now, so there was almost none left for Lep when his turn came—he went last, of course. He was even hungrier than before.

And he had no friends. Sometimes the older monks spoke kindly to him, but none of the ones closer to his age. He felt completely alone in the world.

Worst, he was self-conscious about his singing now. He studied as hard as ever and learned the words to more prayers, but when he sang he kept his voice low. This was the hardest of all—singing was what had kept him able to endure the temple life. He hoped that maybe now the younger monks would accept him.

But they didn't. They still looked away and didn't talk to him, and took most of the food first. And Pra Ong had a very pleased look about him. He was not an especially good singer, and Lep could tell that he just memorized the words, not the meanings. But he was sent out a lot because he was strong and good-looking—people liked having him at their ceremonies. And of course all that extra food that people gave the monks at ceremonies only made Pra Ong all the stronger and more handsome. Lep felt like a scrawny child compared to him.

Lep was so hungry all the time now that he took the enormous risk of picking green mangoes from the trees when nobody was looking, and eating them, hard and sour, in secret. In the evenings, again when nobody was looking, he caught the large insects and gobbled them alive and squirming. He had to be very, very careful about it. If anybody saw him, he could be thrown out of the monastery, and that would be the opposite of merit for his family. It would be disaster and shame.

What if Pra Ong saw him? He shivered at the thought, even in the blazing heat. But he kept taking the risk.

The abbot did not attend all the prayer lessons, but Pra San was Lep's special teacher—and Lep always made sure to keep their room very clean. And one night when Lep was feeling especially hungry, and downcast, Pra San said to him in their small hot cell, "Something is the matter with you, Lep. You don't sing the way you used to."

Lep certainly wasn't going to say anything about Pra Ong. But he had to say something. "I don't want to go above my place," he said.

Pra San looked at him steadily. "It is time for you to be sent out to pray at ceremonies," he said. "But you must use the voice the Lord gave you. If you don't, I can't recommend you to the abbot." He paused, and then added, "Not all the monks feel you go above your place, only some. And to be a monk, to honor the Lord, you must use your gifts to the fullest. Keep that in mind. It is very important."

Lep didn't sleep well that night. He had to make a decision. He thought about Pra Ong and the contempt he felt from him and his friends. He also thought about how much he loved to sing. What was more important than that? It was weak to be afraid of Pra Ong.

Unless Pra Ong caught him eating when he wasn't supposed to.

That made him think of the naughty boy he had sometimes been before becoming a monk, stealing fruit, fooling with leeches and grenades, playing rough games with the other boys. It was better to be like that than to be afraid. He made a decision. He would sing the way he felt. He would not worry about Pra Ong.

And if Pra San was right, maybe then he would be sent to ceremonies, where there would be a lot of food.

And the next day at prayers he sang loud and full. Pra Ong did not look pleased at all. And after prayers, when the older monks were gone, Pra Ong bumped into Lep, and gave him a long, hard stare. Lep could feel the threat in that look.

But Pra Ong had not said anything in front of the group, so Lep continued to sing the way he wanted to. The young monks still avoided him, and whispered when he walked past, and took most of the food. But at least Lep could sing again. He was scared, but he didn't let that stop him. He knew he was meant to sing this way.

Now Lep was more worried than ever that Pra Ong might catch him eating the green mangoes and the insects. But he couldn't control it; he was too hungry.

Two days later the abbot called him to his quarters. Lep was almost shaking. Had Pra Ong reported him for eating when he wasn't supposed to?

"I have a special assignment for you, Lep," the abbot said, and Lep felt weak with relief. "You're young to do a funeral, especially one for an important family, but Pra San is always telling me you have a good voice, and a loud one, and that you understand the prayers. This family might like that. They are very sad and want the best. Their only married daughter, who was going to have a baby, was killed by a land mine. The funeral is tomorrow. Five monks will be going, as usual, and you'll be the youngest, and lower than the others, of course. The family is sending a car at eight in the morning. That's all."

Lep *waied* the abbot, bowing his head and bringing his hands pressed together up to his forehead, and turned to leave his quarters.

"Oh, and one more thing," the abbot said. "This family is rich and they'll have a lot of very special food, as much as anyone wants to eat. And you're so thin. You can use a good meal." The abbot smiled, which was rare.

Lep was excited about the funeral. After six months his strong singing voice was finally getting him somewhere. He would be singing for *real,* not just practicing; he would be helping the spirit of the young woman and her baby go into the next life.

And he would be able to eat as much as he wanted. That had never happened to him before.

This was such an important family that the abbot went, too, and Pra San, and Pra Ong, and Pra Surin, who was just a little beneath Pra Ong—Pra Surin was the one who had spoken nastily to Lep. So two of the monks were his enemies, and the other two were testing him. This was a wonderful chance, but also frightening, not just exciting; this was a lot harder and more important than the singing contest when he was in school.

A man from the family came in their shiny new pickup. It had an extra cab inside, so there was room for the four important monks to sit in the air-conditioned comfort—there was, of course, no air-conditioning at the temple. Lep sat alone in back in the open truck, in the shadeless heat.

Yes, he was a little scared. But he was also very proud to be

going to the funeral. He knew all the songs. And he was especially excited about the food. If the family could afford this
bright new car, they would surely put on a real feast for the
monks—probably better food than Lep had ever eaten in his
life. He had to think about the Lord, of course, not the food,
and not worry about Pra Ong. Most important, he had to sing
his best.

Lep had never been inside a house like this before. His own
house was a collection of old boards and corrugated tin, without windows, and with a dirt floor. This house had an upstairs
of new wood, with many windows with panes of glass in them.
The downstairs was brick and cement, and there were actually
tiles on the floor, bright red tiles, and many more glass windows. The windows were open and the sunlight poured in, and
though there were fans, it was hot—a lot hotter than the cool
darkness of the temple.

And the first thing Lep noticed upon walking behind the
other monks through the big wooden front doors was the
smell. Not the smell of food he had been looking forward to,
but the smell coming from the coffin.

The closed coffin was decorated in a pattern of bright yellows, greens, purples, and reds. It sat on a cart against one
wall—later it would be pulled to the crematorium. Even
though the family was rich, the coffin must have been nailed
together too quickly, because Lep could see that blood was
oozing out of it. Many flies sat in the blood and swarmed
around it. The body had been there probably for three days
already in the tropical heat. There was, of course, no refrigera-
tion, and nobody in this small village knew anything about

treating the body so it would not decompose. The smell of it was overwhelming. Lep stumbled and almost fell as he got closer to it. He gulped, and did his best not to breathe through his nose.

The family and the mourners sat on the floor, filling the room. The monks sat on mats along the wall with the coffin. Lep, being the youngest and lowest, sat right next to the coffin, where the smell was the strongest. The others placed themselves farther away. Did he detect a smug expression on Pra Ong's face? Lep looked away from him and tried not to think about him—or about the smell.

They began to pray. It was very difficult for Lep, because he was used to breathing deeply when he sang. At first his voice was weak. He felt faint. He didn't know how he could get through this.

He thought again of Pra Ong, and that made him want to sing stronger.

But more than that he thought of the young woman who had died. Lep used to go to the jungle a lot—he could easily have been killed by a land mine, like she was. And there was a baby inside her, too!

Their prayers were intended to help her make the passage smoothly into the next life. What was he here for if he couldn't do that? What had he been studying for? Yes, living at the temple was a way for him to keep learning instead of just doing farmwork. But now, at the funeral, there was more to it than that.

It was the smell, the stark reality of it. He was in the presence of human death for the first time since he was a baby. And if he was worth anything at all, then he had to do his best now, *despite* Pra Ong, and *despite* the smell.

He breathed in, he opened his mouth, and he sang. He sang the best that he could. He concentrated on the meaning of what he was saying, how he was helping this poor young woman's spirit—this young woman who maybe had been pretty, and happy about having a baby, and who had now become a thing of disgust.

> *"Oh, Lord Buddha, please listen.*
> *This body has died, and now the spirit is trapped in the body.*
> *Please free the spirit from the body.*
> *Please take this spirit into your hands.*
> *Help the spirit to avoid all the dangers it faces now.*
> *Help to bring this spirit into its next life, better than this one.*
> *Or if this is its last life, please bring the spirit with you to*
> *heaven . . ."*

There was much more to the prayer—it listed all the dangers the spirit faced, and it asked the Lord to protect the spirit from each one of them. It talked about the spirit's next life, and how much better it would be. And it talked about how, if this had been its last life, it would now enjoy all the glories of heaven, and listed every one of them. It went on and on and did not repeat.

Lep sang the long prayer and he did not stop, he did not faint, he did not even feel sick anymore. He was the closest and the smell was worst for him, and for that reason he wanted to sing the best.

Before, at practice, he had *become* the prayers. But something more was happening now. He wasn't just singing to entertain or to show off or for the pleasure of it. He was really doing something for this poor young woman who had died so horribly and unfairly.

And suddenly he believed every word he was singing. He believed he was saving her from all the dangers her spirit faced now. And he wasn't losing himself in the prayer, like before. He felt more that he was finding than losing. This was something he had never known before—something bigger than the words and the song and his worries about Pra Ong. The closest thing to it was the dreams he sometimes had that he was flying. He wanted to pray for real like this again and again.

And when they finished singing the people brought out the food. And indeed it was food such as Lep had never seen before. Rice, of course, but also a curry of golden squash and pork, great plates of eggs with onions and tomatoes, and boiled chickens in rich broth. He had never even *imagined* such food, let alone been presented with it for him to eat!

But now that he was not praying, the smell took over again. They had prayed, the girl's spirit had gone safely to the other world, and now she was just a dead thing, with blood and flies and that powerful stench.

And so there was all this food, but Lep couldn't eat it. The flies from the coffin were crawling all over the rice and curry and chicken on his plate—and it was not for a monk to wave them away. Everybody was watching them eat. Monks had to behave with decorum.

He pretended, he moved his spoon and fork, to be as polite

as possible. But he could hardly eat a single bite. And after they left it would be noon, and he would not have a chance to eat again until the next morning. It was the custom in Thailand not to empty one's plate, so the family and the mourners didn't notice, and nobody thought he was being rude.

The other monks, seated farther away from the smell and the flies, were eating their fill, especially Pra Ong.

Lep was so hungry from eating even less than usual that he hardly slept at all that night.

And the next morning after prayers the abbot summoned Lep and told him, "The family was very pleased with your voice yesterday, Lep. You are the best singer. From now on I will send you to all the funerals. And then you won't be so thin anymore."

WILLIAM SLEATOR

"The Funeral" is a true story.

Lep and I built a house for him and his family very close to the remote village where he grew up in Thailand, near the Cambodian border, and I spend about half the year there. The house is somewhat primitive by U.S. standards, but not in rural Thailand. I relish the fact that when Lep was growing up they were the poorest family in the village, but now have the most beautiful house and garden. Lep supervises the growing of rice and vegetables on the farm and on other plots of land he has bought in the area.

Lep has told me many stories about his childhood. It's true that he decided to become a monk so that he could devote himself to the fun of learning instead of dreary farmwork. Not only did he learn to sing prayers in Pali while a monk, he also learned to read and write Cambodian.

But despite the fact that he did not enter the monkhood for spiritual reasons, he would still be a very different person today if he had not spent four years at the temple. Though he has very little formal education, I have never known another person who knows so unerringly what to do in almost any difficult situation. He saved my life once when I was choking on a piece of food caught in my throat. The Heimlich maneuver did nothing, so Lep, who is a head shorter than me, picked me up, threw me over his shoulder, and banged on my back until the food was dislodged.

His friends and family are always asking him for advice, and his answers are not only based on practical common sense, but also on certain of the Buddhist principles that were ingrained into him as a monk—not to lie or steal and, most important, to try to understand other people who are different from yourself, and to act on that understanding.

He also drinks alcohol and eats meat. Nobody's perfect.

As for me, I have written more than two dozen young adult books, many of them science fiction, which I try as much as possible to base on real scientific principles—as well as to make them exciting. I have also written a very funny book about my own childhood, called *Oddballs*.

But those are not the books I want to emphasize here. If you enjoyed this story, I urge you to look for the two books I've written with a Thai theme—*The Spirit House* and *Dangerous Wishes*. They're both out of print, but you can probably find them online at book-searching places. They are thrillers, full of scary and bizarre and gross incidents—and also full of spirits, since everyone in Thailand literally believes in spirits and spends a certain amount of time trying to appease the spirits with bad tempers. And these spirits really do seem to do things to people. I could tell you stories. That's one reason I love it there.

And that's also why I'm so grateful I had the opportunity to write this story.

THE OLIVE GROVE

BY ELSA MARSTON

Hustling along behind the other boys, Mujahhid stooped to grab a stone, then quickly caught up. About halfway across the open square they stopped. Right next to the military checkpoint was a two-story stone house that the Israelis had taken over. The boys could see the olive-drab helmets of soldiers, behind sandbags, on the flat rooftop.

"Take that, you dogs!" Mujahhid shouted in Arabic, hurling the stone toward them. "Get out of Bethlehem—it's *our* town!"

Shouting with every throw, he then flung whatever he could get his hands on . . . chunks of plaster, pebbles, concrete rubble, worn bricks from the older streets. The soldiers, of course, had every other kind of missile—bullets, stun grenades, tear gas, shells. Today they weren't firing, though, not yet. The boys grew bolder and started making dashes to throw from closer range.

You can get near enough to see faces, thought Mujahhid, *but not what's in their eyes. Anyway, they're all the same . . . they all hate us. Even the young guys, just three or four years older than us, hard as their rifles.*

In a brief lull, Mujahhid heard shattered glass fall to the street with a strangely musical jingle. Then the sound of yelling again filled his ears, some of the boys' voices hoarse and loud, others so high they seemed—like the tinkling glass—to belong to a different time and place . . . like children playing in a school yard. For a moment Mujahhid felt as though he and the others were playing, too, in the warm November sun.

He looked around for Nawar, his best friend. "Come on, Nawar! I can throw twice as far as you!"

In answer, Nawar grabbed a large chunk of plaster and, with a grunt, hurled it in the direction of the soldier. Falling short, it smashed to bits. Mujahhid laughed and Nawar whirled on him, then broke into a sheepish grin.

"Okay," Nawar said, "we'll see who's stronger. We both throw together—*now!*"

Two stones went hurtling toward their target, but Mujahhid's went astray and hit a battered Dumpster. He was just about to let fly another when, above the shouting, he heard the first notes of the call to prayer from a mosque close by. Pausing, he let his arm drop and retreated a few steps. His parents had raised him to take prayer seriously, and his instinctive response was to welcome the call as a moment of peace.

But as he listened to the rise and fall of the chant and the familiar, beautiful words, Mujahhid felt as though a wound in his heart had been torn open afresh. It was near that mosque that his older brother had been shot just a month ago. Killed on his way to prayer—as if he was being denied his right to pray, denied his religion! He'd been given the funeral of a martyr, even though he wasn't a fighter.

The sounds and sights of that day came back to Mujahhid . . . the call from the mosque sounding so sad, and all the church bells in Bethlehem ringing and ringing. Many hundreds of people had stood quietly and listened in mourning, Muslims and Christians together. They were all one in the struggle, Muslims and Christians, all one people. Remembering, Mujahhid's heart felt full of terrible grief . . . and a strange kind of triumph.

Now, for the sake of his brother, his people, his religion, he fought every chance he could. Surely that was what God wanted him to do—help resist the army that had oppressed them for thirty-three years now, so that Israel could gradually take over more and more of the Palestinians' land. Surely God wanted the Palestinian people to be free in their own country. Then someday, everybody—Muslims and Christians and Jews— could get together and work things out fairly.

A new wave of exhilaration gripped Mujahhid. He was helping to bring that day—he was part of the struggle for a better future! After all, hadn't his parents named him Mujahhid, the one who struggles for a good cause? This struggle was the most important *jihad* he could ever hope to fight, a sacred duty to fight for his own homeland. With a yell, he hurled another large stone.

A few of the boys had started to throw Molotov cocktails. The homemade missiles flew toward the army post, but the flames went out in midair. Smashing on the littered street, the bottles added the smell of kerosene to the stench of tear gas drifting over from a few streets away.

Just then, Mujahhid heard an ominous rumble. Tanks? Yes! From the far side of the army post came a couple of tanks, grinding their way toward the boys. The sight and the sound filled Mujahhid with cold fear. It always did, no matter how many days he'd been out in the streets.

"Come on—the next street!" yelled Nawar, yanking at Mujahhid's shirt sleeve. With the other boys they raced back through the broad square, turned and tore down an alley. Reaching another open area, they found a couple of soldiers in a jeep and started pelting the vehicle. The soldiers yelled and gunned the motor but didn't come after them.

Suddenly Nawar jerked upright in a little jump. Then, with a sigh, he crumpled onto the rough pavement. Mujahhid and the others turned, baffled. What was wrong with him? They'd heard nothing. But already blood, from his neck or chest, was seeping into the dust. He lay still, not even a tremor.

One of the older boys let out a hoarse cry. "A sniper—with a silencer! We've got to get out of here!"

Terrified, Mujahhid started to run, looking for a sheltering doorway or another alley. A chip flew off a limestone wall nearby, then another. The sniper was still shooting. Mujahhid wanted to run forever, anywhere to get away from bullets and tanks and grenades.

But—Nawar! . . .

He dashed back to his friend, grabbed an arm, and managed to pull Nawar over to one side of the street. For a moment he thought he heard Nawar speak, and he bent down to look into his friend's face. With a sickening spasm in his stomach, he realized there was no life in those wide-open eyes.

The stone houses on this street were old, their walls rising right at the edge of the paving and their windows tightly shuttered. Would anyone help? Cold with panic, Mujahhid looked around.

Then he heard a woman's voice. "Here—bring him in here!" Twisting his head as he tried to get a better grip on Nawar's limp body, he saw a door open a crack.

Mujahhid dragged Nawar a few meters to the door, over a worn stone threshold, and into a dark hallway. Although he looked as small as a child, Nawar felt heavy. Mujahhid gently let his friend down as the woman hovered nearby, muttering a mixture of curses and prayers in Arabic. Was she young or old?—in the darkness he couldn't tell. Then Mujahhid felt a strong pair of hands pull him away. Dazed, he let himself be pushed through the shadowy first-floor rooms of the house.

"We'll get help—*yallah,* go home." A man's voice. "Go out the back way, I don't think anybody's on that side. Where d'you live?"

Mujahhid told him the street. He barely knew what he was saying and his teeth chattered with shock, but the man understood him.

"Good, not far. Keep low and run like hell. You kids, damn fools, throwing stones at an army—!"

Mujahhid squeezed out a half-opened door and heard it click shut behind him. Heart pounding, he raced up one narrow street and down another, keeping close to walls, expecting any instant to be dropped by an unheard bullet. Soon he reached familiar territory, then his apartment building, and home. His mother, seeing Nawar's blood all over his shirt, welcomed him with screams of horror.

> > >

Everyone in the neighborhood soon knew of Nawar's death, and how he'd been struck . . . the silent snipers gave people a double chill of fear. However dreadful the roar of tanks and helicopter gunships, even more terrifying was the knowledge that death could strike without a sound.

Her gray hair loose and tousled, clothes in disarray, Mujahhid's mother wept all evening. His father silently paced the length of the small apartment, smoking one cigarette after another, down to the butt. Mujahhid sat on the bed in his room, listening to his mother moan his brother's name over and over. Again he heard in his mind the rhythm of the church bells, mingling with the call from the mosque. And it seemed, too, he could still hear the odd little sigh that Nawar had let out as he fell.

He remembered, too, how his mother had wailed when the Israelis shut the schools again, a couple of weeks back. Fearing that nothing would keep him off the streets now, she and Papa had yelled at him, reasoned, argued, threatened. They'd even locked him in the tiny bedroom that he now had all to himself . . . but he'd managed to get out the window easily enough. Well, something was really going to change for him now. He knew he had it coming.

In the morning Mujahhid's parents directed him to the couch in the sitting room. His mother had pulled herself together, and the black blouse and skirt she wore in mourning were once more tidy. Mujahhid sat with hunched shoulders and prepared himself for a lecture.

"No more," said his father gruffly. "We can't trust you. You're going to stay with my sister. You're going to Beit al-Makhfiya."

"What?" Thunderstruck, Mujahhid stared. "I have to go stay

with my aunt? In that miserable little village? When? How long?"

"As long as it takes. You go tomorrow. We've already arranged for a car."

Mujahhid's dismay boiled over. "I don't want to go! I belong here—with the other fighters! And—and to help you, help in Papa's shop. You need me here!"

Mujahhid's mother exploded. "We need you *here*—to worry about you day and night? To wonder when somebody will come tell us *you've* been shot, too? We need that? May God save us! We need to know you're alive! You're the only child we have left, Mujahhid."

"*Ummi*—Mama, listen—!"

"You listen. *Ibni,* my son, we support the resistance—you know that. But we've given enough of our family. It's bad enough to suffer what we have to under *them,* without losing *both* sons in the fight. You're going to stay with your aunt, out of trouble."

"But, Mama, if we keep up the jihad we won't have to suffer forever—"

"Jihad! Don't talk to me about that. Look, Mujahhid *habibi,* go to the mosque to be close to God. Try to understand what He wants of you. But don't listen to talk of jihad!"

Mujahhid glared at her. What did she know? She was just a worker in a textile factory, and his father a sandwich-shop owner. He tried again.

"I have to go on with the struggle—"

She made a sharp gesture, cutting him off. "*Khallas*! Finished! Go to your room and get your books together—you're going to study there, by God. I'll get your clothes ready. The car leaves at seven in the morning, and it may take all day to get there."

Mujahhid pulled himself up from the sagging couch and, at his father's nod of dismissal, headed for his room. *All* day? he thought. *All day to go the twenty kilometers to that nowhere village? What do I have to do—push the car, with the other passengers on my back?* He was glad to have thought of something even slightly funny—it helped him walk away with a scrap of pride. Then, behind the closed door of his room, he let resentment snarl within him.

So this was what became of the great resistance fighter. He got packed off to a tiny village to live with his aunt and his girl-cousin and his grandmother. A house of women. He got stuck out there, away from Bethlehem—his home, his friends, the holy sites. Away from the action, where he was needed. The shame of it! Why should he be safe and sound while his friends were going on with the struggle, fighting for the freedom of their people?

He heard his mother in the kitchen heating water to scrub his clothes, and he knew that one of those garments would be the shirt stained with Nawar's blood. The image of Nawar lying crumpled on the street, his arms so thin, came back to Mujahhid. He remembered how his first instinct had been to run, and again he felt a searing shame. At the same time, another thought hit him, like a stone. He had seen death before, sure . . . he'd wept over his own brother's body. But Nawar—that was the first time he'd seen a close friend go down, so suddenly, so unexpectedly. Mujahhid remembered looking into the unseeing eyes of his friend.

What would it be like to suffer pain, to live the rest of his life a cripple, blind, or paralyzed—or dead, for that matter? Too horrible even to think about! Yes, he felt almost relieved not to face that danger anymore.

Immediately he caught himself. Relieved to give up, to betray the jihad? I *am* a coward, thought Mujahhid.

As they waited for the taxi, his mother had hugged and kissed him until he'd felt steamy with embarrassment. But he'd let her, and accepted his father's one embrace stoically. Somehow, the warm feeling of their clothes and the flesh inside had stayed with him all that long day.

Ten hours for twenty kilometers, packed in with four other nervous, tight-lipped passengers with their bags and bundles. More than nine of those hours had passed as they waited at checkpoints, wondering if the rattling old taxi's gas would give out . . . fearing the scrutiny of the soldiers, who might delay them even further on some pretext or other.

One soldier, in dark glasses, had peered in at him and spoken in Arabic. "Getting out of the fighting, huh? Smart kid."

Mujahhid had wanted to flare up: *You think I want to? I'd throw something at you, if I could!* But of course he'd kept his mouth shut.

Now, at the home of his Aunt Rasheeda, Mujahhid sat with the family at the midday meal. Yesterday she had managed to find some chicken for his first dinner with them, but today they were back to yogurt and rice. Money was scarce, and good food scarcer.

He looked up from his empty plate and briefly studied the faces of the three women at the table. Aunt Rasheeda, tired and sallow, with short hair of a dark reddish color . . . she said little but kept the household going, while teaching at the village elementary school and working a second job in an office. Next to her sat the grandmother, whom they called Sitti, "Granny." Withered but bright-eyed, she wore a head scarf and her traditional long dress richly embroidered in bright colors, the dress she had made many years ago according to the old Palestinian custom. "She'll wear it till it falls apart," Mujahhid's cousin Hanan had told him. "She keeps part of Palestine alive that way."

And Hanan herself, a year older than Mujahhid, with thick black hair in a single braid and a sober face. Too many small blemishes to be really pretty, he thought, but okay. A good student, Hanan was aiming at medical school, and Mujahhid found her serious manner a little intimidating. He hoped she would properly appreciate his past role as a fighter for freedom, but feared she might see him as just a troublesome kid, something more for them to worry about. In general, he resolved to keep out of her way.

The meal was over. Having spent the morning doing odd jobs for his aunt, Mujahhid wanted to go out and see if there was anything interesting in this quiet little place, which he had seen previously only on brief family visits. Sitti, however, in a talkative mood, kept them at the table.

She made a sour face as she reached for the small dish of olives. "Old, last year's crop," she said, chewing with her few remaining teeth. "From our neighbor's trees . . . good enough, but never as good as our own."

Mujahhid allowed his face to show a flicker of surprise. He hadn't seen any olive trees on his aunt's property. The house was a small one built of plaster-covered cinder blocks, with barely enough yard for a patch of parsley and a clothesline.

"Not here," said Sitti, noticing. "I mean in the village. The old village, the one we left in '48. Every year at this time we used to go back—not supposed to, of course, but they didn't watch the back roads too closely then, not like they do now. We'd all squeeze in the car . . . my husband drove. He wouldn't pick the olives, though. Said it made him feel like he was stealing from his own land. He'd sit in the car and cry—I could tell—while the rest of us did the work. God bless him, stubborn old man."

"But," Mujahhid asked, puzzled, "how could you pick olives in the village you left so long ago?"

"Oh, there're lots of villages they never built on. Not yet, anyway. Drove the people out, tore down the houses, but left the trees and gardens. So we could still get the olives and the thyme and even some grapes, for a while." She sighed. "Oh, those olives were tasty, olives from heaven. God wanted us still to have them. God be praised, He still gives us the beauty of the world. He still gives us good, even in our loss. God is merciful."

God gives us olives, thought Mujahhid, *but took my brother and my best friend.* He shifted restlessly in his chair, wanting to say something but not knowing what. Then Aunt Rasheeda touched his arm.

"We have to talk more about olives, Mujahhid," she said. "Our neighbor still has a grove, thanks to God, and we must help him with the harvest. All of us. You'll be a big help, you're young and full of energy."

What was this? Mujahhid stared at his aunt. "But—but I don't know anything about picking olives. I've never done it before. I'd—how can I do that work?"

"You'll learn quickly enough, it's not hard. We need you, Mujahhid. They're ripe now."

Mujahhid pushed away from the table, stood, and with a muttered phrase of necessary politeness, left the room. It wasn't just the idea of physical work that riled him—although he had little experience other than helping in his father's shop. It was the thought of picking olives, something so ordinary, so dull, when he should be back in the city, carrying on the struggle in the name of his brother and friend. The shame of it tore at his insides. What would his friends say, who were bravely facing danger every day?

He went out to stand by the front gate of the house, feeling like a prisoner. In the peaceful quiet he scowled at his surroundings, the soft yellow of the stone houses warm in the afternoon sun. The village was called Beit al-Makhfiya, the "hidden place." Mujahhid didn't know why it was called that, but it was "nowhere" in his eyes, just a few narrow streets of small houses and, a short distance off, the olive grove.

Then, beyond the grove, he noticed something he had not seen before. On a nearby hilltop, overlooking the village homes, stood a tight cluster of new, boxlike buildings—a community of Jewish settlers. It looked as though it had been planted there by mistake, like a military fort in a garden. Anger started to smoke inside Mujahhid.

He heard someone approaching but didn't turn. In a moment Hanan spoke, in quiet tones.

"I couldn't say anything earlier, Mujahhid, it would just upset my mother. But, well, I want to say how sorry I am about your brother. He was so good, such a fine person."

Mujahhid gave her a fleeting glance. Maybe she'd been fond of his brother. . . . His heart felt contracted with his own grief, and now—it surprised him how quickly—with hers.

Hanan let out a sigh. "And sorry about your friend, of course."

Mujahhid's thoughts, forced back to the holes that had appeared so abruptly in his life, became confused and turbulent. He knew it was wrong to question, but he couldn't help wondering why God had let those terrible things happen. His family had always tried to be good Muslims, to love God and live as He wanted them to. But sometimes God made decisions that were very hard to understand.

They stood quietly for a minute or two. Then Hanan spoke again, in a different tone. "I know how you feel," she said. "I mean, about that, I mean, and about the olive picking. It really isn't hard, you know, and it'll take only a few days. The neighbor's old, he doesn't have enough help in his own family. We have to do it, Mujahhid."

"Why?" He turned on her. "To get your year's supply?" It was a rude reply, coming from his pain. But he didn't miss the tightening of Hanan's expression.

"He's generous, he lets us keep a lot," she answered coolly. "But that's not the only reason. Mama owes him money. Every year she has to borrow from him, and he lets her pay it back by helping with the olive harvest. She wouldn't want you to know that, of course, but I guess you need to. We've always had to do it alone and it's hard for us, especially Sitti. We really need your help, Mujahhid."

Stung, he remained silent. After a moment Hanan went on. "Olive trees mean so much to the villagers. Not just for food . . . but they're almost like children, something sacred. We feel that God gives them to sustain us, just as Sitti said."

Mujahhid thought, *sure, I know about olive trees. We have them in Bethlehem, too. But—*

"It's the only grove left around here. So many people in this area have lost their homes and their groves and orchards. Everything smashed and uprooted, to make roads for the Israelis, or because the army says people could hide among the trees. Just to suit . . . them." She finished with a glance and a shrug in the direction of the settlement.

"All right!" Mujahhid snapped suddenly. "I never said I wouldn't, did I? I'll pick a ton of olives, if that's what you want. It's just that—that I should be doing something else."

"What should you be doing?"

"The jihad! The holy struggle to win back our land!"

Hanan drew in her breath. It sounded almost like a sniff, and Mujahhid felt a prick of anger. "The fighting at the army checkpoint in Bethlehem," she said quietly. "I respect that, Mujahhid. But there's more than one kind of jihad."

"That's the only kind I want to fight!" he shot back.

Then, again Mujahhid saw his friend Nawar lying motionless, heard the roar of tanks and helicopters and shells, the earsplitting racket of rifle fire. He felt cold with fear—and hot with the shame of his cowardice. God must find him disgusting.

> > >

Each morning, Mujahhid and Hanan walked several kilometers to a high school in a neighboring village. Afternoons they spent in the neighbor's olive grove. For four days Mujahhid worked alongside his cousin and one or both of the older women. He worked silently, half listening to their chatter and responding only with grunts when they spoke to him. Contrary to what Hanan had promised, it was hard work—beating the branches with a long stick so the women could pick up the olives that fell onto a cloth spread below. Mujahhid's arms and shoulders ached from the unfamiliar exercise. Furthermore, it felt like forced labor. When any of the villagers passed nearby, he kept his face turned away, not wanting anyone to think he was doing this willingly.

At times, however, he let himself weaken a bit. For a moment or two, lulled by the whisper of the silvery green leaves, he would run his hand lightly over the gnarled wood and think about how very old these trees were, the two or three hundred years they had seen on this quiet hillside, the many human lives they had nourished.

But then Mujahhid would catch himself. *Don't get silly,* he thought. *They're just old trees.*

On the fifth day he set out for the grove as soon as he got back from school. He was already tired after the long walk, but now anxious to finish the job. The crop was bountiful this year, and they had harvested only half the trees thus far.

Looking ahead, he saw Israeli soldiers in the road. Some of the neighbors had gathered, more than a dozen, mostly women. Although tired after the long walk, he was impatient to finish the job.

Mujahhid paused, uncertain, wondering whether he dared confront the soldiers. In the streets of Bethlehem he had shouted himself hoarse at soldiers from a distance, yelling every curse, obscenity, and patriotic slogan he could think of. But he had rarely talked with a soldier, except for brief muttered answers when stopped at checkpoints. What would it be like to tell these men face to face: *Get out, leave us alone!*

He took a few steps, hesitated, then quickened his resolve and walked up to the nearest soldier. "What—what's going on?" he asked, embarrassed by the crack in his voice.

The soldier turned to Mujahhid. He looked young, less than twenty, with pink splotches on his cheeks and a small chin. His eyes were not hidden behind dark glasses, and Mujahhid was glad of that.

"These trees must be destroyed," the soldier said in heavily accented Arabic. "The bulldozers are coming any minute. These people must get out of the way."

For a moment Mujahhid could not believe what he had heard. Then he began to sputter, his determination to keep cool completely undone. "These—these olive trees—what d'you mean? Why?" The villagers backed him up with a raucous uproar.

The soldier winced and raised his voice. "I'm trying to explain—if you'd only be quiet! Listen, everyone, this orchard is in the way. A new road will go through here, a road to the settlement up there. The settlement needs a good road to Jerusalem. The olive trees are in the way. They must go." He spoke slowly, as though he were repeating simple information for children, but with a trace of uncertainty.

Mujahhid glanced at the trees nearby—and suddenly he felt that he was seeing them in a new way. Their oddly bent shapes, like old people, their delicate leaves dancing like soft young children, the ripe olives still glistening on the branches like strong, confident youths. They seemed to be speaking to him, and at last he could hear. Sitti's words came back to him . . . *God still gives us the beauty of the world, even in our loss.* At the time, he'd thought it was just old-woman talk. Now he understood. The olive grove was something fine that God in His goodness had made for people. In a way, it was just as sacred as a mosque. The trees must be defended.

"You can't do that!" Mujahhid shouted in a burst of passion. "You can't cut down those trees! They don't belong to you— they're our neighbor's, and they're all he's got." Vaguely he became aware that the chorus of villagers' angry voices was subsiding, and in the quiet his voice rose. "You can't cut these trees! Go away—all of you, go away! This is *our village!*"

"Look, kid!" said the soldier, seeming more uneasy with every word. "It's not my idea. I don't decide to cut down trees—I don't like to cut down trees. I'm just following orders."

"They're bad orders. Go tell the army they're bad orders and you won't do them. We won't let you—we'll fight you!"

Mujahhid saw something like a veil of fear in the soldier's eyes, but the young man quickly mastered it. He was sweating, his hands nervously fidgeting as he held his rifle. Other soldiers, a half dozen or so, now joined him. He seemed to be the main spokesman, probably knowing Arabic better than the others.

"Kid, listen," stammered the soldier, his face taking on a look of earnestness. "It—it won't do you any good. This has to be done. Come on, be reasonable, go on home and let us get on with it—"

One of the other soldiers broke in. In a glance, Mujahhid saw that the man had a superior rank, probably the sergeant in charge of the detail. He barked at the younger man in Hebrew, then turned and gave Mujahhid a swift cuff on the side of the head.

"Get out, Arab filth."

Hurt, furious, Mujahhid staggered and nearly fell. But as he turned away, he caught sight of a flash of color among the more distant olive trees. What could that be? Sitti? . . . Yes, Sitti, in her embroidered dress! And Hanan with her. Somehow they must have gotten into the olive grove unnoticed from a terrace higher up the hillside. In that instant, Mujahhid knew that the battle was not yet over.

He retreated from the soldiers, rubbing his temple where the sergeant had hit him. Head low, he started to shuffle away toward the nearest houses. A moan rose from the crowd, a sigh of disappointment before the women started their haranguing again.

As soon as Mujahhid felt safely out of the soldiers' view, he dashed around the corner of a house and raced back to the upper terrace of the olive grove. Reaching it, he climbed over a stone wall, as his cousin and grandmother must have done, and soon joined them.

They greeted him with nods and promptly resumed their work. Mujahhid fell into their rhythm, the pace at which they'd always worked . . . not so fast as to tire early, not so slow as to needlessly prolong the job. He pulled down and held the branches so Hanan could gather the olives into her bamboo basket. Steadily, calmly, they went on with the harvest.

Suddenly an angry shout went up from the soldiers. Then came a collective cheer from the villagers. Mujahhid tried to ignore both. But from the corner of his eye he could see someone hurrying toward them, dodging around the trees. A moment later the young soldier reached Mujahhid and took him by the arm.

"Kid, get your sister and granny out of here!" blurted the soldier. "They can get hurt—I don't want them to get hurt. Or *you*—and you will, if you—"

Hanan broke in. "The olives have to be harvested," she said matter-of-factly, as though speaking to a grocer. "There's no sense letting them go to waste."

Shooting a look of admiration at her, Mujahhid took the cue. "This is our job. We have to get on with it."

"*Yallah,* young man," said Sitti to the soldier, "make yourself useful or make yourself scarce. We've got work to do." She bent over to pick up a few olives that had fallen to the dry soil.

The Israeli turned back to Mujahhid. "Look, you think I like this? Tearing down trees, knocking people around? Is this right, destroying the world God gave us—"

At an angry shout, he jumped and glanced around nervously. His sergeant and a few other soldiers were hurrying toward them. The young soldier seized Mujahhid by the shoulders and pleaded once more.

"You've got to get out of here! Please, before you get hurt! *Please!*"

But Mujahhid stood motionless, startled and held by the soldier's words: "... *destroying the world God gave us...*"

The men reached them. Hesitating in confusion for a moment, the soldier then turned from Mujahhid, rushed over and stood by the two women, his arms outstretched protectively. Two of the other soldiers shoved him away. They seized Sitti and Hanan, knocked the baskets from their hands, and propelled them swiftly along the stony terraces toward the road.

With a shout of protest Mujahhid started toward his cousin and grandmother, only to find himself again grabbed by the young soldier. This time, however, the soldier seemed to be trying to keep Mujahhid away from the other men. It did no good. Mujahhid felt himself yanked from the soldier's grasp. Holding him by his shirt front, the sergeant slapped him hard several times, on both sides of the head, then threw him face down with full force.

Mujahhid lay on the stony ground, his head ringing from the blows. But above him he heard a verbal battle begin to break out. The younger soldier, impassioned, yelled in Hebrew at his sergeant. The sergeant, equally enraged, shouted back. Although he could not understand the furious words, Mujahhid grasped the meaning and heard the young soldier ordered away.

As Mujahhid tried to pull himself up, someone yanked him to his feet. For a second, before steel-like hands started to drag him through the grove, he caught a last glimpse of the young soldier ... cheeks flaming, face twisted with anger and shame. Their eyes met, and Mujahhid understood something more. He and that soldier were not all that far apart.

> > >

At the washbasin by the kitchen, Hanan helped clean the dirt from Mujahhid's face, gently sponging the dark bruises. No way to conceal them from Aunt Rasheeda, of course. She would learn all about it anyway, as soon as she got home from work. Even now they could hear the growl of bulldozers at the other end of the village, and the death groans of the old trees.

Mujahhid turned from Hanan's hands and studied his face in the cracked mirror over the sink. Battle scars . . . he was proud of them. And thankful not to have a bullet in his throat, like Nawar. He didn't think he really wanted to be a martyr. It was better to live, to go on with the struggle.

And then, as Hanan pulled his face around to apply ointment to the abrasions, her earlier words echoed in his mind. *There's more than one kind of jihad. Yes,* Mujahhid thought, *I guess there is. Like picking olives. Doing what you have to do, no matter what. Maybe that's the kind of* jihad *God wants most from us. From all* of us.

ELSA MARSTON

I remember vividly my first glimpse of olive trees, from a train going through northern Italy. No matter how many I've seen since then—on the terraces of Mount Lebanon, the hills of Tunisia, the outskirts of Jerusalem—I still marvel at the curiously twisted shapes and the beauty of the shimmering silvery leaves. No wonder people have cherished the tree since most ancient times, and that Noah's dove chose an olive twig, symbol of life and hope!

That's why every time I read of the Israelis bulldozing a

Palestinian olive grove, it horrifies me to the core. Whatever the official explanations, the underlying reason of this policy, I believe, is similar to the nineteenth-century American strategy of wiping out the buffalo herds on which the Plains Indians depended. Destroying a resource that gives people both sustenance and spiritual strength is an efficient way to break the will to survive.

The problem goes back to 1967, when Israel occupied the West Bank and Gaza, the last remaining parts of Arab Palestine. Instead of withdrawing, as required by international law, Israel established numerous settlements of armed Israeli citizens on Palestinian land, building highways to connect them. Even during the so-called peace process in the 1990s, the Palestinians increasingly saw their orchards bulldozed and their homes destroyed. Palestinian towns and villages could be isolated at any time by the Israeli army, their people prevented from going to work, school, market, hospitals. These conditions ignited the popular uprising that started in September 2000.

Although Palestinians are Muslims and Christian, the conflict between them and the Jewish state is emphatically not an "age-old" religious battle. It's a contemporary political one. In my story, Mujahhid fights against Israeli *soldiers,* an occupying army; he doesn't fight against Jews as such.

Religious identification does influence Mujahhid's behavior, however, as he believes his resistance is the sort of *jihad* called for by Islam. In the West, the term *jihad* is typically translated as "holy war," calling forth an incorrect image of Muslims spreading their faith by the sword. The real meaning is "struggle, striving," which sometimes includes fighting to defend religious rights and to oppose aggression. More important, *jihad* refers to inner struggle: each person's effort to overcome moral weakness and evil, to strive for justice and compassion. In fact, throughout most of its history, Islam has been a remarkably tolerant religion—and I think Mujahhid's own religious understanding grows a little broader by the end of the story.

With New England origins and a home in Bloomington, Indiana, I've had the chance to travel and live in several Middle Eastern countries. My nonfiction books range from ancient history—*The Phoenicians, The Ancient Egyptians, Muhammad of Mecca*—to modern topics such as *Women in the Middle East: Tradition and Change,* plus two novels set in Egypt.

A DAUGHTER OF ABRAHAM

BY DIANNE HESS

ANNANDALE, VIRGINIA, 1966

"Take out 'Come All Ye Faithful,'" Mr. O'Reilley orders our ninth-grade chorus, "and let's pick it up at the bottom of page two."

Obediently we shuffle through our Christmas music, then we wait for Mr. O'Reilley to raise his baton.

We make it all the way to "Come all ye citizens of Bethlehem," when he interrupts us abruptly.

"This is our last rehearsal before our Christmas concert," he says, wiping the sweat from his face with the back of his sleeve. "Damiano, less volume there on 'Bethlehem'—you're screeching it out like a Jewish mother."

Everyone twitters as we pick it back up and sing to the finish.

The moment the song ends, I close my music book and step down from the bleachers. I notice Christine Harper is leaving at the same time. Quietly we sneak out of the gym and make our way to our lockers.

"Sarah!" she calls after me. "Wait up. Where are *you* going?"

I duck my head and look at the floor to avoid her. Christine is someone I've wanted to get to know since she came to our school in September. But today I don't feel like having a conversation. Still, she is quick to catch up with me.

"I'm going to see a shrink," she volunteers before I can say a word. "My parents are getting divorced." She says this matter-of-factly, as though parents get divorced every day of the week. "Dr. Arnold thinks I'm acting out my anger by doing things with my boyfriend that are inappropriate for a fourteen-year-old." She punctuates *inappropriate* with a sarcastic roll of her eyes.

I look at her with mild shock, but I'm intrigued. My mother often tells me to stay away from people with "divorced parents" and "mental problems." But Christine's boldness attracts me. Because she has confided in me, I feel safe in divulging my own dark secret to her.

"Actually, I'm on my way to see a psychologist," I tell her. "It's my first time."

I've sworn to my mother that I won't breathe a word to anyone as to why I am leaving school at two-thirty in the afternoon. "It's nobody's business," my mother warned me before I left. "And besides, people will think you have mental problems."

All day long I have been feeling nervous and ashamed about going. But now it seems like a funny coincidence that we are both going to therapists at the same time.

Christine and I exchange sly smiles. We have a secret bond.

"What are you in for?" she asks.

"Not that much," I say, disappointed not to have as interesting a reason to go as she has. "My mother thinks I'm not applying myself in school. And my sister and I fight all the time."

The big reason for going, which I don't mention, is that it was discovered that I'd been cutting religious school for the past two months. I'd never seen my father get so mad. The last time I was there, the teacher was talking about the Holocaust. They showed a horrible filmstrip of people dying in the concentration camps. "Anyone who doesn't learn the lessons of history is doomed to repeat it," were the last words the teacher said before I disappeared into the bathroom behind a cloud of cigarette smoke from some other kids who were cutting class. After that, I never went back.

Christine and I promise we won't tell anyone that we're seeing shrinks, and we celebrate our being the misfits of Robert E. Lee High School by breaking into "Joy to the World" and harmonizing in funny falsetto voices. Then we put on our coats, slam our lockers, and continue to sing in the parking lot until our families come to pick us up.

A light blue Nash Rambler station wagon pulls up next to the curb and I get in. My whole family is there—Daddy, Mother, and my older sister, Jane, who is in high school. Grandmother is not there. But that is only because my mother doesn't want her to know where we are going. Not that my grandmother doesn't know we fight. She lives downstairs in our house, so she hears us going at it with each other all the time. Grandmother is from Germany, and her English isn't very good. Even so, the way we fight is fairly universal. People who yell and scream at each other the way we do are fighting in any language.

I begin to hum "Joy to the World" as we drive off, but it makes my sister mad. She tells me what a lousy voice I have, then she shouts at me to shut up. Then the family breaks into World War III. It's kind of like a Greek play, with my mother doing the chorus.

"Can't you live and let live!" my mother shouts. "You are robbing her of all her self-confidence. We are such a small family."

On the word *family* my father stiffens. There is always a kind of silent tension when that word is mentioned.

"Please! No shouting while I drive!" my father shouts. "I'm going to have an accident!"

"You're upsetting your father," my mother shouts. "This is terribly dangerous while we're driving! Don't upset your father!"

"I can't stand her constant singing," my sister continues to shout. "And why do you always take her side."

Ignoring my sister, I continue to sing, and as though nothing is going on, I bring my song to a rousing crescendo.

"Shut up!" my sister screams.

"Please?" begs my mother.

"ENOUGH!" my father barks sharply.

In a jagged counterpoint, everyone shouts at me at once to stop my singing. The car swerves one way, then the other, then we ride the rest of the way to the family counselor in dead silence.

> > >

The next day after school, Christine stops by my locker and asks me to walk home with her. As we walk, she tells me all the intimate details of her life and what kinds of things she does with her boyfriend. She even tells me how her therapist made her tell her everything. I listen intently.

"How did your therapy go?" she asks me when she's done.

"It was kind of weird," I say. "He asked my sister and me all kinds of questions about anger. Then he asked my father if he had any brothers or sisters and to talk about what it was like growing up in his family. But then my parents got really weird and they made us leave the room before they would say anything."

"Why did they make you leave the room?" she asks.

"I don't know." I shrug. "They never talk about his family."

Even though I barely know Christine, I feel comfortable telling her things I normally don't talk about. Right away we are friends, and she invites me to her house for dinner.

Christine's house is about a half mile from mine, and it's almost identical. As we walk up her front stoop, I notice the colored lights that outline her house, and the life-size Rudolph the Red-Nosed Reindeer that blinks from her rooftop. In her living room is a bare pine tree in a stand of water, and she lets me help her decorate it. We put last year's bulbs and tinsel on the branches, and I show her four little brothers and sisters how to make colorful chains and snowflakes from construction paper.

I love the fresh, piney smell of the tree, and I particularly love the red-and-green metal dishes of Christmas candy that sit generously on every coffee table and side table. Christine tells me to help myself, and I can't stop eating the colorful ribbon candy and the foil-wrapped chocolate-covered marshmallow Santas.

As we decorate the tree, Christine's father is downstairs in the family room, drinking beer from a can and watching football on TV. He doesn't seem to notice we are there. Her mother is out somewhere, so we're free to do whatever we want to do. As her four brothers and sisters play noisily with scissors and construction paper and glue, we make a few cans of SpaghettiOs, then dish them out into green plastic bowls for ourselves and the kids. We open a couple of bottles of orange soda, and when we're done, we eat more candy.

When we tire of eating candy, we put on our coats and dart outside. We dash through the neighborhood, and even though it's cold and dark, we cut through the woods along the creek. We sit on a rock and listen to the creek run by as Christine continues to tell me things about herself that no one has ever told me. She tells me more about her boyfriend, Dennis, and how he kisses her, and suddenly I am aching to do all the things she says she has done.

"My mother wants me to break up with him, though, because . . ." She pauses a moment to gain her composure, then takes a deep breath. "She's having an affair with Dennis's father. We accidentally saw them through the window."

I put my arm around her to comfort her, and her eyes fill with tears. I'm not quite sure what to say, so we both get quiet for a while and skim rocks across the creek. Our gloves are wet and our hands freeze in the cold, but we don't seem to notice.

"My mom is making me go to a dance this Friday night at the CYO," she says, fighting back more tears. "She thinks if I meet a nice Catholic boy, I'll forget about Dennis." She skims another rock across the creek. "Will you come with me?" she asks.

The Catholic Youth Organization has dances once a month. It's part of the church school Christine went to last year. Many kids from Lee transferred in from St. Bartholomew, which only went up to the eighth grade. So there will be some kids there from our school, too. I want to go with her to the dance, but I know it's not something my parents will allow me to do.

Suddenly I feel safe enough to tell her something I've never told anyone at school. "Can you keep a secret?" I say.

She nods.

"I'm Jewish," I tell her. My hands are shaking.

She stares at me without saying anything. There is a long silence, and I wonder, in a panic, if this was one secret I should have kept to myself. I hate being the only Jewish kid in my school. It wasn't worth risking Christine's friendship for this.

I can't tell if she hates me, or if she'll be embarrassed by me, or if she's planning to turn me over to the Ku Klux Klan.

Finally she responds. "That doesn't matter," she says. "And besides, I really couldn't tell. In fact," she reassures me, "you don't look Jewish at all."

I let out a deep sigh of relief. "You mean it?" I ask. "I would die if anyone found out. Promise me you won't tell anyone."

She opens her coat in the cold and takes off her necklace. It's a beautiful gold chain with a tiny gold cross. She gestures to me to open my coat, then she puts the necklace around my neck. "You can have it," she says.

"Are you sure?" I ask her.

She nods.

I have always wanted to wear a cross. I used to wear a gold Star of David all the time. But I took it off in the seventh grade when Jodie Simon called me Jew Nose. Already I feel like a new person.

"It's all yours," she says. "I've got another one at home."

"Just don't tell my parents that we're going to a Catholic dance," I say. "They would kill me if they found out."

"I won't," Christine promises. "After all, we're best friends."

I try not to show how pleased I am, but I can't help it. A best friend just doesn't happen every day.

At home I lock myself in my bedroom. I take the cross out from under my sweater and admire my image in the mirror. It's amazing how a cross can transform a person. I twirl around and around. I look like Maria from *West Side Story*. I look Catholic and holy and good. Just like everyone else.

Suddenly someone pounds on my door. "Sarah?"

I jump.

"Sarah. Have you finished your homework?"

I tuck the necklace back under my shirt. I'm back to my Jewish Cinderella self.

"I'm doing it now, Mama," I answer her.

"Don't stay up too late," she says.

"*I won't*," I promise, then I study for my English test until the last light in the house goes out.

When I'm sure everyone is asleep, I sneak downstairs into the living room. When I was eight, I bought my parents a mezuzah as a Hanukkah present at a religious school bazaar. I had nailed it up, right on the living room wall, in between my mother's Picasso and Modigliani reproductions. Now I glare at it. The little finger-shaped object with a blue enameled Jewish star at its center threatens to betray me. Suddenly, I want to hide it. What if I meet someone at the CYO dance? What if they were to come home with me and see it? No one would want anything to do with me if they knew.

I take a little photograph from another wall and hang it on top of the mezuzah, as though it were a nail.

The picture is of a little girl of about six. I've always loved the picture. She's got dark curls and beautiful chubby cheeks, and she wears a lacy white old-fashioned dress. She is holding a bouquet of roses, and she smiles like an angel. She is Ilse Margot, Grandmother's favorite niece.

Grandmother came from a large family in Germany. She loves to show me everyone's pictures and tell me their names. But whenever I ask her anything about where they are now, she quickly changes the subject. And now, I use the mysterious photograph to cover evidence of my biggest shame.

Friday night before the dance, Christine comes over to our house for dinner. My sister is out with her friends, so things are not as insane as usual.

When the doorbell rings, my grandmother welcomes Christine at the front door.

"Ach, yah," she coos. "Come in, come in." Her English isn't very good, and she calls me in to rescue her.

"Grandmother, this is Christine," I say, then I ask if we can look at her apartment downstairs. Grandmother is proud of her things, and she loves when I show them off. She follows us downstairs across Persian rugs that are scattered all around, past large ancient oil portraits of my great-great-grandparents. Then we come to my favorite part. I show Christine all the treasures in the large glass china closet in Grandmother's living room. There are hundreds of small antique pieces: cups and figurines and all sorts of miniature objects. Sometimes I stare inside the case and am transported back to another world. I wonder what these things are and what their other lives had been in Germany. And I wonder if some day, all the ugly modern things in the world will become this beautiful when they are old. As I show her the pieces, Christine becomes as mesmerized as I am. But the moment Christine points to a photograph of a woman from long ago, Grandmother smiles uncomfortably and disappears up the stairs and into the kitchen to help with dinner.

"Did I say something wrong?" Christine asks.

"No," I say. "They always get weird when you talk about the family."

"Where is your family from?"

"Germany," I say.

"No wonder they have accents," she says.

I have never noticed that anyone in my family speaks with an accent, but as she mentions it, I suppose she is right.

My mother calls us to dinner and we sit around the table. She and my grandmother have made one of my father's favorite dishes, bratwurst—a kind of pork sausage with sauerkraut. It is not my favorite food at all. But Christine loves it, and she asks for seconds.

"Is this some type of Jewish dish?" Christine asks my father politely, and my parents howl with laughter that Christine thinks that pork sausage with sauerkraut is Jewish. Then my father explains to her that Jews don't usually eat pork. But since we are Reform Jews, we don't follow the dietary laws.

Just as my grandmother is trying to make Christine eat a third portion of sausage, the telephone rings. My mother answers the phone and begins speaking excitedly in German. She stays on for a while, and when she returns to the table, she continues speaking German. My grandmother looks startled and turns white, and everyone speaks rapidly and with great excitement. Usually my grandmother is the only one who speaks German and my parents answer her in English. They only speak German when they don't want us to know what they are saying. And now they are all speaking German. I ask what is going on, but no one will answer me.

While the excitement of the phone call has everyone's undivided attention, Christine and I excuse ourselves. I tell my parents I'm going to a dance, but no one seems to be paying much attention, so I don't have to explain where it is. From what I can gather, someone is coming from far away to visit us, but my mother just tells me that I must come right home after school on Monday and not to make other plans. Then they continue their German conversation. Before anyone comes to their senses and begins to ask questions, Christine and I charge out the front door and race down the street.

We take a shortcut through the woods. It's very dark, and the ground is hard and frosty. The winds howl through the trees, and we spook ourselves with suggestions that someone is following us. We walk along the edge of the winding creek until we come to the highway. The church is on a big hill facing the highway. In the front is a huge white statue of St. Bartholomew with his arms outstretched before him. He is twice as tall as the tallest man I have ever seen. I feel like a tiny child in front of him. His face is sweet. He makes me feel like one of his children, like I belong here.

The dance is in the auditorium, but I stop in the sanctuary of the church on the way. I have never been inside a church before. Unlike our synagogue, which is a plain gray room with folding chairs, this church is filled with red-velvet pews and paintings and statues and stained glass. All around ghosts of a time long past fill the room with their lively spirits. Surely God will hear my prayers from here as they rise to the ceiling that soars up into the heavens.

Christine shows me how to kneel on a bench. She crosses herself, then we squeeze ourselves between the rows of praying people and we sit down in the pews. The church is the most beautiful place I have ever been. I could be a tiny figurine sitting inside Grandmother's china cupboard, surrounded by her beautiful treasures. If only I could be Catholic. I would sit here all night by the flicker of hundreds of candles. I would wear a uniform, and I could keep my cross out, and I'd be one of St. Bartholomew's children. I would have lots of brothers and sisters and would always be around people who were just like me. And again I am reminded of how much I hate being the only Jewish girl in my school.

"Let's go to the dance," Christine says to me after we have been sitting for a few minutes. Reluctantly I give up my beautiful velvet seat and follow her downstairs into the auditorium.

The speakers are blaring "I'll Be There" by the Four Tops, and the room is crammed with Catholic schoolboys in their St. Bartholomew's uniforms and greasers in black leather jackets from our school who sneaked in to meet "chicks." Christine points out the boys to me that she likes, and makes sure I notice when a particularly cute one walks by. At first I'm anxious, but soon I begin to relax as we develop a code for rating boys. For the really cute ones, we jab each other sharply in the ribs once with an elbow. A very long jab is for an especially cute one. My ribs are beginning to hurt.

Christine and I go to the back table to get Cokes. There's a *really* really cute one behind us. I elbow Christine hard. She elbows me back.

"Hi, John," she says to him. His eyes are so blue I think my heart is going to fall on the floor. He smiles shyly, and Christine and I elbow each other so hard, we almost knock each other over. There will be a bruise from this one for sure.

Christine knows a lot of the kids from having gone to Catholic school her whole life. She talks to John for a while. He asks her if she likes public school, and Christine makes a crude-sounding noise with the back of her throat like she's going to throw up. We all laugh nervously. Christine is really pretty funny.

Another friend of hers comes along. "Buddy!" Christine calls out.

"How do you know him?" I whisper, impressed at all the people she knows.

"He's friends with Dennis," she says.

Buddy walks right over to me. He's much older than the other kids. He's a greaser, like all the popular kids in school, and wears a black leather jacket and slicked back hair. The smells of cigarette smoke and Brut aftershave cling to the air around him.

"Who's your friend?" Buddy asks Christine. He speaks with a very heavy southern accent.

Christine puts on a funny voice. "That's George," she says, pointing at me.

"Yeah, I'm George," I repeat.

"You sure don't look like a George," Buddy says, piercing me with his gaze.

"I'm definitely a George," I say.

"How old are you?" he asks me.

I'm only fourteen, but I tell him I'm sixteen.

Buddy pulls me close to him and we begin to dance. He looks me in the eye with his piercing gaze. We are Tony and Maria in *West Side Story*. As we dance, Buddy kisses me on the lips. I've never been kissed by a boy before, and I melt into his arms.

Suddenly one of the nuns comes over and whacks the table next to us loudly with her palm. I am mortified. I've never been so embarrassed in my life. Christine watches helplessly as the nun escorts Buddy and me out to the coatroom and asks us to leave. Christine shrugs, then she makes a sign to me that she will call me at home.

I walk out with Buddy. "I'll give you a lift," he says.

I've never been with a boy who had a car before. I guess, to tell the truth, I've never been with a boy at all. I'm a little bit afraid of Buddy since I don't really know him. He's very tall and is eighteen years old. He tells me he's from West Virginia.

"I used to go to Lee," he drawls, "but I dropped out before I graduated."

I look at him curiously. "I've never known anyone who has dropped out of school," I say.

"I got me a good job in D.C.—over at the Mobile station on sixteenth Street," he says, tossing his head toward D.C. "I pump gas and give lube jobs to all the Jews in their Cadillacs," he tells me. His joke hurts me, but I smile politely.

Before we go to my house, he parks the car on a deserted corner and kisses me some more. I'm frightened by his intensity, and I struggle to get away from him. He forces himself next to me, but the moment he kisses me all my fears go away. I think I am falling in love. That night when I get home, I adjust the picture that covers the mezuzah.

On Monday, before I leave the house for school, my mother reminds me to come right home at three o'clock. "It's very important," she says. "We're having company."

Monday afternoon is our school Christmas concert. Everyone's parents come but mine. If only I were Catholic, my parents would be there, too. Christine and I are nervous, and we spend a lot of time beforehand putting on grape-kiss lipstick and combing our hair. "You never know who might show up at one of these things," she teases, and then I get even more nervous thinking that Buddy might come. Every time the door opens I look up. I'm hoping he will come to watch me sing Christmas music.

The choir warms up. It's evident we could have used a few more weeks of practice, but Mr. O'Reilley rehearses us before we go on and miraculously we finish without any major disasters. When it's over, we gather around the tree and everyone sings more Christmas carols and eats more Christmas candy.

Christine is waiting for me at my locker. For the twentieth time she makes me tell her about my adventure with Buddy and how in love I am with him, and she listens with great interest. I can't believe I finally have a story to tell that is as interesting as one of hers. But I can't hide my disappointment that he didn't come to hear me sing.

"When are you seeing him again?" she asks.

My knees grow weak. "I don't know," I say.

Christine suggests we have a Coke and French fries at Grant's Five and Dime after school. "Sometimes kids from school are there," she tells me. "And sometimes Buddy hangs around there with the cashiers."

When we get there, Laurie Fanelli asks me for some money to buy some French fries. I don't know Laurie at all, and I tell her I don't have any money on me.

"Just a dime?" she pleads.

"I don't have anything," I say, showing her my empty pockets.

"You're a cheap Jew," she answers, and walks away.

As I reel from the sting of her words, I hold back my tears and take Christine's cross out from under my shirt. I wonder if Laurie really knows I'm Jewish. Then I check nervously around the room for Buddy. It's late, and I still don't see him. Maybe he knows I'm Jewish, too. The crowd thins out, but

Christine promises she'll stay with me. Just as we're about to give up, she jabs me in the ribs with her elbow and stares straight forward. "It's Buddy!" she whispers without moving her lips.

I freeze. I raise my eyes slightly, and through the corner of my eye I see him with some of his friends. I can smell his Brut aftershave from across the store. My heart pounds and my knees shake. "If he talks to me now, I will forget my name," I tell Christine.

Within a minute he is behind me. He puts his hands over my eyes. His aftershave is strong. He offers us a ride home, and drops Christine off first. Then he takes me to the empty lot in the woods. He examines my cross necklace and tells me how beautiful I am. I let out a sigh of relief. He doesn't know. I am still Maria to him. Then we kiss.

It's almost six when I get home. My mother is waiting for me at the door, and she's furious. "Where were you?" she asks. "I told you to come right home today."

"I was with some friends," I whisper weakly. I completely forgot I was supposed to come home early. I wonder if she can smell Buddy's aftershave on my hands.

When I finally get inside, there's a strange woman and a young girl sitting with my family at the dining room table. Everyone is speaking German.

I take a seat next to my sister. She's uncharacteristically quiet.

"Sarah," my father says as he stands up and takes my hand. "I would like you to meet our cousins."

"I didn't know we had any cousins," I say.

He smiles uncomfortably and leads me around the table to a woman wearing beautiful antique gold jewelry. She looks a little bit older than my father.

"This is Ilse Margot," he says. "She came here last week from Rome."

I stare at Ilse Margot's blue eyes and warm smile. She looks just like Grandmother.

Suddenly it dawns on me. "Aren't you the little girl in the picture?" I ask. "The one Grandmother always showed me— the one with the white dress?"

She looks puzzled. She only speaks German and Italian, so my grandmother translates my question into German. Then the two of them speak rapidly to each other in German.

"All my life I've loved to look at your picture," I tell her, but she doesn't understand, so she just smiles.

I am introduced to the young girl with her. She is about my age, and her name is Rachel. She has long, thick dark hair and blue eyes like mine. She is Ilse's daughter, but Rachel grew up in Italy, and speaks only Italian, so we aren't able to talk, either. We all stare at one another for a long time, then Ilse and Rachel hug me, and we stare some more. These are my cousins. Real cousins. I've never met any family outside of the people from our house.

All through dinner, the grown-ups talk intensely in German. There are tears and laughter, and more tears. But since Jane and Rachel and I can't understand what they are saying, we take Rachel around the house. We show her our rooms and our magazines and our funny knickknacks, and we play her our favorite records. She points to a picture of John Lennon on

Jane's bedroom wall and says, "Beatles," and we laugh because we can understand.

For dessert, my grandmother brings in her plum tart, which is the most wonderful thing that she makes.

"Ach, *Zwetchkin Kuchen!*" Ilse says, and talks more in German.

Grandmother explains to me and my sister that this is a family recipe, and Ilse remembers it from her childhood.

Then they start talking about my name. My father translates and reminds me of how my name is the name of Sarah, the wife of Abraham. Abraham was the first Jew.

But Ilse is desperately trying to tell me something else. She tries to speak English. "Sarah mine und Vater's grandmother name," she says. Her speech is slow and labored as she squeezes out words in broken English.

My parents are silent. My grandmother begins to cry.

"Sarah was your great-grandmother," my mother explains. My father looks tense.

I never knew I was named after anyone, and I am surprised that my name has any meaning.

"She had much courage," Ilse says. "Much courage."

Then my mother looks at my father. "You should tell them now," she says, her voice shaking.

My father opens his mouth to speak. At first words don't come, but then he continues. "Our grandmother was killed by the Nazis during the war."

"What war?" I say.

"The Second World War," my father says.

"Hitler's war against the Jews," my mother spits.

Ilse speaks quickly in German and looks at me. Grandmother cries softly to herself, and both my parents and my cousin are having trouble holding back their own tears.

"Your grandmother's mother, Sarah, was very courageous," my father struggles to continue. "She risked her life to save our family. She obtained false papers from a neighbor so that the family could escape over the mountains into Switzerland. But the person who sold her the documents was an informant. So she, three of your grandmother's sisters, my father, and two of my brothers were deported to Auschwitz."

Silence sweeps over the family. It is too much to take in.

Now I remember the filmstrip in religious school about the concentration camps. The war was not so long ago. How can so many people from my family have been killed? The pictures they showed had been so terrifying, I couldn't bear to watch. I left the room and didn't go back again. Suddenly I am holding back nausea as I dare to imagine that anyone in that hideous filmstrip may have been someone from my family. Suddenly I am beginning to understand what no one wanted to talk about.

"Your grandmother and I fled to America," my father continues. "Our good friends were able to get us out of the country, and after the war they sent our possessions. It's a miracle we are here.

"Ilse had been living in Italy," my father continues. "When the war came, she was hidden by nuns in a monastery. We are now just seeing each other for the first time since the war. We had no idea anyone else from our family had survived. When Ilse called on Friday night, she had come to the states to visit a friend. It was by sheer coincidence that she found us here!"

I am stunned that Grandmother and my father had come so

close to death. I had no idea that my father's family had been killed. I can't imagine how I would go on if my father or mother or sister had been killed. I have questions to ask, but I don't know where to begin.

When dinner is over, Jane and I take Rachel downstairs to Grandmother's living room to look at all of her beautiful things. Everyone follows us down.

I show them my favorite pieces and ask Grandmother to tell them the stories she has told me about them. My grandmother talks in German, then Ilse interprets for her daughter in to Italian. My mother then interprets as Ilse tells how some of the pieces have been in the family for generations, and how some are pieces she remembers from her own childhood. Some of the pieces are parts of sets that match pieces she has. Like puzzle pieces that have been pulled apart, they are now beginning to fit back together again.

When the evening is finished, Ilse Margot and her daughter say good-bye.

They will be leaving for Italy tomorrow. I want them to stay, and I don't know if or when I will ever see them again. I look at my cousins and I cry because my family has been stolen from me.

When the taxi arrives to take them back to the hotel, Ilse Margot looks at me one more time and tells my father in broken English that I look like a Simson. That is my father's family name. And now, for the first time, I am beginning to feel like I didn't just land in Annandale, Virginia, from the moon.

As soon as their taxi disappears down the street, I run inside. First I remove the photograph from the top of the mezuzah.

Then I go to my room and replace Christine's cross with the gold Star of David that my grandmother gave me for my birthday when I was nine. Suddenly Maria from *West Side Story* feels very far away. Suddenly I am feeling much more like Sarah; great-granddaughter of Sarah Simson; namesake for a woman of courage; a daughter of Abraham.

DIANNE HESS

Growing up outside of Washington, D.C., in the mid-1960s, I rarely felt connected to my world. America didn't embrace diversity. There was seemingly one culture, and we all tried to fit into it, often with great discomfort. Prayers were allowed in schools and Christmas was treated as a national holiday. We were all pretty ignorant, and we hurt one another with our ignorance.

Back then, being different was cause for shame. Our communities were segregated. African Americans did not live with us or go to school with us. I had seen places where blacks and whites were not allowed to share lunch counters or drinking fountains. I'd never seen a Native person. Or, at least I didn't know the one Latino girl in my third-grade class was part Native. The kids taunted her and called her Juanita Banana and made fun of her accent. We made no effort to get to know her. We thought she was from Spain.

The most exclusive neighborhood and country club in our area didn't allow Jews. There were rumors that the family of my best friend who lived there had changed their name from Rubenstein to Roberts to get in. That was the thing about being Jewish. You could hide if you wanted to.

My father, who had escaped from Nazi Germany, never talked about what happened to his family. Perhaps it was survivor guilt, or perhaps it was painful to be associated with anything German at that particular time. My father didn't reveal his history to me until a few years ago when I knew enough to ask the right questions. One of my greatest gifts has been having my parents with me as I continue to learn enough to ask the right questions. Ilse Margot is based on a real cousin of mine who died last year at age ninety. I only saw her twice. The first time we were unable to speak. The second time I knew enough German to have a conversation with her. One of the most stirring moments of our meeting was the realization of just how much the war had severed my family.

In writing this story for the *Soul Searching* collection, I explored how the discovery of history and the past was something that helped me to connect to my own ongoing spiritual journey. Somewhere in this is the idea that life is eternal; that we are, in mind and body, a continuation of one another. Long after we are gone, our voices and our deeds live on. By feeling our connection to the past, we can more clearly see our place in the universe. And it is from this vantage point that we understand the importance of the gifts we leave to the future.

Dianne Hess lives in New York City and has been editing children's books for twenty-five years.

WORDS OF FAITH

BY DAVID LUBAR

There's nothing that can ruin your day like the words *I expect better from you* scrawled in red across the first page of a paper. Except, maybe, the words *I expect MUCH better from you.* With *MUCH* underlined. Twice.

"Merry Christmas," I muttered as I stared at my grade. To my left, Mr. Sterns shuffled along the aisle, handing out the last of the papers just before the bell rang.

"Have a lovely holiday," he shouted over the noise of twenty-seven students scrambling toward freedom.

I kept looking at the grade, hoping I'd misread the number. No such luck. It was definitely a sixty-five. And it was definitely my own fault. I'd dashed off the paper the night before it was due, figuring I was a good enough writer to get by with a first draft. Bad plan.

This truly sucked. I needed to end the year with at least a ninety. That's what it took to get into the senior honors writing program. I'd managed an eighty-seven the first marking period. I'd been hovering around ninety-one this period. Until now. It was going to be hard as hell to climb out of the pit I'd dug. Maybe impossible.

I had to get into that class. I'd been planning on it ever since I was a freshman. I loved writing. In my humble opinion, I was probably the best writer in the school. But that didn't mean anything without the right grade.

I tried not to obsess about my problem during vacation, but it kept getting in my face. A&E ran a biography of Stephen King. I worshiped him. He had the bug so bad he lived in a rented trailer while he wrote his first book. AMC showed a special on novelists who'd become screenwriters. The Science Fiction channel did a feature on Ray Bradbury. His short stories are awesome.

Despite my misery, the holiday sped by. I read, I wrote, I watched too much television. Christmas Eve, Mom mentioned something about going to church.

"You really want to?" I asked. The idea didn't thrill me, but I'd go if it would make her happy. Maybe I could pray for a better grade. *Dear God, all I want for Christmas is a ninety.*

Mom pushed aside the curtain and looked out the window. "It'll probably be crowded."

"There's always next year," I said.

We rented a movie instead. I think Mom went to church when I was little, but I don't remember much except this room with a picture on the wall of happy pairs of animals boarding the ark. And cookies. They had great cookies.

The next day we unwrapped presents. I gave Mom a boxed set of Audrey Hepburn movies and a really nice scarf. She gave me a fountain pen and a blank journal bound in leather. On the cover, stamped in gold, it said *The Early Works of Michael K. Ellison, Famous Author.* Aunt Jill renewed my subscription to *Writer's Digest Magazine,* and Aunt Leona gave me a book store gift certificate. Dad sent me a football.

Weighing down the fun of Christmas was the knowledge that I'd blown the one thing that mattered the most. But the first day of school after vacation, I found hope. That was also the day I met Julia. My homeroom teacher had sent me to the office to drop off some papers. On the way back I noticed this girl wandering the hallway. She moved from door to door, staring at the numbers as if they might eventually change. I knew from my own experience with Mr. Sterns's grades that such miracles never happen.

"Lost?" I asked her.

"Once." She gave me an odd smile, as if we'd just shared a joke. "I can't find room 307."

That explained it. Whoever numbered the doors had screwed up and skipped 307. Instead of doing it over, he'd just changed the last number on the floor from 329 to 307. "That's where I'm headed. You just move here?"

She nodded, sending the ends of her red hair kicking across her shoulders. "Last week. Right after Christmas."

"Where'd you come from?" I asked.

"Paris."

"Wow." I hadn't noticed an accent. Damn, a redhead from Paris. My eyes dropped to her sweater, wondering what was hidden behind the loose draping of wool. I looked away as a dozen fantasies flashed through my mind and a guilty warmth spread through my cheeks.

"Paris, Texas," she said.

Not France, though still pretty far from Pennsylvania. I slowed my pace. Even so, we reached the end of the corridor too soon. "The mysterious room 307," I said.

I followed her in, and dreamed of other ways I could help her feel at home. But all thoughts of learning more about Paris were set aside that afternoon when Mr. Sterns dribbled a crumb of hope into my dismal pit of failure.

"It's time to start your writing projects," he said. He outlined the requirements. Then he explained his grading system. And there I found salvation.

"In order to encourage writing and discourage sloth," he said, "I'm awarding an extra credit of one point for every five hundred words in your finished project. So feel free to knock yourselves out."

There were the usual protests from those who'd rather crawl through ground glass soaked in vinegar than write a hundred words. But to me, five hundred words was a warm-up.

"Any limit?" I asked. I was already running numbers in my head, figuring out what it would take to bring my grade back from the dead.

"You can get as much extra credit as you want," Mr. Sterns said. "No limit." He probably figured that only a complete maniac would try for more than three or four points.

I planned to get fifty.

That meant I had about a month to write 25,000 words. Rough, but doable. Dean Koontz produced a couple thousand words every single day of the year. Alexander Dumas wrote three hundred novels. Big, whopping mothers. All by hand with a quill. Hell, I had a computer. I thought about using some of my old stories, but I'd already showed the good ones to Mr. Sterns. I'd have to start from scratch. The moment I got home from school, I hit the keyboard, so eager to start that my hands were shaking.

Almost immediately, the demon—the one who reveals the dark side of every plan—whispered words of failure in my ear. I could get a great grade in the project and still blow my average by screwing up some stupid little quiz. I wasn't going to let that happen. No way. I studied hard. In a week, I wrote four stories and aced a tough test. I spent so much time hunched over my computer, mushrooms sprouted from my flesh. I hardly saw my friends. I talked with Julia in homeroom, and thought about her a lot as I was drifting off to sleep, but she wasn't in any of my classes, which made it tough to get to know her.

Julia, on the other hand, found a way to get to know me. I was heading out of homeroom at the end of the second week of my writing marathon when she said, "Hey, Michael, got any plans for tonight?"

"Not really." I had a hot date with a PC.

"Want to go to a concert?"

Somehow, I gained control of my nervous system before I leaped in the air. "Sure. That would be nice," I said, trying to sound eager but not desperate. "How much are the tickets?" Christmas had wiped out most of the money I'd earned last summer making French fries in hell.

"Good news—it's free," she said.

"Free?" Bad news. Usually when people gave away music, it was stuff nobody liked. But I figured I'd happily sit through almost anything if I was sitting through it with Julia. Except opera. Good god, don't let it be opera.

That gave me a plot idea—guy goes to an opera with a beautiful girl. It's so unbearable, he leaps from the balcony to end his suffering. As he dies, she reveals that she hates opera, too. She only went because she thought he wanted to go.

"It's not one of those classical things, is it?" I asked.

Julia smiled. "No. There'll be plenty of guitars and amps. Drums. Bass player. The works. You'll like it."

"Great." We arranged to meet at my place since it was on the way to the concert.

That evening I had an early dinner with Mom, then went to my room to write. But my mind kept drifting to the concert, and especially to the walk home afterward. It would be cold. Maybe we'd huddle together for warmth. Maybe she'd forget her gloves. Maybe . . . I must have fallen deep into the daydreams, because the next thing I knew, Julia was knocking at my bedroom door.

"Hi. Your mom let me in." Julia pointed at the computer. "Am I interrupting something?"

"No, I was just working on my English project." *And thinking about you.* "I'm writing a book of short stories."

"A whole book?"

"Yup." I tapped the bottom of the monitor, where the display showed the page count.

"Wow," Julia said as she leaned over my shoulder and read the number. A fresh smell—shampoo?—teased my next deep breath. I wanted to touch her hair. Instead, I got up and followed her out.

We walked through the center of town, then took a side street past the library. After a block and a half, she stopped in front of an old brick building with a wide wooden door.

"This is a church," I said.

"Yup," she said. "It's a church."

I read the sign by the steps. *El Shaddai*. That sounded like Hebrew. "Are you Jewish?" I asked.

Julia laughed and shook her head. "No. I'm a Christian. Though my dad says we're adopted Jews." She started up the steps, then turned back. A half-formed word dangled from her lips.

"What's wrong?" I asked.

Her eyes shifted toward the door. "The crowd might be kind of enthusiastic. So don't get spooked by anything. Okay?"

"Spooked? Me? No way. I read Edgar Allan Poe for bedtime stories." I followed her up the steps, wondering what kind of spooky enthusiasm waited on the other side of the door. How wild could things get in a church? My mind answered that question with a story idea about a guy who thinks he's on a date but ends up being a human sacrifice. I stashed that plot away before I spooked myself. Time to stop dreaming up disastrous dates.

The inside was far from scary. It was the plainest church I'd ever seen. No pictures or stained glass—just a wooden cross on the wall. We found a spot at the end of a pew about halfway down the aisle. After we sat, I checked out the instruments up front. The band's name was painted on the bass drum. *Tarsus Express*. Weird. That sounded like an anklebone. Two guitars and a bass leaned against Marshall amps, flanked by an electric piano and three floor mikes. Definitely enough gear to make some noise.

A moment later the band came out. They seemed pretty clean-cut for musicians. One guy picked up a guitar, hit a chord, then moved toward a microphone and said, "Praise God."

He hit another chord and the rest of the band joined in. The first song was about someone named Emmanuel. The next song was just like the sign out front—*El Shaddai*. Even though we were in a church, I hadn't really expected religious music. The Unitarian church across town had concerts all the time, and those never had anything to do with religion. But the band was good, so I didn't mind.

Around me, kids were standing, clapping along. Julia grabbed my wrist and gave a yank, pulling me to my feet. I didn't mind that, either.

After a couple more songs, the guitarist said, "Okay, let's get some testimonies. What's Jesus done for you?"

Huh? I felt like I'd suddenly found myself in German class after taking three years of Spanish. I didn't even understand the question. *Testimonies*? A dozen hands shot up. I hunched down in my seat and listened as kids spilled their sorrows.

"Man, I was all messed up," this guy in a torn denim jacket said. "I was on drugs, living in my car. I stole from my parents. Got kicked out of the house." He told how he'd been saved by Jesus.

A thin girl with haunted eyes confessed she'd tried to kill herself three times before she'd found salvation.

I felt funny listening to the testimonies, sort of like I'd snuck into an AA meeting.

When the music started up again, everyone got back on their feet. The air grew so warm from all the clapping bodies that Julia took off her sweater. As she pulled it over her head, her T-shirt lifted for an instant, revealing a glimpse of the smooth flesh above her belt. The shirt fell back, but the memory stayed. It was the sexiest thing I'd ever seen.

I tried not to stare at her. Plenty of other distractions fought for my attention. Kids were hopping in the aisles. Others raised their arms and swayed to the music. A girl behind me kept screaming out stuff that sounded like her own private language. It made me think of the doo-wop lyrics they sang in the sixties . . . shamma ramma lamma damma, shoo-bop-awooo.

The band stopped a couple more times for testimonies, and once so the drummer could preach a sermon about going where God sent you. At the end of the concert, the lead singer put down his guitar and said, "If you want to accept Jesus as your Savior, come forward."

Whoa. Back to German class.

A handful of kids left their seats and walked toward him. I couldn't imagine doing that—not in front of all those people.

The guy who'd preached started laying his hand on people's heads and yelling about fire and the Holy Spirit. One kid fell on his back and flopped around. Nobody seemed concerned. More came forward, and more fell. The floor looked like the deck of a fishing boat right after they dumped the net.

The place was so warm now that I could barely breathe. Up front, the sounds shifted to quiet voices mixed with sobs. Finally, the crowd began to filter out.

"Well," Julia asked as we merged with the flow heading through the exit. "Like it?" The air had grown crisp. She rubbed her hands together and put them in her pockets. No gloves.

"Yeah. It was kind of fun." *Except for that stuff at the end,* I thought. Orion hovered ahead of us, bright points marking his outline. "So . . ." I said.

"So?"

"You're into this?" I flinched at my clumsy wording.

"I serve the Lord," Julia said. "I've been born again."

The silence grew painfully obvious as I searched for a suitable response. *That's nice,* seemed far too shallow. *Holy shit* struck me as totally wrong. I wasn't used to being around religious people. I figured I'd probably broken all sorts of rules I didn't even know existed. As hard as I tried, I could only remember a couple of the Ten Commandments.

Other memories were much clearer. Every thought and fantasy I'd ever had about Julia shot back to me like evidence at a trial. That brief glimpse of her flesh taunted me. Forbidden fruit. I wanted to hold her. And I wanted to run.

"Hey, what's wrong?" she asked. "Never met a Christian before?"

"Yes. I mean, no. Sure I have. My mom's one. I mean, she was. So I guess she still is. And I celebrate Christmas. Easter, too." I tried to think of other religious holidays.

Julia's smile tickled at the edge of her lips. As my own words echoed in my mind, it dawned on me how ridiculous I sounded. "I'm babbling. Right?"

"Maybe a little."

"Sorry. I guess I don't know anyone who's really religious," I said.

"You might be surprised. We don't wear signs. Not every Christian goes around shouting Scripture. That's no way to win souls. My life is my testimony."

There was that word again. "The stuff they talked about. You know, the people who told how messed up they were . . ." I paused, afraid to pry.

Julia answered my unspoken question. "I've never suffered those things. Some of us come to the Lord more easily," she said. "I've been a believer all my life."

A believer all her life. That seemed so foreign. And so permanent. "What kind of church is it?" I asked. The sign out front hadn't offered any clue.

"Pentecostal," Julia said. "Some people call us *Holy Rollers.* But we're just enjoying the gifts of the Spirit."

"You go around knocking on doors?" I asked.

"That's not us. Mostly we stand on street corners shouting about the end of the world. I love to scream 'repent' real loud. It saves tons of souls."

"You're kidding?"

Julia nodded. "Yes, I'm kidding. But that's what people think. They think all kinds of weird things." She touched my shoulder. "Why not come to church with me some Sunday? Then you can see for yourself. I know you'd enjoy it."

"I can't right now. I'm pretty busy with my English project."

"Maybe another time?"

"Sure." We'd reached my house by then. I think if I'd lived closer to the church, I'd have just walked her home. But the strangeness of the evening had faded with distance. And the flesh and blood Julia was still by my side. "Want to come in?" I asked.

"That would be great."

We were cold from the walk, so I nuked two mugs of milk for cocoa. Mom peeked into the kitchen, said hi, then left us alone. We talked for a while. Just about school and stuff. Nothing heavy. Nothing spiritual.

"Let me walk you home," I said when Julia got up.

"You don't have to."

"Yes, I do. It can get a bit rough around here at night."

So I walked her home, and we talked some more. When we reached her house, she said, "Have you ever read the Bible?"

I wanted to impress her by saying yes, but I realized it wouldn't exactly be the best thing to lie about. "Not really."

"Here." She pulled a small red booklet from her front pocket. "It's *The Gospel of John,* in modern English. Give it a try."

We said good night. She stepped away before I could think about kissing her, and I watched her glide up to her porch.

"Nice girl," Mom said when I got home. "Very pretty. You have a good time?"

"Yeah. I did." Mostly.

Mom sniffed, then scratched her nose. "I think I'm allergic to her soap or something." She scratched again, then laughed. "You remember what your grandma always said?"

"Yeah. If your nose itches, it means you're going to kiss a fool."

Mom gave me a kiss on the forehead. "See, it's true."

I watched TV with her for a while, then went upstairs. It was too early to go to sleep, so I looked through my stories. I'd written nine, but two of them stunk, so I really had seven, several of which were just first drafts. I needed at least ten stories to reach my goal of 25,000 words. No problem. It wouldn't be hard to come up with three more.

As I stared out the window and thought about Julia, my mind invented a scene. A guy sees a beautiful girl drift past. He follows her. Wait. Reverse it. What if it was a girl who saw a guy? Yeah. Much better. He's wearing clothes from a different era. And carrying something. What? I traced a dozen branching possibilities as I let the story evolve in my mind.

I wrote the first paragraph, finding the viewpoint by reliving the moment when I watched Julia walk up her porch. I moved to the next paragraph, where the fiction began. And the next. The writing filled me so deeply that nothing else existed. No world. No room. No chair. Just words.

I didn't stop until I'd written the whole story. By then, I was beat. I fell into bed and picked up the booklet Julia had given me.

In the beginning was the Word . . .

Cool start. Words were one of my favorite things. If this had been a movie, or one of my stories, I guess I'd have been instantly converted by the power of the written word. But this was life. *The Gospel of John* was interesting, but I wasn't ready to believe a story just because someone had written it. In a way, I envied Julia. She was able to accept things she hadn't seen. I could never do that.

God, I thought as I drifted toward sleep, *why is it so hard?* Would it hurt for God to give people one little sign? A familiar line floated through my thoughts. *Ask and it shall be given.* Maybe God just wanted people to make the first move.

"God . . ." I said aloud, the word hanging in the darkness, barely louder than a thought. I wondered about the crowd at the concert. All those believers. They seemed so happy. Were they mindless sheep? Or had they found something I could never understand? "If you're listening to me . . ." I stopped again, realizing how stupid that was. If God was God, he heard everything. "Do something," I said. "Just something little."

What kind of sign could I ask for? Any god who could create a universe could certainly give me some small signal. I blurted out the first idea that came to mind. "Make my nose itch."

"Stupid," I whispered at myself. I couldn't believe I'd just asked God to make my nose itch. I was such a moron. Even so, I held still, waiting to see what would happen.

Nothing.

I wondered what I'd have done if I'd felt the slightest of itches, a sensation so subtle that I couldn't tell whether I'd imagined it. Maybe that's what faith was—just a form of imagination. Was that the secret of the universe? Was faith an imaginary itch? My last thought, before I fell asleep, was that, real or imaginary, it must be nice to have faith.

It would have been even nicer to have faith at six that morning when the policeman came to the house. Mom had driven to the corner store. I guess to buy milk for her coffee because her selfish idiot of a son hadn't left any. She'd been mugged in the parking lot. She tried to fight the guy off. The cop told me this while he gave me a ride to the store. Our car was there. A smashed carton lay next to it, the puddled milk tinged with blood.

"She's at the hospital," he told me. "You okay to drive?"

I nodded and he left. Then I closed my eyes and saw all the ways this was my fault. If I hadn't used up the milk, Mom would still be okay. If I hadn't gone out with Julia, none of this would have happened. What if I'd gone forward at the end of the concert? Would God have stopped the mugger? Was I being punished for not believing? A worse thought hit me. Maybe I was being punished for my fantasies. Punished because the whole time I'd sat in that church I'd wanted to pull Julia close to me, run my hands under her shirt, and touch the warm soft skin of her back. Kiss her neck. Bury my face in her hair. If only I'd walked out when things started to get weird.

Last night, all I'd heard was *God is good* and *Praise the Lord*! I wished one those grinning believers was here right now. I'd have pushed his face into the blood and asked if this was how his God worked.

I drove to the hospital, then waited a couple hours before I could see Mom. She had a broken wrist and a deep gash on her forehead. But she'd be okay. A cop came by later to tell me they'd caught the guy.

When I got to school on Monday, everyone had already seen the news in the paper. There were lots of questions and lots of sympathy. I handled things okay until Julia came up to me.

"You all right?" she asked.

I thought I was just going to say, *Yeah, I'm fine.* But something else shot out. "No, I'm not all right." I hadn't slept in two days. The whole thing kept looping through my mind, echoing like a nightmare. I'd punched my bedroom wall hard enough to knock a hole in it. My fist still throbbed. "Is this what your God does?" I asked. "Hurts people for no reason?"

Julia backed off a step. "God does everything for a reason.

But we don't always know the reason."

"Well, there was no reason for this. If you think there is, you're crazy." I walked away. She was wrong. Life was random. Good things happened. Bad things happened. I couldn't believe I'd tried to talk to God.

That evening, I picked up *The Gospel of John* and wrote in red pen on the first page, *Good start, but no follow through. You fail to convince the reader.* I added a grade—seventy two—then tossed the booklet aside.

Life got hectic. While Mom healed, I handled the housework. I couldn't believe how much stuff there was to do. Over the next couple weeks, I felt like I was watching myself from a distance. I was sorry I'd gotten angry with Julia, but I didn't want to hear any more about God, so I avoided her. Once again, she didn't avoid me.

"How's your mom?" she asked me one morning as I headed out for first period.

"She's getting the cast off on Monday," I said.

"That's great."

"Hey. About that day. Those things I said . . ."

Julia gripped my shoulder. "I forgave you the moment you spoke," she said.

Bad choice of words. I backed away from her as a wave of fury swelled through my body with such strength that I lost the power to breathe.

"What's wrong?" she asked.

I forced air into my lungs. "I wish you wouldn't act so damn perfect. Don't you ever get angry? Don't you ever hate? Don't you ever just feel freaking miserable?"

Julia flinched. "Every single day," she said. "I'm human. There was only one perfect man. And they crucified him." She put her hand over her heart. "I'm just like you inside. Probably nowhere near as strong. I'm weak. I have daily battles with hate and envy and pride."

She dropped her eyes for a moment, then looked back at me with an embarrassed smile. "Lust, too."

That caught my attention. But she quickly stepped away from the subject. "Sure, life is tough. But it's easier when you have something to believe in."

"I don't get it," I said. My body sagged against the emptiness inside of me. Why couldn't I have faith? What kind of God would create people who weren't capable of believing in him? It seemed like the cruelest joke in the universe. "I just don't understand."

"Then come to church with me," Julia said.

"How can I go when I don't believe?"

"Faith comes from hearing the word of God. Give it a chance. Open yourself to the word. Sunday morning. Ten thirty."

"No, thanks." I rushed off, knowing that anything else I said wouldn't do either of us much good.

That afternoon, Mr. Sterns reminded us our projects were due on Monday. I'd fallen behind schedule when Mom got hurt. But I figured I'd be okay. The first eight stories were all set. I only needed two more. It was Friday. I could write both stories by Saturday night, then polish them on Sunday. No problem.

I got started right after school. Nothing came at first. But I didn't worry. I knew I'd get an idea sooner or later. I'd have bet my life on it. I typed a couple sentences, then deleted them. Tried another opening. Killed that one, too.

Friday evening came and went. Saturday morning, after having breakfast with Mom, I returned to my room. Two stories. Due Monday.

Nothing.

I waited.

Still nothing.

I took a walk around the block. That often helped kick my mind into high gear. I came back, out of breath from the fast pace.

Nothing.

Lunch.

More time staring at the monitor. Nothing.

Dinner.

Back to the computer.

Something.

An idea, fully formed. A gift from the creative regions of my skull. I loved when that happened. Usually, I just got an idea for a scene, a character, or a chunk of the plot. Sometimes I started with nothing more than a line of dialogue. Not this time. The whole story rose into my mind—plot, characters, setting— blooming in one glorious piece. It was all I could do to type fast enough to keep up with the images flooding my head. Wow.

It's the greatest feeling in the world. I'd created a whole story, a miniature universe, from nothing. And I saw that it was good.

One down.

My brain was fried. I decided to get some sleep. I'd write the other story Sunday morning. It would come. I knew that beyond any doubt. I slept deeply but woke early.

One to go. I let my mind wander, trying to pluck an idea from the stream. Time passed. I thought about going out for another walk.

The phone rang. I ignored it.

"Telephone," Mom called from downstairs.

Damn. Any interruption could kill the flow. I picked it up in my room. "Hello?"

"Hi. It's me. Julia. I wanted to see if you felt like coming to church."

"I can't," I told her, relieved to have a ready-made excuse. "I have to finish my project."

"Oh . . ." There was a pause. Then she said, "How's it going?"

"Not bad. I wrote a story last night. One more and I'm done." I felt a bit of the barrier between us dissolve as I talked. I'd built the wall. It was my job to remove it.

"You're amazing. You've got a true gift."

"Not really." It didn't seem special to me. I wrote stories. Big deal. I had a hard time understanding people who claimed they weren't creative. It was like hearing someone say he didn't know how to breathe.

"Where do you get all those ideas?" Julia asked.

"They just come. I don't try to examine it." That was as good an answer as I could give. The ideas always came. Sometimes, like last night, I had to wait awhile. But, sooner or later, I knew I'd get an idea. I couldn't explain how it worked, but I was sure it always would. The words were there when I needed them. The words never failed to come.

My word . . .

The random pieces of the universe came together. If I hadn't been sitting, I might have fallen to my knees. As it was, I let the hand holding the phone drop to my lap. It took me a moment to notice that Julia was still talking. I raised the phone back to my ear.

". . . guess I'll see you Monday, then."

"Yeah. Bye." I put the receiver down. "Faith," I whispered, giving voice to my revelation.

I couldn't see or touch the source of my ideas. But I believed in it. It had no name, and no face, but I knew it was an endless fountain. I had faith. Rock solid faith. Not religious faith. But faith in something unseen. Faith in something mysterious and magical. Something wonderful.

All these years, I had true faith, and never saw it for that. It was so simple. I'd been a believer all my life.

I put my fingers back on the keyboard. One more story. Piece of cake. My eyes drifted to my clock. Ten fifteen. I could just make it. I rushed down the stairs, said bye to Mom, then hurried out.

I ran into Julia outside the church. She grinned when she saw me. "I'm so glad you came. You finished your last story already?"

"No. I'll do that this afternoon."

"You sure?" she asked.

"Absolutely."

"Great. Come on." Julia grabbed my hand. We ran up the steps and into the church. Once inside, she let go. I guess church wasn't the place for hand-holding. But the warmth of her touch lingered.

On the way down the aisle, I stopped for a moment as

another sensation hit me. I couldn't help laughing as I realized what I was feeling.

"What's so funny?" Julia asked.

"I'll tell you later." I reached up to scratch my nose, then let my hand fall. I was in no hurry to get rid of this itch. Maybe it was a sign. Or maybe it was just my hormones kicking into high gear from the touch of her hand.

We sat and waited for the service to begin. I didn't know what lay ahead, but I was open to anything and eager to discover where this new plot twist would lead me.

DAVID LUBAR

Goodness, how'd I end up in such a monumental collection? I am, for the most part, a fairly shallow person. My thoughts tend to center on food, beverages, the TV schedule, and other primitive essentials. My books often have monsters on the cover. I leave the heavy thinking to trained professionals— priests, rabbis, bartenders, and the like. But I did have one grand revelation. Here's how it happened. On a Sunday in 1995, I realized I hadn't written any fiction for a whole week. So I sat at my computer, determined not to leave empty-handed. Eventually, an idea came and I wrote a story. While describing the experience to a friend, I was struck by the same insight that Mike has in "Words of Faith."

Later, I used this revelation as the core of another story. That story was about a girl named Faith. When I submitted it to our fearless editor, she told me that the girl sounded like a boy. She suggested I switch to a male character, and recommended a variety of other excellent changes. Lisa gets credit for pulling a solid story from the mishmash I'd created. Just to prove how difficult her job was, here's the original opening: *It's ironic that Mom named me Faith, since I don't seem to have any. Too bad she hadn't named me Excess Fat. I'd certainly love going through life without any of that.* In hindsight, I can see where this was a bit heavy-handed. Thank God for editors. (And for other writer friends. The stunningly talented Dian Regan also provided some crucial suggestions.)

As for my own beliefs, I've already mentioned that I'm not very deep. But, since I've been given this space to share my thoughts, let me peer into my soul and see what's brewing. Hey, I found some insulin. Wait, that's my pancreas. Let me check over here. Okay, I found some sound bites. Here goes. Faith is good, as long as nobody gets hurt. Be nice to people whenever possible. If it feels wrong, it probably is. The universe is very big. See—pretty shallow. I warned you. Hard to believe I was a philosophy major.

If you've gotten this far, I have to assume you're someone who compulsively finishes anything you start, so I guess I can safely make a transition to the part where I talk about myself and give a couple of plugs for my books. I've been writing since way back. I live in Pennsylvania with my wife, daughter, and three cats. I've also designed scads of video games. You can visit me online at www.davidlubar.com. My latest books include *Hidden Talents* (an ALA Best Book for Young Adults), and *Dunk* (October 2002). *Dunk* is a novel about the healing power of laughter. I think it's the best book I've ever written, even though I didn't get any help on it from Lisa.

That's all. Except to wish you faith, peace, and happiness. And maybe a cat or two.

THE EVIL EYE

BY DIAN CURTIS REGAN

I notice her on my first day of high school at Escuela de Puerto La Cruz.

How can I not? We sit at opposite ends of a palm-lined court-yard. I watch her as she watches others. Her near-black eyes and permanently-tanned skin match other Venezuelan *chicas* I spent the weekend gaping at on Lido Beach—hotties every one.

The majority of girls here at EPLC in Puerto La Cruz, Venezuela, are American, not dark, exotic beauties. A few South American kids attend this international school, which caters to families sent overseas by oil companies, but no one turns my head the way she does.

After three weeks I've seen her only a few times—odd in such a small school, but she isn't in any of my classes. Usually she's hanging around the guardhouse outside the gates, having a smoke and flirting with hired vigilantes toting sawed-off shotguns. I don't know her name, but it doesn't stop me from giving her one: Diosa. Spanish for goddess.

Today is Friday and I've stayed after to watch a video in the library on trekking to Angel Falls. Dad promised we'd go.

Mom and Jules, my taking-a-break-from-college-to-work-on-her-tan sister, won't join us since the only way in is by single-engine plane.

Gack, Ben, a total guy trip, Jules told me. *May I have your CD collection after you plunge to your death in the toy plane?*

"Hey."

I glance up from the TV screen.

It's *her.* Diosa. Ohmygod. I hit the "Stop" button and stare. "Are you talking to me?" Immediately, I am mortified by my stupid response.

She smiles in that *you're an idiot, but I'm too nice to tell you* way as she perches on a tabletop like she owns the library. "Your face is frowning."

Frowning? Oh, right. From recalling Jules's "plunging to your death."

"You okay?" the goddess asks.

I am smitten by her charming accent. "Sure," I answer, laughing for no apparent reason as my nervous fingers attempt to rewind the video.

"Well," she continues, "I wish you peace."

Odd thing to say. Reminds me of Father Jacoby back home at St. Monica's.

Diosa stands and studies me as if I'm her science project. "You're new."

"Yeah. My dad transferred here a few weeks ago. Mid-November."

"Any friends yet?"

My BS meter tilts toward high. She's asking if I've made friends? Like she cares? No way.

I grab my backpack and follow her through the courtyard, waving at Rafael, the janitor. "Haven't gotten to know people— yet." I shrug as if it doesn't matter that I've left all my buddies behind in Houston. I don't mention Mike, a guy who's befriended me in homeroom. He's quite the geek; I doubt she knows him.

Look who you're calling a geek, Ben Munger.

I hate it when my inner voice sounds like Jules.

"Hey," Diosa says. "A few meet for church on Friday nights. Want to come? I go now to catch the bus."

Church? She's asking me to go to CHURCH?

I'm still in shock that she's even noticed me, and now she wants to hang out? My inner wiring is about to boing.

She is soooooo out of your league.

I know, Jules. Get out of my head.

"Well, come if you want. Oh, and *perdóneme,* my name is Ludy."

"Ludy," I repeat, filing "Diosa" away for later. It'll be my pet name for her when we become an item at EPLC. Ha. "I'm Ben."

She shakes my hand, causing my socks to ignite. "*Mucho gusto,* Ben."

Reluctantly, I release her hand and watch her walk away. "Yeah, okay, thanks," I call.

Yeah, okay, thanks? What kind of lame response is that? GO, you idiot. Say YES.

I watch her disappear through the school gates. My engineer-to-be brain is a jumble of Brand New Information, trying logically to sort it out. Choices for Friday night:

1. Dinner with family. Watch local TV and try to figure out what the hell they're saying. (Assignment for Spanish class.)

2. Go with the goddess who obviously WANTS you.

"Ludy!" I holler. "Wait up!"

The vigilantes at the guardhouse hoot and whistle as I rush past.

Wanton lust needs no translation.

While we wait for the bus, I call home on the mandatory cell phone expat kids with Orion Oil must carry. No one is there, so I leave a message: I am going to church (ha) with a friend (HA) and don't know what time I'll be home (whoo hoo).

Ludy drops her cigarette into the gutter and squishes it with one sandal. I notice three toe rings, an ankle bracelet, and *azul* nails, the same shade as the Caribbean on cloudless days. Above her ankle is a tattoo of a coiled snake wearing a crown.

There is nothing worse than dead air space between a *diosa* and a geek. My mind flounders for an intelligent conversation starter. "So, how did you get so good at English?" I ask, hoping the question isn't insulting.

"My father is Canadian. He live in Montreal," she answers in a clipped tone.

Sounds like a touchy subject. Before I can ask more questions, a rickety city bus arrives. Stumbling down the aisle, I ignore stares. My light hair, Nikes, and University of Texas T-shirt all shout that I'm American. (*North* American.) I wonder what the locals are thinking.

They're not looking at you.

Oh, right. I watch Ludy choose an empty seat with the

least-ripped vinyl, and remind myself I'm with her. I want to shout it to everyone on the bus, but my Spanish sucks, hence the effect would be lost. Instead, I comment on her tattoo and she tells me it's an anaconda.

As the bus lurches forward, it occurs to me I have no idea where we're going, yet still, I'm thrilled. *Pathetic!*

We barrel down a back street to avoid traffic jams through Puerto La Cruz. No air-conditioning. Great. I try a window, but it barely opens, letting in humid air that does not cool me. Peering out the smudged glass, I see dirty concrete buildings, stray dogs, and too many people loitering late afternoon for me to believe they're employed.

This whole city needs a coat of paint. I shudder at the depressing sight of garbage, graffiti, and raging poverty. The scenery is the same around our fancy apartment building. I am used to Houston's clean streets, lined with glitzy strip malls. Landscaped boulevards. Fancy dogs on leashes. No tattered women on street corners, frying *arepas.* I wonder where Ludy lives, but don't know if I should ask.

The bus leaves the city and starts up a narrow road into the mountains. LOS ALTOS DE SUCRE, a sign reads. *Hey, where are we going?*

"Uh, Ludy, about the church. Where exactly is it?" I cannot believe how asinine this question sounds, but I'd assumed she was taking me to Mass somewhere near the school. In this Catholic country, any number of cathedrals would be a short bus ride away.

"Oh," she exclaims as if she's forgotten to fill me in. "We meet on the mountain. At Mundo Nuevo. You will see."

Even I know that Mundo Nuevo means New World, but it tells me nothing. The bus twists and turns up steep grades. I figure the vehicle was purchased—used—forty years ago. I hope they've serviced the brakes since then. I try not to remember movies in which buses in South America plummet over cliffs.

Hail, Mary, full of grace. The Lord is with thee. This time, my inner voice sounds like Father Jacoby—not Jules.

I cannot help but admire the lush mountains in the fading light. I can see them from our apartment. The range borders the city, roller coastering along the horizon, trailing to a stop on a flat Caribbean beach.

I hate awkward silences. Why isn't Ludy talking? Chatter is so much easier for girls. I can smell her Patchouli perfume—the current rage at EPLC. I try not to let the sexy scent affect me. She is incredibly adorable in her tight shirt, with ceramic beads circling her perfect neck. But her face is pinched by unpleasant thoughts. (Hence, the silence?)

Why can't I ask what's wrong? I am tongue-tied. I am a wimp. A wimpy geek. I am *beyond* pathetic.

I pretend we are boyfriend and girlfriend. Her dainty hand is gripping the seat. I want to casually pick it up and hold it, but not even a galleon of macho Spanish conquistadors could talk me into it. *Get real, Munger.*

Why is she gripping the seat? Something is definitely bugging her. I hate myself for not having the nerve to make her tell me.

The bus squeals to a stop. My head whips around, trying to see what's going on. I tense at the sight of Guardia Nacional soldiers hoisting rifles, swarming like flies around the nose of the bus.

"An *alcabala*," Ludy explains. "Check point. It's okay—routine stuff. *Tranquilo.*"

Any time guys with machine guns board a bus to inspect the passengers, it is not okay. I slump, attempting to remain tranquilo and try not to look so American. They leave me alone. I wonder if it's because I'm with a Venezuelan.

The trauma-drama ends quickly, yet Ludy's tense silence still sits between us. I don't understand. Did I do something dumb? Say something wrong? I want to hurry and get to the church so we'll have other kids to talk to. Maybe then Ludy will relax.

The bus turns off the main road, stopping along the way to let people off and on. Ludy grows more agitated, which totally befuddles me. Finally she opens her waist pack and pulls out a red ribbon with a charm on the end.

"Put this on," she whispers, shielding it from curious eyes.

Confused, I take the charm—a tightly closed fist, carved from a red seed. "What is it?"

Her brows furrow, as if she's deciding how much to tell me. A sudden urge to kiss her makes me lean close. The unexpected surge of hormones startles me. I restrain myself. Ha.

"It is called an *azabache*. We pass the gateway into the commune of Maria de la Noche. Up here is much spiritualism. I give you protection."

My good Catholic upbringing triggers alarm at the word "spiritualism." Communicating with the departed? That topic was a no-no back at St. Monica's.

Ludy slings the red ribbon around my neck, tucking the

azabache beneath my shirt, out of sight. "The fist will catch the *mal de ojo*—the evil eye—so no harm will come. The red seed turns black when it snatches wicked energy."

I cannot believe what I'm hearing. "Uh . . . the evil eye?"

Exasperation drops her voice to an irritated whisper. "I am not meant to tell you this *or* give the cure. But if any who possess the power of the evil eye use it against you, the fist will capture the curse."

"Curse?" I hoot loud enough to make people stare even more.

Ludy shushes me, and I feel embarrassed.

The bus *bump bumps* to a stop in a small *pueblo*. We hand the driver a thousand *bolivares*—a little over a dollar. Now we are alone on a hilly street lined with concrete *casas* painted in vivid blues, greens, and yellows.

Five seconds later, niños and niñas swarm from every *puerta*, buzzing like mosquitoes, picking and poking at our clothes. I hand out coins and am immediately sorry. The circle tightens until I cannot move. It rattles me. What if they strip me of my money, ID, and cell phone as quick as a school of piranhas?

You're afraid of children?

Pissed, I snatch back my Nokia from a small hand and shove it deep into my pocket. "Can we get out of here please?"

"¡Metase en la casa!" a woman shouts. The children melt into doorways and we are alone again in the street. The woman recognizes Ludy and begins to make the sign of the cross over and over. *"Salga de aqui,"* she growls.

I wonder if the woman is disgusted by Ludy's tight clothes, tattoo, and heavy makeup, but something tells me it's more.

She's encountered Ludy before; I can sense it. The woman tells us again to get out of there. Ludy obeys but stares her down.

The exchange chills me. I wait for Ludy to explain, but she says nothing.

We hike into the rain forest. The mountain air feels cooler than city air. In the dusk, mist lingers over the vines, casting silvery streaks on every leaf. I breathe in the freshness of the virgin forest as I slap at mosquitoes. We are following a path overgrown with wild red poinsettias. I wish Mom and Jules could see them; they'd go crazy and want to pick basketfuls for the holidays.

Thoughts of my family jerk me back to the present. What am I doing? Following a stranger into a forest in a foreign country? On the pretense of going to church? Am I crazy? *Think with your head, Ben, not other body parts.*

Jules, again.

"Hey, Ludy, stop. We need to talk."

She scrinches her face, as if wondering why it's taken me so long to question her.

"When you invited me to church, I assumed you meant Mass—with other kids from school. That's *not* what's happening here. What's the deal?"

Hesitating, she plucks a mango-colored blossom from a vine and absently rips off the petals one by one.

He loves me; he loves me not. I think. Ha, like that's what she's wondering.

"There are many ways to worship," Ludy begins. "Our beliefs are based in your Catholic Mass, but flavored with other religions in the West Indies. The Church of Maria de la Noche offers a peace you've never known, love, acceptance, and total revenge against your enemies."

Her halfhearted presentation sounds rehearsed; the English perfect. She's got me with the peace, love, and acceptance stuff, but . . . revenge? Is that in the Bible? My answer springs from memories of sixth grade with Sister Rachel: " '*Vengeance is mine,*' saith the Lord." I can hear the sister's drawly voice adding an emphatic: "What the Lord *means,* people, was that *we* aren't supposed to avenge our enemies, *He* is."

"Do you know Rastafarianism?"

"Sure. Bob Marley and the dreadlocks thing. Reggae music." What they actually *believe,* however, I haven't a clue.

"Do you know Santeria from Cuba?"

"Um, no."

"The Kali cult in Trinidad and Tobago or the Maldevidan cult in Martinique?"

I squint at her in the dusky light. Is this still part of the presentation? What happened to my sexy Diosa and her Spanglish?

"The Earth People in Port of Spain?" she continues. "Voodoo in Haiti? Pocomania in Jamaica? We have adopted the best ideals of each belief, making ours a superior religion."

The word *voodoo* shakes me. What ideals could they possibly adopt from a religion based on black magic? To lighten things up, I say, "Pocomania? Isn't that Spanish for 'a little crazy'?" I give her a playful nudge. "You're inventing these religions, aren't you?"

Ludy glares at me. "What you do not know about spiritualism can hurt you. Badly. I see unwanted babies die because of the mal de ojo—an easy solution for the mother. I see members send illness and *mal* fortune to any who cross them. To any they envy. Or send death to a man so they can take his wife." Whirling, she starts off down the path.

Whoa. She's creeping me out. This is not going the way I'd hoped.

"Hey, wait," I call after her. Annoyance overrules my desire to impress her. "Why did you bring me here? What are these things you're not supposed to tell me? And why *are* you telling me? What am I not understanding?"

Stopping again, she covers her face with both hands.

"Ludy?" I pull her hands away. Tears moisten her eyes.

"Look," she says. "Forget it. We go back and catch a bus to the city. Come."

Relief gives me hope that the night can be saved. We'll go back to Puerta La Cruz, to Plaza Mayor for a *hamburguesa*. Do something totally normal for a Friday night.

Before we take one step, a man in a multicolored poncho blocks our getaway. "Bueno!" He seems very pleased to see us as he herds us back up the path. *"Un recluta!"*

Recluta? I do not know the word, but I hate how much it sounds like "recruit." Am I being recruited? By the Church of Maria de la Noche? Mary of the Night? How anti-Catholic does that sound?

Hail Mary, full of grace, the Lord is with thee. This time, the voice is mine and I mutter the complete prayer three times. A sudden need for spiritual protection strips me of any delusion I had of being cool enough to attract this girl.

We come to a circle of huts built of palm fronds and pale slabs of rock. In the center a fire leaps and crackles. A goat, stuck through with a bamboo stick, is roasting—head and tail attached. I want to barf.

The man steers me into a candle-lit hut. It smells of wet clay. Pottery and ceramic figures line the walls. Figures of snakes.

Ludy disappears. I do not want her to disappear. A señora beckons me to sit at a table carved of redwood. Bangles adorn her bare arms. On her shoulder is a tattoo of a coiled anaconda wearing a crown, identical to Ludy's.

Curiosity, plus an insane eagerness to please Ludy, are the only things that keep me from bolting. Those, and the fact that it's dark and I do not know the way home.

I am pissed at myself for getting into a situation I do not understand.

The señora serves tea and *cachitos.* This is good because it's dinnertime and I am starving. The tea is sweet and thick. I cannot nail the flavor, nor can I stop sipping it. She begins to speak in a soothing voice—in English, which amazes me. "With us, you will find your heart's desire," she says. "With us, you will find comfort."

The word "cult" slams me in the gut. Ludy had used it earlier. This time I pay attention, yet it just doesn't seem like an evil word. Didn't all great religions begin as cults? As small groups following Jesus? Or Muhammad? Buddha or Confucius? Hiding out in mountains like these?

Cults aren't necessarily evil, I tell myself, trying to be rational and calm myself at the same time. Then it hits me like the delayed punch line of a bad joke. Ludy's earlier rant about the horrors of spiritualism was about *this* cult. She wasn't giving me vague warnings or hearsay, but telling me things she'd actually seen: Members sending illness to enemies, death to unwanted babies, destruction to men whose wives they coveted.

These people are dangerous. That voice was mine, chorused with Jules and Father Jacoby. Mom was in there. And possibly even St. Monica herself.

Where is Ludy? I glance out an open window. People are gathering around the fire in the misty gloom, dressed in earth-colored ponchos. They are chanting in Spanish. My mind shifts into denial and focuses on the bus ride home. I want to leave, yet I dread riding in the dark on the steep, winding road. I so wish I hadn't come.

Between the heat and the tea and EPLC's ridiculously early bell, I feel drowsy. *What's in this stuff?* I force myself to stop drinking.

My brain is synapsing in slow motion, yet I replay the past few hours. Ah, *now* I understand Ludy's questions: *"Are you new here? Do you have any friends?"* The truth strips away the rest of my teen-guy delusions. She was looking for a loner. A loser. I was the weak antelope, separated from the herd by the tiger.

Panic counteracts my slowed reflexes, jump-starting my pulse. The señora is joined by two men in panchos. They gaze intently into my eyes, mumbling in Spanish. I try to look away, but cannot keep from glaring back at them. The words *evil eye* slither like an anaconda into my brain. I want to lift the table and shove it into their faces, then get the hell out of here, but I can barely command my eyes to blink.

I grasp the azabache beneath my shirt, then jerk my hand away, not wanting anyone to notice and take it from me. *Hail Mary, hail, Mary, hail Mary.* Forget the stupid seed charm. I'd rather rely on the word of God to battle whatever nightmare they are trying to plant in my mind.

Ludy betrayed me. Man, I'm gullible.

The señora offers more tea, but I shove it away, angering her. She gets into my face: "Do you not want unconditional love? Total serenity? Absolute freedom?"

I am picking up venomous vibes from her I cannot explain. The air pulses with a black energy that feels alive. It coils around me, intent on burrowing into my veins. I think the floor is crawling with snakes, but I'm not sure if I'm imagining it. Hissing voices swirl around my head, spoken from fanged jaws with forked tongues.

I drop my head onto the table and doze. My mind is filled with rain forest mist. I think of home, yet can barely picture my mother's face. When I wake, it's completely dark and I'm alone. Flames from the fire outside lap through the window, glimmering menacingly on the walls. How many hours have passed? I've *got* to call home. By now, Mom has probably notified security at Orion Oil. I'm in deep trouble.

I reach for my cell phone, but it's gone. So are my wallet, watch and ID. How could I have been so stupid?

Whatever drug they gave me is wearing off. I slog to the window, kneeling on the dirt floor to watch. People are swaying and chanting. Some are dancing close to the fire, half naked, whirling in a frenzy. Cages of snakes—anacondas?—are stacked everywhere. Then I notice some of the dancers entwined with the glistening serpents. Gross!

What do they want with me? A virgin to sacrifice? I try to laugh at the absurdity but cannot. I watch a man rear back his head. Blood arcs from his mouth toward the fire. The flames explode, sparking higher. Now I can see the wispy image of a naked woman, blood red, writhing in the flames.

"Holy shit!" I leap to my feet, shaking my thick head to look again. I swear the image is still there. The blood has turned into a fire spirit.

Beyond the flames, a girl tears at her clothes and drops onto all fours. She howls like a wounded wolf, then lopes off into the rain forest. Demon possessed?

Terror backs me against the far wall. *I've got to get out of here.*

The door is locked. I am breathing so hard, I think everyone can hear me. I cannot crawl out the open window because it's in full view of the fire. The other window is locked from the outside.

While numbed brain searches for a plan of escape muffled noise stops my heart. It's Ludy, at the back window, giving a sign to stay quiet. Seeing her does not calm me. She no longer looks like my diosa; she looks like the instigator of my worst nightmare.

Ludy unhooks the window lock and I shimmy out. She is wearing a poncho like the others. I do not know whether to thank her or run from her.

She shoves a tiny bottle at me. "Ben, drink this."

"What? How stupid do you think—?"

"Listen! This will cancel what they gave you. You must stay alert to get away."

I gape at her. "You got me into this and now you want to rescue me? What kind of weird game are you playing?"

"My heart change," she shoots back. "Now, *drink.*"

Cursing, I take the bottle and chug a liquid as sweet as the poison tea. "I am trusting the enemy," I mutter.

Ludy grabs my hand. "*Vente conmigo!*" she hisses. "Come with me!"

We stumble through underbrush. I am hoping we don't run into any anacondas now that I know there are plenty about. Minutes later, we intersect the path, lit by torches. Ludy slows and walks beside me. "I need to explain," she begins.

My insides are still dashing down the pathway. "Explain *later*. Let's hustle."

Ludy remains calm. I cannot *believe* she's stalling. "Look," I yelp, "they're gonna notice I got away and come after me." I hate the way my voice is quivering.

She grabs my flailing arms. "*No problema.* They know you leave. Black magic is strong. The eyes of a snake are always open."

She pauses while I let that sink in.

"They no come for you because they know you are with me, and they know I will not let you get away."

"But you said—"

"Yes, and I mean it. I help you. They want me to start process on the bus to open your soul to their trickery, but I cannot. I do not want to be part of the church anymore. I run from them, too. They brainwash me—they think. I let them believe it."

We hurry on in silence, putting space between us and them. I stifle my fight-or-flight instinct, still unsure if I can trust her. "So, why did you join such a wacko church?"

She pushes hair back from her face as she considers the question. "I believe their lies. They help me with the betrayal I feel when my father leave. My mother, she move us from our villa to a hut. She clean houses for food until two months ago when she . . ."

The sudden tears tell me what Ludy is trying to say.

"Wait a minute. Your mother is . . . is gone and your father's in Canada?" *Bingo.* I am slowly figuring it out. "You don't even go to EPLC, do you? You just hang around the school, looking for victims."

Ludy flinches. "I had no place to live, so I stay at the commune. I—I see things, Ben. Horrible things. I cannot stay."

The eyes holding my gaze now look far older than sixteen. "But you're leaving the church," I remind her. "That's good. You'll be fine." I feel empowered to be the one comforting her.

She begins to walk faster. "My plan was to bring the church a new convert to distract their suspicions away from me so I could disappear. I do not recruit; you are my first."

How ironic. "I'm honored to be your only victim," I say, but the jest falls flat.

Ludy stumbles on the path. I grab her arm and she places a hand over mine. "I am sorry, Ben. Yes, I pick a . . . a *victim* as you say. When you did not come out from the school this afternoon, I went to look for you. First time I am ever inside the building." She glances at me to let me know my theory about her not attending EPLC is correct.

"In the bus," she adds, "my . . . what is the word? Conscience? It would not let me go on with deception. I mean, you are a nice guy."

I listen, finding it hard to hate someone I am so attracted to.

"Where will you go?"

"My father send a ticket to come for Navidad after he learn of my mother's death. I will beg him to let me stay in Canada."

"Wait a minute. Why would your dad not let you stay?"

Ludy is quiet for so long, I start to repeat the question.

"My father, he want me to visit, but not stay. He has an American wife and niños. I do not fit with his family. He wants me to live here with my aunt in Caripe, but if he send me back, the church will find me, and . . . and they punish . . ."

I start to ask *how* they punish, but she gives me a *you don't want to know* look.

We leave the rain forest and enter the pueblo. "Where can I find a phone?" I ask.

Ludy actually chuckles. "No phones here. No service in the mountains."

I sigh. Just my luck. "Well, then, where do we catch the bus?"

"Ben, there is no bus until morning."

"What?" I cannot imagine the hell I'm putting my family through. "Then, how—" I forget what I'd started to say because the same woman who ran us off earlier is suddenly walking toward us. It's the middle of the night. What is she doing out here?

She and Ludy exchange words in Spanish. Ludy's tone is pleading; the woman's voice is gentle. She beckons us to follow her.

"Come," Ludy tells me. "She is a curandera. She can chase away black magic and break the power of the evil eye."

I scoff but follow. "How'd she know we were coming?"

The woman stops. *"Perdone mi Inglés,"* she says. "The Lord—He tell me."

A mixture of awe, respect, and fear straightens my spine. Is there really such a thing as good spirits battling bad spirits? I want an answer, but I'm afraid to know.

We follow the woman to her tiny *casa,* a one-room hut, sparsely furnished. An alcove in one corner is a gaudy shrine to the Virgin Mary. Benevolent glass eyes beckon us. Incense sweetens the air. Candle flames reflect off bare walls, reminding me of the fire spirit. I shiver.

Ludy stays outside the door and refuses to come in.

The woman makes me kneel in front of the shrine. She prays.

Honestly, I feel fine. Not bewitched or cursed or damned. Do I credit all those Hail Marys? Surely not the azabache. Touching the woman's arm, I interrupt. *"No necesito,"* I say. "I'm okay. *Estoy bien.*"

She looks at me as if it's understood. "*Si,* you have faith. I no pray for you, *mi hijo.* I pray for *la chica.*"

Whoa.

I realize Ludy is crying. Rising, I move to the door. She's huddled on the step, shaking and sobbing. "Ludy, come inside."

"I can't," she whispers.

"She wait on the Lord," the woman says as if she's prepared to settle in for a long night. Her prayer voice segues into a rhythm as she begins to sing praises.

I may have been slow to realize what was happening at Mundo Nuevo, but I realize what's happening now. The curandera is exorcising Ludy—not me.

I sit on the floor, unsure what to do—except pray. I pray

every memorized prayer I learned at St. Monica's, then make up new ones of my own. I'm so buzzed from whatever Ludy made me drink, it's hard to sit still.

As the hours pass, Ludy inches toward the altar. The tears and trembling never subside. I want to hold her, yet I sense that what I'm doing is a lot more helpful.

Finally, the woman rises and extends her arms. Ludy falls into the embrace, whimpering as if in physical pain. The woman anoints her with oil, blessing her in the name of the Father, the Son, and the Holy Spirit three times.

I am exhausted.

We are safe. We are free. The cult of Maria de la Noche has no power over us.

The sun is rising by the time we settle in to sleep, Ludy and I, on mats on the floor. I hold her hand and whisper calming words to my diosa. I know that when we wake, the bus will come and take us down the mountain. Then, a plane will take her away. This does not make me sad because I want her as far from here as possible.

I think how this night has changed me. Put my faith to the test. Verses memorized in Sister Rachel's class seemed so remote at the time, but their truth blazed bright in the darkness of a horrible night: *I shall fear no evil for thou art with me.*

In a few hours, I'll return to the life of an average expat kid—yet a lot less trusting. Especially of pretty girls. I squeeze Ludy's hand, wondering if, perhaps, there will be a trip to Canada in my future, too.

In the leaf-dappled light of early dawn, I pull the azabache from beneath my shirt. The red seed has withered and turned black. My engineer-to-be brain tells me that any seed plucked from a branch will wither and darken. The part of me that believes in the mal de ojo has an entirely different explanation.

DIAN CURTIS REGAN

The fictitious Church of Maria de la Noche is loosely based on a real cult in the mountains of Venezuela: the cult of Maria Lionza. All other religions and cults mentioned are real. Even Pocomania.

Venezuela is considered the "least religious" of the South American Catholic countries. A strange mix of Catholicism and spiritualism exists. For example, a prayer to Maria Lionza mentions Jesus as well as encouraging one to say three "Ave Marías." Many followers consider themselves Catholic, yet attend rituals to obtain spiritual and material help by entering into agreements with spirits and offering "blood sacrifices."

In addition to praying over a mal de ojo victim—a Curandera might also rub a fresh hen's egg over the body to absorb negative energy. Afterward, when the egg is broken, the yolk is scrambled and the white is smoky from the absorbed evil.

As for those who possess the power of the evil eye, if their negative energy is too strong, they must look at their own children through a mirror so as not to inadvertently put a curse on them.

In Caracas, there is a statue to honor the "Protector of the waters; the Goddess of the harvest," Maria Lionza.

Special thanks to: Maria Zerpa Scaglia de Rocha
and Zorny Machado Decan de Hilton

> > >

Dian Curtis Regan (Diana Curtis French de Regan) is the author of many books for young readers, including *Princess Nevermore,* and the *Monster of the Month Club* Quartet. While researching this story, she acquired her own azabache after learning more than she wanted to know about the presence of black magic, spiritualism, and the evil eye in her own neighborhood in Puerto la Cruz, Venezuela, where she lived for three years.

She encountered expats who believed the evil eye had been used on them. She met educated Venezuelans who put azabache bracelets on their babies and went to Mass to protect themselves and their families.

In addition, her cat, Poco, was not surprised at all to learn of "his" religion, Pocomania. Dian (and Poco) have repatriated to the United States of America and presently live in Kansas. Visit her at www.diancurtisregan.com.

THE SEE-FAR GLASSES

BY MINFONG HO

As the school bus rounded the corner, Ling could see the water of Rockaway Islet through her window, glinting blue-gray in the late afternoon sun. Even before it had come to a complete stop, Ling had edged her way to the front and was the first one out when the doors swung open. Once on the pavement, she hoisted her backpack across one shoulder and breathed deeply, as if clearing out the stale air of the classrooms at the high school.

There was a strong breeze blowing, and the air was cold and moist, slightly brackish from the sea. *Perfect sailing weather,* Ling thought, and decided to take the familiar detour home that would give her a view of the open sea.

Waving a casual good-bye to her schoolmates at the bus stop, Ling walked toward the park near Long Beach. It would add a good half hour to her walk home, but the view from the beach would be worth it. She could see two sailboats flitting across the water, white sails taut against the wind. Farther away, a tugboat was pulling a barge along, and there was a chartered fishing boat, plying its way across the whitecaps. Squinting her eyes against the sun, Ling looked west toward the Manhattan harbor, and in the distance were the outlines of two freighters and a luxury cruise liner. Four, five, six, seven, Ling counted silently. Seven ships at sea, a lucky number. She smiled—her grandmother would like that.

Taking a last look at the ocean, she turned and started walking home.

It was a breezy spring afternoon, the last of the snow still crusting the tidy front lawns of her neighborhood, with the first few patches of grass already showing through. At the front yard of her house, Ling paused to examine the buds of the plum tree growing by the front door. Plumper than grains of cooked rice, each bud was still tightly furled. They had planted that tree years ago, shortly after their family had moved from southern China to New York. The first spring when the plum blossoms had burst into bloom, Ling's grandmother had stroked the tree trunk tenderly. "I wonder if it's springtime in Sun Wheay, too," she had said.

Carefully Ling snapped off a twig of plum tree now. *Maybe Ah Po can make it bloom,* she thought as she walked through the front door.

"Ah Po, *ngo fan doe lay leh!*" she called. As always, Ling announced her homecoming to her grandmother as soon she walked in the house, this reversion to Cantonese almost like a password to the familiar domesticity so separate from the world outside.

"Over here!" There was a low call from the kitchen, which Ling recognized as her grandmother's greeting. Ling followed the sour smell of yeast into the kitchen and found her grandmother, elbow deep in soft white dough, kneading rhythmically.

"Grandma, I'm home," she said again, slinging her backpack onto a kitchen chair. "The snow's melted through in places, now. You can see bits of grass again."

The old woman smiled. "And the ships? How many did you count today?"

"Guess!"

Her grandmother shut her eyes in concentration. "Three," she said.

"Seven!" Ling said, and laughed. "I win!" It was a game they had played ever since Ling could remember, as they sat on the park bench near the beach and looked out to sea. One of them would guess at the number of ships out there, and the other would count them. Even now, long after the old woman had become too frail to walk to the park, and her eyes too dim to make out the passing ships, they would occasionally play at it.

"And the plum tree, is it in bloom?" her grandmother asked now.

"Not yet," Ling said to her. "But almost—see? I brought you a branch." Often, when she switched back to Cantonese after a day's usage of English, she felt a little tongue-tied, even shy.

The old woman lifted her head at the sound of Ling's voice and nodded. But her eyes stared unseeing at the flower. "Very nice," she said.

Ling sighed. It was hard to tell how much her grandmother's eyesight had deteriorated in the past few months. The cataracts in both eyes had become like opaque bits of sea-smoothed glass, but the old lady knew her way around the house so well by touch that she herself seemed hardly to notice her fading eyesight.

"Can you really see it?" Ling persisted. "Can you see the buds on it?"

"Nice buds," the old lady agreed happily. "Offer it to your grandfather."

"But . . . I meant it for you."

"And I want it for your grandfather. Go, put it in a vase and set it on the altar."

Ling knew better than to argue. There were some things that her grandmother was totally unyielding about: The family altar was one of them. Ling did as she was told, careful not to spill the water in the vase as she stretched up on tiptoe to set it on the altar.

"Did you remember to bow?" her grandmother asked when Ling came back from the little alcove in the pantry where the altar was kept.

"Yes, Ah Po."

"And did you light some incense?"

"Yes, Ah Po," Ling lied.

The old woman sniffed at the air. "I don't smell it," she said.

Ling rolled her eyes in exasperation, but she slipped off to light some incense and stuck it into the ashes of the brazier.

"Smell it now?" she asked her grandmother.

The old lady nodded in approval. "Your Ah Gung would be pleased," she said. "He always liked plum blossoms."

"I know," Ling said.

"He always insisted on picking the first plums of the season himself."

"Yes," Ling said. And offer it to his father, on the altar, she continued silently.

"And offer it to his father, on the altar," Ah Po said. Ling had only the vaguest memory of her grandfather, but she knew so many details about him that it seemed as if she had practically grown up with him.

"Go wash up and set the table for dinner," the old lady was saying now. "Your parents will be home soon."

"Wait, Ah Po," Ling said, opening up her backpack. "I have something else for you." She delved into her backpack and pulled out a pair of binoculars. They felt cold and heavy in her hands.

"Look, Ah Po," Ling said. "I have something to give you, something special."

"What you can give me, I don't need," the old lady replied. Her voice was low, almost guttural, but with that tonal lilt particular to Cantonese when it is spoken gently.

"But you don't even know what it is," Ling countered.

"I don't need to know. Everything I need, I already have."

"Everything, Ah Po? What about better eyesight? Wouldn't you like to see better?"

"Who says I cannot see now?" her grandmother asked sharply. "Is it that doctor with the hairy hands? Just because I wouldn't tell him what shapes were drawn on that silly wall poster of his?"

"But you do want to see better, don't you?" Ling amended quickly.

"I am not, absolutely not, having my eyes sliced open," the old woman said.

"I know," Ling said.

"Like a clove or garlic or what . . . talking about peeling them."

"That's why I brought you these . . . these glasses. If you can see with these things, maybe you won't need to have the cataract operation tomorrow."

The old woman tilted her chin up. "Show me," she said. "What is it?"

"Glasses . . ." Ling said. She groped for the Chinese word for binoculars. It was on the tip of her tongue. "See-far glasses, Ah Po, that's what they are! Try them!"

"See-far glasses? I've never heard of such a thing. What do I want to look at faraway things for?" She lifted her eyes and stared blankly at Ling. Cloudy with the pale thickness of accumulated years, her eyes stared at everything the same way— calm and blank like windows draped with thick curtains.

Ling stared back at her, this papaya-shaped old woman whose womb, like the seed cavity of the fruit, had held countless seeds within it. Mother of nine, grandmother of thirty-four, great-grandmother of seventeen, her seeds had burst out from her and planted themselves in ripples of huge concentric circles that extended over Asia, Europe, North America, while she, riveted at their center, held them all together. Now, in the kitchen of her eldest son's house, she spent her evenings kneading bread dough. What, after all, would she need these binoculars for?

Ling sighed, and started to slip the binoculars back into their case. She had joined some bird-watching group at the high school, just to have access to these things, *but I needn't have bothered,* Ling thought, turning away.

Sensing her retreat without even looking up, the old lady suddenly called out after Ling. "Wait!" she said. "Those see-far glasses of yours—can they see the ships at sea out there?"

Ling walked back to her, the eagerness growing in her again. "Let's try it! We could go up to the little park at Sand's Point, near the bus stop, and look out at the ships through those see-far glasses. You could count the ships for yourself, again."

"Not just the ships," the old woman said. "I want to see the shipyard, too. I haven't seen it for so long." A wisp of gray hair, worked free from the bun at the nape of her neck, dangled across her face.

Ling took a deep breath. "Ah Gung's shipyard? You mean back in China?"

"In Sun Wheay," the old woman said patiently.

"But . . . but that's so far away."

"Well, you did say they were 'see-far' glasses," the old lady chided.

"Oh, Granny . . . ," Ling murmured. "They can't see that far . . ."

Outside the kitchen window it was getting dark. The bare branches of the plum tree scraped against the windowpane as the old woman stared unseeing at it, her arms hanging limply at her side. "What good are these glasses of yours, then?" she said. "Who needs them anyway? I can see Sun Wheay well enough, shipyard and all." She smiled faintly. "Behind my eyes."

As she spoke, the glare of headlights shone into the kitchen window, briefly throwing the branches of the plum tree into silhouette against the opposite wall. Then the garage door rolled up, its metallic hinge creaking noisily.

"You haven't set the table," Ah Po said, bending down to knead the dough again, "and here we've been talking about Sun Wheay!"

The kitchen door swung open, and Ling's father stepped into the room, setting his briefcase in its usual place on the counter. "What's this about Sun Wheay?" he asked as he shrugged off his overcoat. He looked tired; his tie was loosened and his collar unbuttoned. Still, like many of his peers in a culture where aging can still be a studied grace, Mr. Li looked only as old as he chose to, his hair carefully dyed black except at the temples, where the streaks of gray gave him a distinguished look, as if he had inherited his wealth rather than made it. "Are you talking about the old days again, Ma?"

The old woman brightened at the sound of his voice. "You remember the shipyard, don't you, Ah Wah?" she asked. "You used to climb inside the empty hulls of the fishing boats your father was building, playing hide-and-seek with your sisters."

Mr. Li grimaced very slightly, but enough to signal his exasperation. "That was long ago, Ma. I don't remember."

"Maybe . . . maybe if you look through those see-far glasses Ling brought back, you could see it all again," his mother said, kneading a lump of dough in one hand.

"What glasses?" Mr. Li said, then he spotted the binoculars in Ling's hands. He frowned and turned to his daughter. "What's this for?" he said to her in English.

"I . . . I thought if she could see with these binoculars . . ." Ling faltered. It suddenly seemed a stupid idea.

"You thought that she wouldn't need to have her cataract operation tomorrow—is that it?"

Ling nodded.

"You keep out of this," he said sharply, still in English. "It's all been arranged. We're checking her into the clinic at 8:45 tomorrow. She'll have the right eye operated on first, then the other one the day after."

"But . . ."

"She cannot see anything . . . anything at all right now, with or without binoculars—don't you understand?" Abruptly he turned and left the room.

Sensing the tension, the old lady had lapsed into silence. She broke off a piece of the raw dough and shaped it into a ball. Then another, and another.

Ling joined her at the table and transferred the buns into the steamer. She knew by the slump in her grandmother's shoulders that she was feeling sad and remote. "Ah Po, about the shipyard I . . . I think I remember," she said, trying to help.

The old woman shook her head. "You," she said, "you weren't even born."

The next morning was a Saturday, so Ling could have slept late if she had wanted to. Instead, she got up even earlier than usual, feeling a vague need to help her grandmother prepare for the long-dreaded trip to the hospital. Not that there was much left to prepare—her overnight bag had been packed for days beforehand, and all the medical forms already filled out by her son. Still, Ling knew that the old lady would be nervous, and she wanted to just be on hand.

She found her grandmother where she had expected to—in front of the small family altar in an alcove between the kitchen and the dining room. From the doorway Ling watched the back-bent old woman putter around the altar. Doing everything by touch, she had dusted the altar shelf, replaced the wilted flowers on it with the yellow crocus Ling had given her yesterday, and was now sweeping the tiled floor. Carefully now she unlocked the top drawer of her mother-of-pearl inlaid cabinet, where she kept all the paraphernalia of tending the altar: tiny porcelain cups, gold-leafed sheets of ceremonial money, candles and joss sticks and countless packets of incense.

"*Jo-sun,* Ah Po," Ling said.

"Good morning," her grandmother replied. "You're up early. Why?"

So the old lady had realized it was a day she could have slept in. *There isn't much she misses,* Ling thought. "Just wanted to see if I might help with anything."

"As a matter of fact, yes," her grandmother said. "Can you fold some paper money for me? And fill the wine cups?"

"Yes, Ah Po, but it's almost eight o'clock. We'll have to hurry."

"Some things cannot be hurried," the old woman replied.

With a small sigh, Ling started to fold the gilt sheets of paper into the horned bars of traditional Chinese money, just the way she had been taught to do since she was old enough to walk. There had been a time when Ling had loved to help her grandmother tend the family altar, gleefully setting the gold and red paper money on fire so that the spirits of their ancestors would have money at their disposal in the afterlife, then smothering its ashes with cups of fragrant rice wine. But in the last few years, Ling had become embarrassed by it, especially after a visiting schoolfriend had said lightly, "All this ancestor worship stuff—it's so quaint." Ancestor worship? That sounded so stilted and unnatural to Ling. It wasn't really that Ah Po *worshiped* the spirits of her dead ancestors but that by sharing her thoughts and her food with them, she was simply including the dead in the world of the living, so that the generations of family could be linked together through the ages. Ling could not articulate this to her classmate, and she had started to distance herself from the family altar.

Yet here she was, enjoying the familiar smell of the incense and the feel of the crisp paper in her hands. She glanced over at her grandmother and marveled at how small the old lady had become. When they had first moved to America, her Ah Po had seemed to loom over her, the long loose sleeves of her shirts barely within tugging range. She had been so competent and confident then, and so available—especially when Ling's parents had been preoccupied at work, with setting up their business. Always her grandmother had been on hand, providing hot porridge, good stories, and quiet laughter in equal measure, so that there was a comforting thread of continuity between the life that Ling had known in southern China and their new life in this cold, strange land.

Gently Ling took three joss sticks from the package and lit them from the candle at the altar, just as her grandmother was doing. In synchronized motion, the two of them bowed before the wooden tablet with the names of her grandfather and great-grandfathers written on it. If the old woman was surprised that Ling was taking part in this ritual, she gave no indication of it.

"Hear me, respected father of my son," she intoned with the loud solemnity that she reserved for her conversations with the spirit world. "Tomorrow I will not be lighting you any incense, nor the day after that because I am being taken to some foreign hospital, to have my eyes sliced open, so I can see better. Your son, he wants it done, you know how insistent he can be. Yes, I am scared, just a little, but your son says it will be safe, and it will not hurt, and there are some things I so much want to see clearly again." She paused, and in the moment of silence the tendril of smoke from her joss sticks curled up sinuously. "Like your ships in Sun Wheay, the way the morning light shone on the waves there—I want so much to see that," she murmured. Then, she bowed again, and reached out to jab the joss sticks firmly into the small bronze urn.

Like her, Ling bowed again, and set her joss sticks in the urn as well. As she stepped back, she wondered softly, "Do you think he can really hear you, Ah Po?"

The old woman snorted. "Who knows? What matters is that I really want to talk to him!" Then, carefully, she shuffled back to the cabinet to put away the matches and incense, and locked the drawer up.

She had not been able to see any of the ships at Sun Wheay, of course, not even after both cataracts had been surgically peeled away, and the bandages around her eyes removed. The overnight stay at the hospital had been extended another two days, because the slight cough she'd come in with had developed into bronchial pneumonia, and the doctors had wanted to monitor her just a little longer. Instead of getting better, however, she had weakened noticeably with each passing day, so that by the time Ling and her parents came to visit on Monday afternoon, she had to be helped out of bed by Mr. Li, who supported her by her elbow as she inched her way to the window in her hospital room.

"How are you feeling, Ah Ma?" her son asked.

"I want to go home," she said.

"Soon, Ah Ma. Tomorrow, or the next day. They just want to make sure the antibiotics for your cough work. Then we'll leave."

Ling came up to the window and stood beside them.

"Do you see the view, Ah Po?" Ling asked. "We're on the nineteenth floor here."

Her grandmother squinted at the window. "It's lovely," she said without conviction. A few clouds grazed across the blue sky, and beneath them a scattering of freighters steamed across the Long Island Sound.

"There are ships," Ling said. "Can you see them?"

Ah Po straightened up with interest. "Where?" she said.

"Over there—near the wharves," Ling said, pointing.

Her grandmother turned to look in that direction, but her eyes remained blank, unfocused.

"Wait—I'll get those see-far glasses," Ling said. "Those should help." She had set them on the windowsill of the hospital room as soon as Ah Po had checked in, and left them there, almost as a talisman, a sign of faith that her grandmother would be able to use them after her cataract operation. She lifted them up now, and held them carefully against the old lady's eyes. Her veins pulsed green beneath the black lens, near her temples.

"What can you see, Ah Po?" Ling asked.

"Nothing."

"Here, try looking over this way." Ling tilted her grand-mother's head slightly, so it was angled downward toward the harbor. "Can't you see the ships? You should—these glasses are powerful, Ah Po!"

There was a long pause as the old woman blinked behind the binoculars, her eyelashes brushing against the lens. Then she smiled, and reached up to hold the binoculars for herself. "Oh yes," she whispered. "I can see, I can see it now."

"What?" Ling asked.

"The beach, the waves against the sand," she said, her voice trembling. "A skinny little boy, in torn shorts, barefoot, walking on the beach. Skipping pebbles, throwing stones at the fishing boats out at sea." She laughed, and her laugh was vibrant, subtly teasing. "I see you, Ah Wah. I see you when you were a little boy."

Beside her, Ling heard her father's sharp intake of breath.

"Mother," he said, and tried to pull the binoculars away from her. Her grip only tightened.

"I see our little house by the sea, next to the shipyard, among the half-built hulls. And there . . . there I am. My pants are rolled up to the knee, and there's that old rattan basket on my arm, filled with the little crabs that I've caught, scuttling between the seaweed on the sand. You're running along beside me, on all fours like a crab yourself, digging into the sand after them!"

"That's enough, Mother," Mr. Li said. "Let me have those things now."

Without resistance this time, the old woman handed the

binoculars to him. And when she raised her eyes back up, they were as blank as the windows of the skyscrapers nearby, blindly reflecting the afternoon light, and the smile had faded from her wrinkled face.

She never opened her eyes after that. The next day when they visited her, she had been transferred to the critical ward. The antibiotics weren't working, a doctor said. She had a particularly virulent strain of pneumonia, which was generally found only inside hospitals, and which had developed a resistance to most antibiotics. Ling listened to the buzz of medical personnel near her grandmother's bedside, but their words slid off her like water off a plastic raincoat. All she knew was that her grandmother had changed, had perhaps even disappeared somehow—and that this old woman lying there was just a shell. She lay propped on a pile of pillows, in a bed with iron railings around it—like a big crib. *My grandmother, the baby,* Ling thought, and felt her heart contract. There was a splint on Ah Po's inner arm, strapping tubes of mauve-cool blood into her veins. Another tube, hooked up to a metallic tank, fed oxygen into her nostril; yet a third was connected somehow beneath the white blanket, and dripped out tea-colored urine into a plastic bag. Amid it all, her face seemed small and shrunken—like a piece of pomelo left on the pavement to dry. Her eyes were closed, and she seemed drained of energy.

"She's asleep," Mr. Li said uncertainly.

"No, she's not," Ling said. "She's squeezing my hand right now. I think she just doesn't want to open her eyes. Please, call her. Talk to her."

"Ah Ma . . . Ah Ma . . . did you sleep well last night?" Mr. Li looked at his daughter for guidance.

"No, Dad," Ling said in English. "Talk about something that matters. Please."

Taking a deep breath, Mr. Li tried again. "Ah Ma . . . those crabs we used to catch together—didn't you use to cook them? With bits of scallion and chili?"

The old woman's eyelids fluttered open, then closed slowly. Had they imagined it, or did she almost nod?

He reached through the bars of the railing and took his mother's other hand in both of his.

"Go on," Ling whispered.

"Didn't you have a big wok," Mr. Li continued, "shiny on the inside, black with soot outside. And a charcoal fire underneath. Didn't you use to make me fan the fire as you cooked?" At first his words were halting, but then they picked up speed and strength, like the first spring drizzle turning into a hard rain.

"And didn't you carve toy boats for me, with scraps of wood from Father's shipyard, with patches of blue cloth for sails? And wasn't there some game we played—with the ships at Sun Wheay as we walked along the beach?"

This time there was no mistaking the nod. "We counted them," the old lady said, her voice barely audible.

"I remember, Ma, we would guess how many there were, before counting them."

Ling felt a shock of recognition. *That's my guessing game with her,* she almost blurted out. *So Ah Po used to play it with you, too?*

And, Ma, we . . . we will count them again," her father was

saying, "The ships at Sun Wheay. We will go back to Sun Wheay, I promise, and we will walk on the beach there again. As soon as . . . as soon as you get well. . . ." His voice broke. Abruptly he turned away, and walked over to the window staring down at the harbor below.

Ling looked at her father's slumped shoulders. She felt a surge of anger and sadness toward him so strong that she felt like shaking him. Why only now? She wanted to demand. Why hadn't you talked to her like this before? Why hadn't you taken her home to Sun Wheay, all these long years since we left? Can't you see it's too late now?

But, raised as a good Chinese daughter, Ling kept her feelings to herself. In the silence a low moan from her grandmother startled her. Ling felt her hand being squeezed tightly by the old woman. She looked down at her grandmother.

"Ah Po, what? What is it?" Ling asked.

"The key . . . ," Ah Po said with difficulty.

"What key? The key to what?"

The old woman turned her head from side to side, as if that movement might spill out the words inside her.

"The key to the altar? Ah Po, are you talking about the key to the cabinet? Where you keep the altar things?"

Opened and closed, her eyes: Yes.

"You want to tell me where it is? But I know, Ah Po. I've watched you enough. It's under the incense brazier, isn't it?"

The eyes fluttered open, and looked directly at Ling. *Maybe the cataract operation had worked,* Ling thought. *She's looking at me like she's actually seeing me.* "What else, Ah Po? Is there anything else you want to say?"

In the deepening twilight outside the hospital window, the sea was merging with the sky, with only a single thread of silver at the horizon.

Her grandmother stared at her, unblinking, and Ling thought she could detect a flicker of urgency in those glazed eyes, as she struggled to say something. Her lips quivered, moved, but there was no sound. Still, Ling felt she understood. "Yes, Ah Po," she said gently. "I will. I will tend the altar for you."

Like blinds being slowly lowered over windows, Ah Po's eyes closed, and remained closed.

The funeral was as it should be—or at least as traditional as it could be in this foreign wilderness, exactly on the other side of the world from where Ah Po had been born and raised. As the eldest son, Mr. Li took care of the arrangements, discreetly deferring to the bevy of his sisters and cousins who had flown over from Hong Kong, Singapore and Taiwan because they seemed to have such definite opinions about how things should be done. His third sister had brought a set of burial clothes, of iridescent brocade from Hong Kong, in which the old lady had been duly dressed. His wife had remembered to have the jade bracelets and earrings slipped on her mother-in-law. His second sister and two nieces had chosen the casket, selecting one that even looked vaguely Chinese, as if it were carved from a single teak tree trunk. The wake had lasted for three days and three nights, with a large photograph of the old lady propped up on a makeshift altar where her descendants could light joss sticks and bow deeply before it.

Ling looked into the casket now, and—in the midst of all these strange proceedings—she felt comforted by the familiarity of the face lying inside. Ah Po looked just as she always did, imperturbable. Her ivory skin was as delicately wrinkled as damp onionskin paper, stretched taut over her high cheekbones, and loosely over her mouth. Even in the casket, with her eyes closed, she looked as if she was frowning, worried. "It's all right, Ah Po," Ling told her silently. "I will take care of everything. I will tend the altar for you."

But how? How many times must I bow, and how do I say what I want to say? Which candles do I light; what wine do I offer; what incense do I burn? Ling pulled opened the little drawers of the cabinet by the family altar, confused by the jumble of the contents inside. Her grandmother had seemed to know exactly where everything was, and her movements in front of the altar had always been precise, almost spare. *I should have watched her more carefully,* Ling thought. *I should have asked her.*

But it's too late now, Ling thought. The funeral was long over, the cremation carried out, all the guests gone. Instead of the constant buzz of relatives and friends milling around, the house was silent and empty again. More empty than it had ever been.

Two weeks it had been now, since her grandmother's death, and still Ling was not used to this void, this awful stillness in the house when she came home from school. She had taken to staying after school or following some friends back to their houses or taking long walks along the beach—anything to delay the pain of homecoming.

Today Ling had spent a particularly long time at the beach-front park, sitting on a bench as she watched the sailboats and steamers pass by. Fifteen of them, she had counted—a record, because she had been there for so long. Only after the sun had slipped past the horizon did she get up and slowly make her way home, dragging her feet.

At the front door, she had seen that the plum tree was in bloom, its buds just starting to unfurl. Ling had twisted off a branch and brought it into the house with her. Inside, the rooms stretched out, quiet and empty. In the late twilight everything was shrouded in darkness and silence. Aimlessly Ling roamed through the house—past the living room, the dining room, the kitchen—until, without really being aware of it, she found herself at the little alcove.

There it was—the altar. There between two candles was the tablet with the names of the ancestors on it, flanked by the old photograph of her grandfather, and now her grandmother, too. The thin red stubs of burned joss sticks poked out of the incense brazier, and beside it the single plum branch, long since dried out, in its small vase. An air of neglect hung heavy over it all.

Groping through the cabinet, Ling found some matches. She lit the candles. Then she took out three joss sticks from a packet and lit them, too, holding the delicate sticks between her palms. A tendril of smoke curled up from them. Awkwardly she stepped in front of the altar and bowed three times. "Ah Po," she began, then faltered. How was she supposed to address her grandmother now that she was dead? What should she say, how was she supposed to bow afterward?

"Ah Po, I counted the ships at sea today," Ling said softly, "Guess how many there were?"

The photograph of her grandmother looked impassively at her from the altar, more stern now than she had ever been in real life.

"Fifteen," Ling whispered.

The silence surrounded her, thick and dreary.

Ling held out the branch of delicate plum blossoms toward the altar, and suddenly, with a longing so sharp that her eyes stung with it, she wished she could place it directly into her grandmother's outstretched hand.

Instead, she reached for the small porcelain vase on the altar, pulled out the dried twig from it, and carefully replaced it with the fresh one. "Ah Po, here—I picked this for you," Ling said. She swallowed, hard, then turned and walked away from the altar. Behind her, the candles cast a flickering light on the altar, lighting up the faces of the ancestors, as a tendril of incense smoke curled up around them.

MINFONG HO

I left home early—at fifteen—and was halfway around the world from my grandmother when she died in Singapore, at the ripe old age of eighty-two. I could not go back to attend her funeral, and so I did the next best thing: I wrote about her. My grandmother, whom I called Ah Po, had always kept an ancestral altar, even though her own children and grandchildren tended to scoff at her old-fashioned ways. Still, out of respect for her, and later out of habit, we all took part in the various rituals of "praying" to our ancestors.

It is in fact the act of communicating with one's ancestors, and not worshiping them, that seems crucial to me. The Western term *ancestor-worship* to describe this is very misleading, since what we are engaging in is basically a secular activity—the strengthening of the family unit by acknowledging and including everyone in it, even those who have died. It allows the living members of a family to forge a bond with the dead ones, so that the chain between us all will remain unbroken, generation after generation.

It is an outgrowth of Confucian tenets, to place such emphasis on the family and on ritual, and yet there is no contradiction between practicing that, and believing in Buddhism and often also Taoism. Most Chinese in fact have traditionally integrated the beliefs and practices of all three philosophies into their own lives. Neither Confucius, Buddha, nor Lao Tse ever claimed to be endowed with any special ties to the sacred or the divine, and none of them ever claimed a monopoly on the truth. Although all three men were—and are—revered, none of them ever professed to be anything more than a teacher.

I would like to think that it is in deference to their wisdom and humility that there have never been any wars fought in the name of Confucius, or of Buddha, or of Lao Tse. At the risk of drastic oversimplification, one could say that Confucius taught us how to behave ethically; Buddha taught us how to feel compassionately; and Lao Tse taught us how to be aware of a natural order. There is very little in any of their teachings that can be made into dogma, much less into holy causes that should be fought over.

I am grateful that, being born in Burma, raised in Thailand, and educated in Taiwan and the United States, I have absorbed—without really having been conscious of it—the live-and-let-live flexibility inherent in those societies, and which I think is the underpinning of religious tolerance. As a child, I used to be awakened at dawn by the slow beating of drums from a Buddhist monastery in Thailand; as an adolescent, I often heard the evening call to prayer from Muslim mosques in Singapore; and as an adult, I am used to hearing the tolling of Christian church bells on Sunday mornings. Different as the three sounds may be, they have always filled me with a sense of deep joy and awe, and an abiding hope that we can all coexist peacefully on this fragile earth.

In addition to this short story, I have written several others, as well as four picture books, and three young adult books set in Southeast Asia, *The Clay Marble, Rice Without Rain* and *Sing to the Dawn*. I live in Ithaca, New York, with my husband (who is of Irish Catholic descent), our three children, and one golden retriever.

GOING TO KASHI

BY UMA KRISHNASWAMI

ey, Bhagvan! Mallika sighed a little prayer in Hindi, as she did sometimes when an English version simply would not do. Oh, God—Krishanji, Ganeshji, whoever's listening—did you have to stick me in that World History class? She tried not to look too pained as Mr. Allen cranked into India gear this Friday.

The textbook wrapped the world into bite-size pieces of eye candy, and Mr. Allen treasured every nibble. India was a naked holy man covered with ashes, a group of kids throwing colored powder on one another, traffic winding its way around a cow. "What's with the dots on the forehead?" someone asked. Mr. Allen launched into an explanation about the *bindi* worn by Hindu women in one of the pictures. Mallika felt curious glances darting her way.

I'd rather be anywhere else but here, she thought. *I'd rather be—I know, I'd much rather be at the TheaterWorks audition!* She'd looked forward to the community theater audition for months. She allowed herself to sink comfortably into thinking about it. She saw herself going on stage, taking a breath. At the precise moment she was about to begin her reading, Mr. Allen's voice broke into the daydream. "And what can you add to our picture of India, Ms. Parmar?" he quipped, and everyone laughed.

In the weekend that followed, Mallika's pot of resentment filled some more because Mom got an e-mail message from Mr. Allen. "Something about owing him homework." She waved the printed message at Mallika. Worse, she insisted Mallika finish every last scrap of the homework before heading out to the TheaterWorks audition, on what would otherwise have been a perfect Sunday afternoon. "Homework first, TheaterWorks later," said Mom in triumph. She said it a couple of times, as if she'd discovered a rare form of poetry. Mallika finished the homework, hating Mr. Allen and his class with every savage stroke of her pen.

Of course, she was late to the audition, and she fumbled her reading. Louise, the artistic director, was sympathy in black silk. "Darling, you're good, but you need to relax." Louise had no last name. She signed herself Louise! with an exclamation point. Her sympathy got Mallika a tiny role—three lines, a smile, an exit. It was better than nothing, but not by much.

"Relax, it'll come to you," Louise told her. "You're giving out so much nervous energy it could turn on the spotlights. Relax and the universe will come to you. Trust me."

Louise's penciled eyebrows arched at her, and Mallika had to smile.

universe, of course, has seen many stories—some sad, some joy- some just logical. For instance, long ago when time was young, the god Shiva cut off one of the heads of Brahma, the creator, to punish him for telling a lie. And since no deed, whatever its intention, can be released on the universe without a consequence, an old woman with crooked teeth began to shadow Shiva. She dogged his every footstep, ranting and cursing and laughing at him until at last he took her to the sacred city of Kashi, where the holy Ganga flows. There she disappeared, and he, god of the dance and of the dissolution of worlds, was cleansed of his dark deed.

They say going to Kashi does that.

The first time the universe brought her and the old woman into the same place at the same time, Mallika wasn't paying attention to questions of living and dying. Mom and homework and the audition failure still rankled.

Mallika's brother, Vijay, had agreed to meet her at the India Grill restaurant downtown and give her a ride back home from rehearsal. Grudgingly, because his girlfriend, Suniti, was along. But Mom had said, "Nothing doing. How can you leave Mallika to take the subway from rehearsal when you're going to see a matinee two blocks away with whatsername?"

"Anything you got for me today?" The woman leaned against the restaurant counter and tugged with crooked hands at a pendant on a black string about her neck, as if tugging helped the words out. Her face was carved into wrinkles, her mouth all squashed in for lack of teeth.

"Anything you got for me today?" Louise would have tilted her head and studied the old face, mentally nailing the lopsided gestures. ("Character, darling, it's all part of shaping yourself as an actress.") But rehearsal was done for the day and Louise was nowhere within eavesdropping distance.

Mallika stared. Vijay and Suniti, of course, saw only each

other, so that left her free to gape at anyone she liked while they waited for *masala dosa* and hot *chai*. The woman's eyes roved around the room, seeming to see only in snatches. They rested lightly on Mallika's face, and stayed there a moment in a quiet flutter, the way a moth might. Then they took off again, skimming ceiling, plants, and fake Rajput miniatures against gold-speckled wallpaper.

The restaurant owner whispered across the counter, "I've told you before—please use the back door."

Mallika couldn't hear the woman's reply, but she could tell her accent came thickly from places of roadside shrines and neon-colored billboards, far from this gray cityscape. The woman's eyes flitted around the room again, and again they lighted on Mallika in what felt like recognition.

But the man ushered the woman into the back, behind the counter, and she sagged off obediently enough through the double doors. He called after her to the kitchen, "*Arre, budhiya ko thoda dal-chaval de do, yaar.* Give the old woman some rice and lentils." He scanned the room in quick embarrassment. Mallika pretended to be fascinated by the rubber plant.

The dosa arrived—crisp, fragrant rice-flour crepes filled with spiced potatoes, with little stainless steel cups of chutney and steaming sour *sambar* on the side.

One of us, Mallika confirmed to herself with a small shock. Someone from India, homeless and waiting for handouts at this restaurant. Her family knew lots of people of Indian origin— they were all doctors or engineers or computer scientists. Or they were small business owners like the chatty couple who owned the Indian grocery store, and this man who presided over the fennel seed trays and cash register. And yet here she was, this homeless woman. Tidy her up, put a sari on her, and she'd look like one of the grandmas of kids in the Hindu temple's youth group.

"Hey, let's go." Vijay and girlfriend, Suniti, were done, temporarily distracted from the business of gazing into each other's eyes. The check had been brought and paid, the tip left on its little black tray.

"Oh, sorry." Mallika shook herself back into the here and now, and followed Vijay and Suniti past a potbellied statue of elephant-headed Ganesh, out through etched glass doors into the street.

Something lay fallen on the sidewalk—a tarnished metal pendant. Mallika barely avoided stepping on it. She bent to pick it up. Vijay and Suniti were back in communion. She could have hefted dead bodies up and they wouldn't have noticed. She slid the pendant into her pocket.

Back home, she scrubbed it with a daub of toothpaste—Mom's old household trick—and watched a silver sheen emerge. She squinted at it. The Sanskrit letter *Om* was faint from years of metal rubbing against skin. On the flip side, Lakshmi sat cross-legged on a lotus, goddess who gives and gives, and keeps on giving. For some strange reason Mallika found herself thinking of Louise. She felt Louise was watching her with amused eyebrows. Darling, just think. Is this a story or is this a story? The thought of Louise made Mallika smile, and the polishing took on a rhythm of its own. She rummaged in Mom's sewing box, found black yarn, and strung it through the silver loop, knotting the ends. All through the week that followed, the pendant rested warmly in her pocket.

"I haven't heard from Mr. Allen for a while," said Mom on Friday morning, as Mallika got ready for school. "I'm assuming everything's back on track."

Mallika pretended she hadn't heard.

"Hmm?" Mom never let a question go unanswered.

"Yes," said Mallika. "Yes, okay?"

After school that day, she made her way to the subway station. She took the train downtown three stops and feeling oddly nervous, walked across to the India Grill. The man greeted her, "*Namaste, ji.* How are you?"

"I'm looking for someone. The old woman I saw here last time?"

He snapped to the defensive. "Has there been a problem, miss? She hasn't been bothering you?"

"Oh, no, no." Relax, she told herself. "I just wondered—she dropped something. Where can I find her?"

"She'll be back here soon, I'm sure. I can give it to her if you wish." He hesitated. "*Bichari,*" he said. "Poor thing." But he drew a little map on the back of a takeout menu, marked an arrow on it, and pushed it across the counter. "Try there, just outside the subway station. I've seen her there. See? You're right here, on this corner."

"Thanks," said Mallika. "Thank you."

She paid for a plate of *samosa* to go, then hurried off, following the directions he'd sketched on the menu. The escalator shaft yawned up from underground. A low gray wall provided some shelter from the wind that blew in sudden spurts and belches through rows of buildings, whirling out of rancid little back alleys.

The woman greeted Mallika as if she'd been waiting for her. As if Mallika were an old friend.

"Ah. You got for me today anything?"

Mallika held out the pendant. Clawed hands snatched at it in amazement, rubbed its new shine. The woman tugged it over her head, cursing when it snagged, then caressing the new black yarn with gnarled fingers.

"Have a samosa?" Mallika peeled back the foil from the take-out. *What would Louise say?* Mallika wondered. She had to suppress a sudden laugh that rippled up.

What would Mom say?

They ate together, comfortably, like old cronies. A small silence hung over the street corner by the subway stop. It was a lull in traffic, in pedestrians, in train trembles from underfoot— a still point at the heart of the city.

Then, "I'm going to Kashi," offered the woman.

"Oh?" Mallika was taken aback. Kashi, Varanasi, Banaras, City of Light—why was it everything in India had a million names?

Mallika had once seen a videotape about places of pilgrimage in India in which Kashi had figured, home to hundreds of temples. People came there in droves, bringing worshipful hearts. The old and the destitute went there to live on the charity of pilgrims.

"People say Kashi is not of this world," the narrator had said in his polished voice. "It's not even on this earth, really, they say, because it balances on the tip of Shiva's trident. The real city of brick and stone is just *maya*—the shape divinity has to take so we can see it. Only form, not substance, like the rest of this absurd world. Take it too seriously and you miss the truth beyond."

Kashi. It's a long way from here. Mallika didn't say it.

"Hiya, Vee. You gotta friend?" A thin woman in a flowered dress joined them, propping herself against the wall, staring at Mallika, scoping her out.

"My name is Vidya," said Mallika's friend, sharer of samosa, owner of a newly polished Om-and-Lakshmi pendant. "I own the Super Ten on Huntington Street."

"I'm Amy," Flowered Dress confided. She added, gathering courage, an afterthought, "She don't own no Super Ten. That's just her crazy talk."

Mallika offered Amy the last of the samosa, but Amy said no thanks, she didn't care too much for all them spices.

Vidya cursed softly under her breath, then burst into laughter, waving her arms about. The laughter turned to coughing, and Mallika dug in her purse for a mint.

"Thank you, bless you," said Vidya. "Got more?"

She popped and sucked the mints till wintergreen fumes choked the cough into submission.

"You got for me anything?"

All around them the universe hummed and went about its business.

It seemed a logical thing to go back, so Mallika went several times, after rehearsals. The show was moving along nicely, and that meant rehearsals were twice a week after school and on Sunday afternoons. One time Louise commented on her rush to leave early. "Where's the hurry, sweetheart? I'm not done telling you what a wonderful job you did today!"

Mom and Dad assumed the rehearsals were long. "How's World History class?" Mom asked.

"Fine," said Mallika.

It wasn't, and it got worse. Mr. Allen showed a film about India, full of peacocks and percussion. He pressed, "Mallika, you've been there. Tell us more."

Mallika wanted to say: It isn't right. Here we are talking about India like it's some kind of Disneyland, and I'm some kind of ambassador. She wanted to say, I'm American. What do you want from me?

Then, just for a moment, Louise's words came to her. Relax and the universe will be yours. Mallika said, a new voice rising defiantly, "Sorry, I don't know any tiger stories and I've never been a dancer in a maharaja's harem." Another e-mail message was surely on its way.

Sometimes, on her trips into the city, Mallika took crackers tucked into her backpack, sometimes a sandwich, or whatever came to hand. Sometimes Amy was there, but at other times old Vidya sat alone, trying to catch the eye of a passenger or two with loose change. And she talked to Mallika, although calling it a conversation was possibly an overstatement.

"I won't be here long. I'm going to Kashi. I'll sing at the feet of the Lord."

"What will you sing?" Mallika asked once.

"*Tulsi ke dohe.*" Couplets by the poet Tulsidas—she said it as if the words were precious gems, as if even speaking of them was a prayer.

Tulsidas, Mallika knew, had written poems and songs in Hindi, in the fourteenth, or was it the fifteenth century?

"He lived in Kashi," said Vidya. "He wrote about Kashi."

"I didn't know that," said Mallika.

Sometimes Vidya let fall fragments of her own life, just the way she'd dropped the pendant on the sidewalk. "My husband, he's a useless, drinking man."

Mallika tried to make a sympathetic gesture and ended up just knocking her purse off her shoulder and tip-tilting its contents all over the sidewalk. "Ah, forget him."

Vidya cackled with laughter at the thought, and Mallika, not knowing what to say, picked her possessions back together. Vidya helped herself slyly to a roll of mints and a quarter.

Another time Mallika took a book, a tour guide to India, and showed her a picture of Banaras. The wrinkled face softened and melted. She grabbed the book, flattened the page open, and stared so hard it seemed she'd burn it up.

"Kashi. My ticket will come tomorrow. I'll go to Kashi."

Mallika took hold of both her hands. "Of course you will. You'll go to Kashi."

Amy of the flowered dress yawned and said, "You'd better go to dinner at the shelter if you want any. Sign in for the night or there won't be no room."

It was another world all right.

At a time when this world trembled with the weight of evildoers, the goddess gathered in her the combined powers of all the gods. Shiva gave her a trident. Vishnu gave her his shining discus. And Himavaan the ancient, king of the snows, gave her a lion to ride. She took their weapons. She fought the demon who could take many shapes, but preferred above all to be a huge black water buffalo—Mahishasura. No man or god could kill him, and so he thought that he was safe.

Out of the north, like a shuddering wind, whirled the goddess. She stood before the demon, and just her presence was challenge enough. She fought him with all the divine weapons she held in her thousand arms. Each time he thought he'd pressed her back, she turned, and turned again with the strength of mountains. When she slew him, her face remained calm as a lake.

"Rotten bastard," said Vidya.

"Who?"

"My husband. Drinking, drinking, all the time. But it's all right, he's dead." She laughed out loud.

One day the pendant was gone. "Where is it?" Mallika asked.

The old face crumpled. Tears rolled down the gullies of her cheeks. "Somebody stole it off her," Amy volunteered. "She went around showing it to everybody, see, telling 'em all it was silver."

Oh my God, thought Mallika.

"That ain't so smart," Amy pointed out. "You get all kinds around here."

It was my fault. I polished it up, didn't I?

"I'm sorry," she said to Vidya, seeing visions of her mugged and helpless, left for dead. "I'm so sorry."

Vidya nodded her head, side to side to side. "I'm glad," she said. "I'm glad he's dead." She comforted Mallika. "It's all right, don't worry. He won't come here and beat you anymore."

"Who?" For a moment Mallika was startled. But Amy pointed meaningfully to her own head and rolled her eyes, and

Mallika realized it was like talking to a broken windup toy. The answers matched the questions only randomly.

"Don't worry." Vidya stroked Mallika's sleeve with sandpaper hands. "Don't you worry."

"Don't mind her." Amy was commentator and director of their interaction. "Don't mind her crazy talk."

"I'm crazy?" Vidya jolted briefly into battle mode. "You're the one talks crazy talk." She shook her head impatiently and turned to Mallika. "Kashi. You know I'm going?"

Mallika thought, *Seeing her that day back in the restaurant has led to this moment, like a needle pulling a thread through fabric, stitch by stitch.*

Louise would say, "When life happens to you, you gotta just let it flow."

Mallika couldn't begin to think what Mom and Dad might say, but they would probably say it at some length. Old Vidya would almost certainly call for a family conference.

Divali, the Hindu festival of lights, rolled around and landed on a Friday. Mallika paced till Dad said, "You're making me nervous, Malli, what's up?" In a Dad kind of way, he didn't hang around to hear the answer.

"Mallika," said Mom. "What's wrong?" She peeled a little sticky felt *bindi* off its sheet and stuck it on Mallika's forehead, then turned to get a platter of flowers and fruit ready to take to the temple. There would be singing. A priest would make an offering at the shrine of your choice, with a lighted oil lamp and burning camphor, and flowers and sugar candy. There would be food. There would probably be a dance performance by kids, something colorful and bright, with flaring skirts on

the girls and turbans on the heads of the boys and jingle bells
on everyone's ankles. There would be fireworks for which the
temple would have gotten special permission from the
county. Oil lamps would flicker up and down the long row of
steps, light calling light, invoking the presence of the goddess
Lakshmi.

She heard Dad in the dining room say, "Vijay, will you get
off the phone please? It's time to go."

Mallika looked out at the darkening day and felt doubts and
tugs inside her. Then she looked at Mom on the sofa, full of so
many unasked questions they practically trembled in the air.
But for once Mom didn't push it. She just waited, and all at
once Mallika knew this was it. This was the universe doing its
thing.

"Mom," she said. "I have to tell you something."

And that was how the story of Vidya flopped out like a fish
yanked from a stream, gasping for its breath. There was no
coherent way to tell it, just whichever bits came out first.
Mallika finished and waited for the objections.

To her surprise, Mom sighed, but said, "Okay, I'll come with
you. You're not going off on your own." To Dad she said,
"Ravi, let me deal with this. We'll meet you at the temple,
okay? Just go on ahead."

Mallika gathered up a package of spiced milk sweets, *mithai,*
and orange sugar-sticky *jalebi* without which no holiday could
possibly be complete. She put a little clay lamp, a *diya,* in the
bag, filled a small bottle with oil and capped it tightly, tucked it
in. She rolled a wick for the *diya* and tossed a book of matches
on top. She felt full to bursting with gratitude.

"Thanks, Mom. I'm ready."

You'd have thought racing off downtown looking for crazy old ladies was just another thing to do on Divali night.

A poor washerwoman sighed because her house was never bright enough on the night of Divali, festival of lights. She could only afford a single small lamp, so all the lights of the kingdom outshone hers. One day, a ring belonging to the king turned up in the clothes she washed for the palace.

Being honest, the washerwoman returned it, and the king said to her, "What would you wish for your reward? Ask anything and it shall be yours."

"O king," said she, "grant me only this. That on Divali night, in all your kingdom, only I may be allowed to light a lamp in my house. All other houses must remain dark."

"What a silly wish," said the king. But he kept his word. He sent his messengers out, forbidding everyone, but everyone, to light a single lamp. Of course, the washerwoman's feeble light shone like a beacon, and so hers was the only house the goddess could visit that year.

The goddess was miffed. "How can I find all these houses in the kingdom," she demanded, "if you insist they all stay dark?" But the washerwoman said, "Promise me this. From now on, come first to my house, every year, for my lifetime and the lifetimes of generations to come, and I will tell the king we can brighten our land again."

And so it turned out. Lakshmi came each Divali night to the washerwoman's house, and prosperity remained there through the years.

Mom drove Mallika through the descending twilight, on the freeway, off again, into the city. The corner by the subway station was empty, but Mallika spied familiar figures shuffling up the street toward the soup kitchen.

"Wait," she called. "Wait."

As always, Vidya didn't seem a bit surprised to see her. "For me you got anything?"

"Yes." She opened up her bag, showed her the contents. "Happy Divali. It's Divali today!"

She had expected excitement, maybe even gratitude. But Vidya's hands, reaching in to touch the little clay lamp, began to tremble as if they had been struck by lightning. She opened her mouth to speak, and no sounds came out.

"Don't you like it? Are you all right?" Mallika began wondering if she'd made a terrible mistake. They walked in tandem toward the soup kitchen and shelter, Mom bringing up the rear.

Then Vidya found her voice. "Light. Light it up." Her old eyes shone. Her hands fluttered like shadows, up and around each other, twisting and tumbling in a frenzy of movement.

By now they were outside a big brownstone building with a blue sign, THE HEARTH: ALL WELCOME, DINNER AT 6:00 P.M. People milled around, waiting for the doors to open—people of all ages and shapes and shabbinesses.

"Here? On the street?"

"Light it up," Vidya commanded.

An audience had gathered. They had come to catch dinner and, with luck, a bed at the shelter next door. But this was an unfolding drama, and they weren't about to miss it. A mother and two grubby kids watched openmouthed. A woman with a bundle of bags, so many she had to tie them all together to lug them around, edged her way closer. Some whispered among themselves. Others watched silently. A staff person peered out anxiously, asking, "What are you gonna do with those matches?"

Mom hung back a bit, waiting and listening. Mallika explained about Divali, self-consciously at first, then hearing her voice grow lighter and stronger, feeling herself settling into this role on this strange stage. She marveled that she knew as much as she did, that she could tell it so this gaggle of people stayed and listened in silence. Darkness to light. Evil to good. Chaos to order, and Lakshmi invited into every home, every workplace, everywhere. Even, maybe, here?

The staffer nodded, obviously satisfied she didn't have an arsonist on her hands. "Oh, all right, go ahead and light it, honey. That's nice." Mallika tipped the oil into the *diya,* positioned the rolled wick.

"Like Christmas," someone said. "It's like their Christmas. Whaddaya call it?"

"Divali." Vidya flapped her hands delightedly, then hugged herself against the evening's chill. "Divali *mubarak,*" she called out to anyone who cared to listen. "Divali greetings. Happy, happy."

The match scratched into a flare. Vidya's crooked old hands came together, fingers twisted in their own peculiar directions, palms managing to clap like the palms of a little child, smacking together almost accidentally. Then, on those steps, against the coffee-stained sunset sky, in her hoarse, tuneless old voice, she began to sing. She sang and sang. Her toothless mouth slurped out verse upon verse. Vidya sang in the quaint old

Hindi of the poet Tulsidas. She sang of Kashi. *It is a place for all, she sang, a place that grants wishes like a gentle magical cow, making sorrow and sin and disease disappear. The words dissolved into the silence of the oil lamp's flicker.*

Mallika's mother knew a food moment when she saw one. She offered the box of *mithai* around. "You have to sweeten your mouth today. Come on, try one." The jigsaw assortment of people sweetened their mouths for Divali, murmuring varying degrees of like or dislike for the strange flavors suddenly rambling over their taste buds. On the step outside the soup kitchen, the oil lamp flame alternately wavered and sparked.

"Happy, happy Divali." Old Vidya licked stray crumbs from the corners of her mouth, measuring the words out with care. "Tomorrow I go."

"Where you gonna go, Vee?" someone asked. They knew one another the way city pigeons know the feet of passersby, just from the habit of sharing space.

The old woman patted Mallika's arm with her contorted hand whose fingers couldn't sit straight anymore. *"I go,"* she said, her look of mild surprise seeming to say, *Didn't you know? "To Kashi."*

After the soup kitchen doors opened and everyone vanished inside, Mallika and Mom drove away slowly, leaving the city behind, heading to the temple where Dad and the others would be waiting. "I wish I could think of some other way to help her," said Mom. "I wish she didn't have to hang around the streets like that, sleeping at that shelter. It's so wrong. Such a rich country and still there are people like this."

One of us. The phrase hung unspoken.

Mallika waited for Mom to talk this through with herself. "Maybe I can speak to one of the trustees at the temple," said her mother at last. "Maybe there's something we can do for her, find her a place to stay, get her into some kind of program, something." After all, this was America. All things were possible.

"Thank you," said Mallika.

Mom darted a quick warm glance at her. "No," she said. "Thank you. That was a really nice thing to do."

Mallika realized with a little start that there weren't going to be any qualifiers. No explanations needed. *It's the first thing I've done in a long time,* she said to herself in wonder, *that she's really understood.* It was a pleasing thought.

"It's so unfair," said Mallika.

"Many things," said Mom, "are unfair. Including, I imagine, World History class."

Mallika stared at her. Mom said, "Mr. Allen sent me another message, something about attitude, but he didn't say what the attitude was all about. What is it that's so terrible about this class?"

Mallika sighed. "Mom, you have no idea."

"Want to try telling me?" suggested Mom.

It was surprisingly easy. Mallika told her about the world—Europe and Australia in large, friendly panorama, South America as ruins and revolutions, Asia and Africa in tight little wads of strangeness. India, loud and wild and weird, and would Mallika tell us more? Mom nodded and chuckled. At the maharaja's harem bit, she laughed out loud.

"It's hard to have to be a cultural ambassador at fifteen," said Mom.

"No kidding," said Mallika.

"Although," her mother pointed out, "the United Nations could have taken tips from you, the way you did that Divali show-and-tell at the shelter."

It was Mallika's turn to laugh. The universe settled comfortably around them, like an old friend on Divali night.

UMA KRISHNASWAMI

Hindu traditions and beliefs are so often seen as exotic and distant, happening in some faraway place, certainly some place other than America. I wanted to do a story that was grounded in a Hindu worldview, but set squarely in the contemporary United States. That is how Mallika came to be. She became the carrier of that voice, searching as much for answers to larger questions about the unfairness of things as for a place of comfort for herself.

There are parts of this story that I left deliberately ambiguous, with mythology and reality interweaving, leaving room for exactly the questions that Hindu philosophy raises—what is the reality of the universe, and what is *maya,* divine illusion? What does duty really mean? In a way this story blurs those boundaries in Vidya's person, and so of course in the rational world she's seen as crazy. It's a story of differing worlds, perceptions, points of view in conflict, with Mallika growing to the understanding that in her own way she can take action to create change.

Uma Krishnaswami was born in India and has lived in the United States since 1979, first in Maryland and now in north-western New Mexico. She is the author of several books for young people including two collections of folktales from the Indian subcontinent, *The Broken Tusk: Stories of the Hindu God Ganesha,* and *Shower of Gold: Girls and Women in the Stories of India.* She is married and has one son.

DUST TO DUST

BY NANCY FLYNN

The world is given to pleasure, delighted with pleasure, enchanted with pleasure. Yet, there are beings whose eyes are only a little covered with dust: they will understand the truth.

—the Buddha

I.

Sunday morning and no bells ringing for church because no churches were back in business yet. No cars, no people in front yards, not even the birds back, all the trees cut down when the men dug up the street to take out the water and sewer and gas lines wrecked by the flood. The *whirr* of a fan in the window of my mother's bedroom the only sound on the street.

I tossed a wad of pink fiberglass insulation on the growing pile of mud-covered trash on the curb next to the fire hydrant, half on the sidewalk, half in the street.

Albert's ugly plaid La-Z-Boy, my mother's upright Hoover, Grandma Malloy's treadle sewing machine. Clare's crib and her playpen and her high chair that used to be mine and before that Paul's and before that a Malloy cousin Paul and I never knew. My mother's jewelry box, its lid warped from water, on top of the high-chair tray. There were several unrecognizable mounds of junk that had fallen out of the boxes Albert made us haul from the cellar. Albert said the Meander borough trucks were finally supposed to come and haul everything to the dump on Sunday, which was today.

My brother, Paul, and I had moved back to our house, our stepfather Albert's house really, as soon as the waters receded, five days after the flood. Albert and my mother and my half sister Clare were living in a two-bedroom furnished trailer wedged into the parking lot behind Broderick's Funeral Home across the street.

"Better than nothing, Irene," my mother said when she found out they met HUD's qualifications because Albert's house had water on the second floor. "Electricity, water from a tank on the roof, and chemical toilets that flush."

There wasn't enough room in the trailer for Paul and me. Even if there had been, we wouldn't have moved in.

Back up the front steps, and across the board Paul had nailed to what was left of the porch and through the propped-open door. The living room of the house was our makeshift kitchen, a green two-burner Coleman stove on a piano bench that, miraculously, survived the water with only minor damage to the varnish on its legs. We had two glass bottles of Glen Summit spring water, one on the floor and the other slung in the cradle of a stand that tipped the bottle forward so we could easily pour the water out. There was no ice because there was no refrigerator because there was no electricity because the house wiring hadn't been replaced, so Paul and I used the red metal cooler like a cupboard instead. We filled the cooler with the nonperishable items they gave us each week at the disaster relief center at Central School: Quaker Oats and Kool-Aid, Campbell's tomato soup that we ate thinned with the spring water, French's potato sticks.

"Better than nothing," Irene, my mother had said as Paul and I carried two boxes of handouts down the hill from Central to their trailer, and took a few cans of tuna to the house for ourselves.

The only words my mother ever said.

Three more loads pulled from between the joists and the ceiling in what used to be the house's real kitchen before what used to be breakfast time, and the tiny pink strands of insulation itched everywhere I had skin. The morning air was hot and thick, syrup down my neck. I sat on the top porch step.

I pulled a dirty red bandanna from the side pocket of my fatigues and wiped the sweat from my face. The bandanna folded into a neat triangle and I wrapped it around my head, tying a knot in back, where the bones bulged out at the base of my neck. Untied my work boots, loosened the laces, straightened my socks so they fit snugly around each heel. I tied my boots again, pulling the laces tight. Dust—from the eyelets, from the laces themselves, from the creases in the leather near the toe of each boot—flew into the air.

Dust down my throat.

The worst thing about the heat wasn't working in it, wasn't all the dust in the air so you'd have to cover your mouth and nose with a scarf or wear a dust-protection mask while you worked.

The worst thing was the smell. Of the mud.

Mud in the walls, the cellars, the cracks of every sidewalk—even now, two months after the flood. A smell sour and suffocating and dead, like milk left out on the counter and a backed-up toilet and the rotting body of a deer on the side of the road, all these mixed into one. A smell everyone said you learned to live with, that you actually got used to, like they said the cleanup crews over at River View Cemetery got used to the smells from the two thousand bodies washed from their graves.

I wasn't used to it.

I'd never get used to it.

Never learn to live with it, even though that's what Albert and my mother said I needed to do. Needed to learn to live with what Our Lord and Savior Jesus Christ gave us, not to expect any more than that.

My best friend, Amy Alder, was off at college, Columbia University in New York City. My best friend, Amy, doing the normal things a seventeen-year-old, straight-A high-school graduate is supposed to do, unlike me. Amy whose house sat high on the bluff at the end of the Anthracite Avenue bridge, around the corner from where we used to live with my father until my father died, and my mother married Albert, whose family owned Broderick's, and we moved to Albert's house on the flats.

There was water running in the bathroom of the trailer across the street and I thought I heard someone, my mother, gagging, and then another sound, throwing up. Then the sound of a toilet flushing, and more gagging and another flush.

I covered my eyes with my hands.

Dry, callused fingers brushed my bare neck, then a foot

kicked the toe of one of my boots. Paul stood on the sidewalk, his hair sticking up in the back from where the edge of his hard hat had been. Paul drove a Caterpillar D-6, eleven to seven, down at the dike where the Army Corps of Engineers were moving piles of rock, dirt, and shale to fill in the hole the river made the night the water came over the top of the dike and into the Meander streets.

"You're up early," Paul said.

"Couldn't sleep," I said. "The heat." I blinked in the glare of the too-bright morning sun.

A gray cottony mask hung around Paul's neck, his mouth and chin where the mask had been the only clean spot on him. Dirt in every fingernail, in the crease of every knuckle, in streaks across the backs of both of his hands. The legs of his jeans wet all the way up from slogging in the river, so Paul had that sour mud smell, too.

I pointed to the pile on the curb. "Already got most of the insulation."

"I can help a few hours before I have to sleep," Paul said.

Paul sat down on the step beside me, his knapsack on the step below his feet. Paul's blue eyes clean and shining, too. The eyes of our father everyone who saw him said. Paul undid the straps that held the top flap of the knapsack in place over the small front compartment and reached deep inside.

"Look what I found," Paul said. "Not here, but down the street. In front of Tweet's."

Paul held up a 33rpm record, the orange and yellow of its cardboard cover warped from being in water, the picture a muddy blur.

"*Oklahoma!,*" I said, taking the record from Paul's hand.

This record wasn't from my collection or Paul's. Paul and I had already salvaged ours. Me peeling away the muddy jackets and inner sleeves, handing each record to Paul who dipped the record into a galvanized metal tub of water, then laid it on a towel in the sun. When all the records were dry, I put them in alphabetical order by title—*Abbey Road, After the Gold Rush, Blind Faith*—separating each LP with jacket-size squares we cut from a roll of old wallpaper Paul found on an upstairs closet shelf.

I wiped the mud off on the record jacket's front with the sleeve of my flannel shirt. Gordon MacRae and Shirley Jones in a horse-drawn carriage, Gordon with one hand on the reins and the other on Shirley's shoulder. The name VINCENT MALLOY still visible, carefully formed letters in the upper left corner, like on all our father's LPs, blue ballpoint pen.

Paul ran his dirt-creased fingers through his stuck-up hair, trying to smooth it down. "There's a whole box of them down there," Paul said. "Albert must have dumped them, the box would be way too heavy for Mom to lift."

I slid the record out of the jacket and set the jacket next to Paul's knapsack. The record had wavy lines of silt covering some of its grooves and the black vinyl was cracked, the silver curlicue writing on its dark red center label split in two.

Oklahoma! on the floor next to the hi-fi, my father lifting me in the air. I can still hear the words, something about a beautiful morning.

Sweat dripped through the knot of my bandanna and down

the center of my back. A pounding on both sides of my head loud as summer thunder in my ears.

"He didn't ask you about these records?" I said. "Didn't even ask if we wanted them; I mean after all they did belong to us."

I didn't wait for Paul to answer.

"No, why would he? It's all about hauling and cleaning and throwing every single thing from her life before away. Starting fresh like it never happened. Everything sanitary and clean, clean as the marble of that table where he tries to make dead people look not dead," I said.

My eyes on the pile on the curb.

"I wonder what else he's thrown away," I said.

"Do you want me to get the rest of them?" Paul said. Paul leaned back, his body the length of the board on the front porch floor, the stretched-out folds in his jeans the smell of him now, mixed with mud and river and dust.

"You know, Paul, he's the one making her sick," I said.

"Irene, that isn't true. We saw the reports from Dr. Myers," Paul said. "She's got cancer."

"I don't buy it," I said. "I mean, why all of a sudden, why now? Christ, she had a perfectly healthy baby when she was thirty-seven, not even two years ago."

Paul's eyes were closed. He looked like he was about to fall asleep.

"Don't be stupid, Irene," Paul said.

My teeth pulled at a piece of skin loose on my lower lip.

"I don't know. I think it's him," I said.

I stood up and, record in hand, walked over to the trash on

the curb. My mother's jewelry box, with the green velvet lining muddy inside, its side split from being tossed on top of the pile, sat on Clare's high-chair tray. I leaned *Oklahoma!* against the back of the high-chair seat.

I touched the mud-caked lid of the box, traced the dragon design on the lid with the fingers of my right hand. When I was little, if I was very good, my mother would let me play with her necklaces and bracelets and clip-on rhinestone earrings while she got herself ready for when my father came home from work.

"Sit here, Irene," my mother always said. Her face in her vanity mirror all lit up, the shape of a pale pink heart, rosy lipsticked lips and cheeks and her shiny black hair combed into perfect rows of curls above her ears.

"On the carpet, next to the bed," she said. "Be very careful. That's a special box from your father. You were born while he was in Korea. He brought it back for us."

When I lifted the lid of the jewelry box, one hinge twisted, and the other bent back so far the hinge came loose from the wood.

I picked up the record.

I can still hear my father's voice, extra loud, when he got to the part about everything going his way.

I brought the record down whack! on the open jewelry box lid. Picked up each piece and, one by one, snapped them into smaller and smaller pieces until my father's favorite musical was nothing more than black splinters on green velvet, shiny as the anthracite coal he'd mined.

Years of praying for God to keep disaster from visiting our

family hadn't worked. *Now I lay me down to sleep, I pray the Lord my soul to keep.* God, please don't let our house burn down, don't let there be a tornado or a hurricane, don't let me be struck by lightning or my parents get in a car wreck or any of us fall in a cave-in in the backyard. But our father died when I was four and Paul was eight, and then his mother, our grandmother Malloy, died, too, the next year after that. And now it was our mother, with a lump in the hollow of her armpit the size of a peach that by June, the month of the flood, had supposedly spread, like the waters of the Susquehanna River, to her lungs and her stomach and her head.

Prayer didn't work.

Even though Reverend Allabaugh sat on the ugly brown couch in the narrow living room of the HUD trailer and held my mother's black-and-blue hands and told Albert and her and even little Clare who didn't understand that it would. That God hears our prayers, that the prayers of the faithful rise up and stop the rains and save the sick and awaken those who sleep in the dust of the earth to the joys of an everlasting life. Said all my mother needed to do was trust in the mysterious Plan the Lord has for us, including the flood, which somehow included her getting sick.

Prayer didn't work any of the other times—not for my father when the mine buried him at the age of thirty-two. Not for my grandmother who had a stroke after mass that snowy December Sunday, home alone. Didn't stop a wall of water from coming over the top of the dike, didn't send me to college with the other smart kids in my graduating class.

Prayer didn't work.

II.

I climbed the trailer's plywood steps and opened the screen door as quietly as I could. My mother sat at the kitchen table already set for dinner, stirring a cup of coffee with the wrong end of a spoon. No lipstick on her lips, no rhinestone clip-ons, what hair she had left now white gray tufts twisted around a few pink spongy rollers scattered along the back of her head. A wadded-up hankie in the hand that wasn't stirring the coffee and dark lines like run mascara above and below her eyes. Her fuzzy blue bathrobe buttoned up to her neck.

"Get the casserole out of the oven, will you, Irene?" she said.

The casserole dish so hot the pot holders weren't helping and I burned my hand.

"Ouch," I said. "Where's Clare?"

"In the bathroom with Albert. He's giving her a bath," my mother said.

"You mean he actually knows how?" I said. I dropped the hot dish in the middle of the tiny kitchen table. "Sorry, Mom, I promise I'll stop."

Paul was the next one through the screen door. He went over to the sink to wash his hands. At the miniature stove—which was next to the miniature sink, which was next to the miniature refrigerator and the table and everything else in the trailer—I ladled peas from a shallow puddle of water in the bottom of a chipped porcelain saucepan and dumped them in an oval serving dish.

"Hey, Mom, how are you?" Paul said.

"Today wasn't too bad," she said.

The sound of a toilet flushing, and more gagging and another flush.

Running water hit the metal sides of the kitchen sink as Paul lathered his hands, tried to get them clean. "Irene and me, we got all the insulation out today and started taking up the hardwood floor in the foyer off the front room," Paul said.

Clare in Albert's arms now out of the bathroom and in her summer pajamas, her yellow hair clumped and wet.

I carried the bowl of steaming peas over to the table and set them next to the macaroni casserole dish. "Hi there, Clare," I said.

"Reen," Clare said. "Pole." Clare at two just beginning to talk.

Clare reached for Paul. Paul finished drying his hands. He took Clare from Albert and wiggled her short toddler legs into her booster seat.

"How much you get done today, Paul?" Albert said. Albert brushed at invisible dirt on the shoulder where Clare had just been, adjusted his shirt collar, straightened his navy and red striped tie. Every fingernail on every finger on Albert's fat white hands manicured. I could see his perfect half-moons.

"All the insulation from the walls in the kitchen and some of the hardwood floor," Paul said. "The cellar's all cleared out, too."

"You're saving the wood, aren't you, Paul?" Albert said. "For kindling."

No words from Albert for me.

We had our assigned seats for meals in the trailer. Albert across the table from me, on one side of my mother, Clare between the two of them in her seat, and Paul on the other side of Mom.

"Everyone serve yourself," my mother said. Everything in miniature in the trailer, the table so small and everyone crowded around so all you could do was reach and serve yourself.

Green peas that came from a can with a white label and black block letters on the side that said GREEN PEAS rolled around on my white plastic plate. There were Ritz crackers instead of bread and Tang instead of milk and lumps of oily tuna on a chipped china plate. I lifted a helping of macaroni and cheese out of the casserole in the center of the table.

"Reverend Allabaugh said he'd stop by later," my mother said. "Nice of him to do that, don't you think?"

"It's part of his job, Margaret. It's what he's supposed to do," said Albert. "Minister to the sick, pray for the dead."

Albert pushed his plate to the center of the table, the fingers of both hands on top of the table edge, the thumbs underneath. Albert always finished first.

"She doesn't need praying," I said. "She needs treatment, better doctors than they've got around here." I shook the spoon and watched as the gooey macaroni dropped in sticky lumps on my plate.

"Dr. Myers was good enough for my mother," Albert said.

The crinkling sound of cellophane as Albert unwrapped a White Owl, his fat hands, his ring finger puffy on both sides of his thick gold wedding band.

"And your mother, Albert, is dead," I said.

The only other sounds in the room were the *clink-scrape* of Paul's fork touching his plate, the *clink-scrape* of my mother scooping up a spoon of macaroni and peas to feed Clare, the scrape of Clare's teeth as she closed her mouth around her Winnie-the-Pooh baby-size spoon.

Albert's fat hand squeezed the cellophane from the White Owl into a ball. He set the ball on the table in front of Clare. The ball was already starting to stop being a ball.

"Gimme," Clare said, macaroni and peas hanging from her mouth.

Albert's purplish lips were around the unlit end of the cigar, the middle of his fat cheeks all sucked in. He flicked the wheel on his silver Zippo. Even with the windows open, a smell like burning tar filled the trailer. Then the cigar was out of Albert's mouth and in his hand, the lit-up end smoking, smoke in the air in front of his face.

"And since you've obviously been to medical school, Miss National Merit Scholar, what do you recommend?" Albert said. The cigar pointing at me, Miss Markovich's menacing ruler when Ralphie Denson acted up in class.

"Maybe you could quit smoking around her for one," I said. "You're the one making her sick."

Paul pushed his chair back. He gave me a look like you're on your own with this one. "See you in the morning," Paul said.

Paul carried his plate to the kitchen sink. Opened the screen door slowly, stepped on the trailer's plywood steps, held the edge of the door, let the door close slowly so it wouldn't slam. Paul got along better with Albert than I did. Paul knew enough to walk away. Knew enough to go to Kuni's and sit at the bar until it was time for his shift.

I put the serving spoon back in the dish in the center of the table. Was about to take my food and follow Paul out the door when Albert's lit cigar arced through the air and landed on top of the macaroni on my plate.

My thumb and finger careful to touch the cigar only in the middle—not the part all slobbery from being in Albert's mouth—I picked up the cigar. My eyes locked with Albert's, as I stubbed the lit end out in the macaroni left in the casserole dish. White Owl cheese smoke drifted up, a sizzle sound in the room.

Albert got out of his chair, fast, his body across the tiny table, his white starched shirt stomach spreading like a pancake where he leaned. Albert's hand touched my hand still holding the cigar, still in the casserole dish. His fat fingers spread like marshmallow around my wrist, then clamped and twisted hard.

"I won't have you acting *this* way," Albert said. "In front of *my* wife, *my* child."

Albert's face was red and puffy and his mouth puckered up. "Get out," Albert said.

My mother never spoke. Only got out of her chair, big dark eyes, and I could see wet streaks underneath them and a blue vein I'd never noticed before sticking out on her neck. The cellophane ball cigar wrapper still in Clare's fist, she heaved Clare from the booster seat to her shoulder and walked down the hall to her room. Her, and Albert's, room.

I backed slowly to the trailer door, taking my time so Albert would remember my face. Wanted him to see me despise him, to see my eyes curse him for what he'd done, what he was doing to my family, what he was doing to me.

Back at the house, I moved the army cot I used for a bed under an open window. I sat on top of my sleeping bag in a thin cotton slip I'd found in a carton of donations marked WOMEN'S INTIMATE at Central School. Worked my fingers through my hair like a comb, then separated my hair into three strands and threaded one strand over the other until a thick single braid fell down the center of my back. Retrieved my one and only rubber band from the windowsill where I'd put it next to the piece of broken mirror I'd rescued from the door of the bathroom medicine chest. Twisted the rubber band around the end of the braid.

I stared at myself in the mirror.

It was not the face of the girl who gave the National Honor Society speech on the Eternal Light of Knowledge, not the girl who won the Lex Greenberg English Prize at graduation, not the face of a college freshman staring back.

I lay awake for hours, looking at the rising moon, looking at the stars, smelling the mud smell and the river smell, calculating what it would take to get far, far away. How much I had in the bank, how much I'd earn between now and winter when the flood cleanup stopped. The $112.79 per month in social security from my dead father ended in October, the month I turned eighteen. Albert would surely throw me out then. Maybe I could get a scholarship to a state teachers college. Maybe I could say I was an orphan. Wouldn't I get help then?

III.

The Welsh Baptist Church was at the lower end of Meander, on Main Street, not far from the town baseball field and the river and the dike. The Welsh Baptist had been hit hard by the flood, unlike Albert's church, Grace Episcopal, up on Avondale

Hill. That last night, the minister and the church elders and even some guys from the dike sandbagging crew carried everything they could upstairs to the sanctuary, but the water had reached there, too.

It was cool inside the sanctuary, a relief from the heat outside. There was so much dust in the air from everyone walking back and forth, hauling rubbish out, it was hard to see who else was working in the room. The bigger guys on our crew—L. D. and Tommy Flanagan—took turns swinging axes to break up what was left of the pipe organ. A piano with all the ivories on the keys popped up from sitting under water had floated across the sanctuary and crashed into one of the mahogany pews and ended up standing on one side. The pew had a row of splintery marks where the edge of the piano had banged up against the wood.

My mother said they poked her arm with a needle twenty-two times while they tried to find a vein to put the 5-fluorouracil in for her treatment last week. They made her stay in the hospital overnight and hooked her up to an IV until her vein finally collapsed. When she came home, it looked as if another chunk of hair was missing from the side of her head, and her whole face, even the white parts of her eyes, had turned a yellowish orange.

My mother touched her head. "Better than nothing," she said.

My partner for the week was a girl named Rhonda. Rhonda was older, nineteen, maybe twenty; before the flood, she'd been studying to be a nurse. Rhonda had hazel eyes and freckles across her nose and cheeks. She wore her long red hair hanging straight down and a heavy hooded sweatshirt no matter if it was hot outside or cold. An earplug in her right ear was plugged into the side of a transistor radio she kept in the sweatshirt's front pocket pouch.

Our crew leader, Joey Lipski, and a kid I knew only by the name Darnell walked past with a chair from the altar held between them, its red velvet seat a stripy green with mold.

"Start with the choir loft, girls," Joey said.

"Grand Funk Railroad," Rhonda said, her head bobbing up and down to the music as she balanced a stack of still-damp hymnals in her arms. "Closer to Home."

My boots made crunching sounds on the dried mud that covered the orange wall-to-wall carpeting. I walked down the sanctuary aisle with a load of sheet music and stuck-together programs from the Father's Day service, June 19, 1972.

"Toss the small stuff out that window," Joey yelled. He pointed to a floor-to-ceiling stained-glass window in the vestibule next to the front door whose lower panes had been removed.

All that was left of the stained-glass window was Jesus from the waist up, pieces of glass cut in shapes to be a dark purple robe, his right hand in the air, his chin lifted and his eyes half closed, Jesus waist deep in the waters of the flood. He had a halo of white pearly panes, rays shooting out from his head, and above his head a milky ivory glass cut in shapes to make three puffed-up clouds. The palm of Jesus' hand was a single piece of glass, painted with fuzzy black lines, a small red dot at the center where the nail to the cross had been. The hand looked too large and swollen, like it didn't belong to him, like it was a rescue raft about to float off.

I wished I was that hand. Wished I could float downstream.

I hadn't had anything to eat since the night before when Albert grabbed my wrist and I'd backed out the trailer door, leaving peas and noodles and ash from a smoking cigar on my plate. My mouth watered for the cheese, lettuce, and mustard sandwich I'd gotten at Dudek's Lunch on my walk to the church. Even though it was the same government-issue cheese Paul and I got at the center, the same government-issue bread, the Dudek's version always tasted better. They had lettuce.

I bit my lower lip until I tasted blood.

My mother threw up so much she had cracks and bloody scabs on her lips.

My head fit out the opening of the half Jesus window. Joey Lipski was on the curb, talking to a guy in a yellow hard hat who pointed at what was left of the church's coal furnace sitting in the middle of Main Street.

Amy at college could eat whenever she wanted, could walk to a coffee shop on Amsterdam Avenue, or Broadway, order scrambled eggs and hash browns, a toasted bagel with cream cheese on the side, any time of the day or night.

I looked around the sanctuary for Rhonda. She hadn't come back from her hymnal load.

I couldn't wait for Rhonda, couldn't wait for noon.

I walked over to where Tommy and L. D. were trying to crowbar the wooden pulpit from the altar floor.

"Tell Joey I'm taking lunch early," I said.

L. D. lifted his shoulders and shrugged. I picked up my knapsack and headed for the sanctuary's back stairs.

> > >

Next door to the church was the parsonage, and next to that a two-story house remodeled to be a neighborhood center set up by VISTA volunteers before the flood. The VISTA workers had come to Meander the summer before. They started a day-care center, so the women could work at the Atwater Throwing Company and the Mar-Cee dress factory, and built a playground out of truck tires and railroad ties behind the center with help from neighborhood kids. They counseled the men who lost their jobs when the Pompey mine closed, helping them fill out applications for work at the sewage treatment plant under construction across the Anthracite Avenue bridge, in Plains. They were just starting to rebuild the bleachers and the concrete walls behind the dugouts at the Ash Diamond when the Susquehanna flood waters hit.

Albert didn't like the VISTA volunteers. He said they were draft dodgers, rich kids with silver spoons who felt guilty, wanted to play at being poor for a year. Albert said Meander didn't need handouts, didn't need any outside help, said we did fine on our own, like we'd been doing for over a hundred years.

There was a towering sugar maple behind the church, between the neighborhood center and the playground the VISTA volunteers had built, the only shady spot between the street out front and a grove of birch and willow along the river's edge.

Rhonda without her sweatshirt and her earplug sat on one of those scratchy woolen blankets the National Guard gave flood victims for free. Next to Rhonda was a guy with a blond ponytail I didn't recognize from our crew. The guy wore dark airplane pilot sunglasses with a shiny coating so you couldn't see his eyes. He had one hand on the hem of Rhonda's shirt. His other hand waved a paper fan attached to what looked like a wooden tongue depressor in front of Rhonda's face. There was a picture of Jesus holding a white lamb and a shepherd's staff on one side of the paper fan.

Rhonda's shirt was wrinkled, a white cotton smock, with red and gold stitching around the neck and sleeves and small mirrors sewn between the stitches that flashed in the sun, blinding my eyes, making it hard to see her face.

"Hi, Rhonda," I said. "Mind if I sit?"

Rhonda moved closer to the blond ponytail guy making room for me next to the blanket's edge. I dropped my knapsack on the grass and knelt down.

"Irene, this is Jack," Rhonda said. Jack waved the hand with the fan.

"Nice to meet you," I said.

I took my cheese, lettuce, and mustard sandwich out of my knapsack, careful not to crackle the waxed paper bag too much. Mustard had oozed out the sides of the sandwich, making a bright yellow puddle in the corner of the bag. I tore a piece off one corner of the sandwich.

A girl in a gauzy blue summer dress with no bra and no shoes walked over from the VISTA center and stood on the grass next to Jack. Her eyebrows arced thick and fuzzy above her eyes and her mouth was a narrow, straight line. The girl tapped Jack on the top of his head, like she was searching for the stud in a wall.

Then she reached over Jack's head and Rhonda's body.

"Hi, I'm Camille," the girl said. The silver bracelets on Camille's outstretched arm fell forward on her wrist and made a jingling sound.

I swallowed the sandwich corner in the back of my mouth.

"I'm Irene," I said. "I work with Rhonda."

"Where's Henry?" Camille said. "I need him to help me with the SBA loan applicants this afternoon."

Jack lifted the hand that had been touching the hem of Rhonda's shirt. He flicked his thumb in the direction of the playground.

I squinted in the direction of Jack's thumb. A bald man in cutoff shorts with no shirt and no beard and curly black hair covering his chest like a gorilla sat cross-legged on the top of a giant wooden spool that had been turned on one end to make a table where the playground kids could eat. The man's eyes were closed like he was praying and the fingers on both of his hands touched at the tips, an empty bowl in his lap.

"You mean Buddha?" Jack said. "He's over there meditating. Said he didn't want to be disturbed. All day."

Senior year in A.P. history we did a unit on religions of the world. Amy's mother had a book about the life of the real Buddha that I read for my final class report. A regular man named Siddhartha who never claimed to be the one and only God, never claimed he would answer your prayers. Just sat under a tree with his legs crossed in a knot and closed his eyes and listened to his breathing in and out.

"I'll give him an hour," Camille said. "You, too, Jack. Nice to meet you, Irene."

I took another bite of my sandwich. Jack's fingers were back on the hem of Rhonda's shirt and Rhonda lay flat on her back.

I felt the way I used to feel when my brother Paul would bring his girlfriend, Tina, over to the house, after our mother and Albert went to sleep, and we'd all be in the living room watching TV, me in the rocker, Tina and Paul sitting on a single cushion on the couch.

The Buddha in the book made his mind so quiet that he was able to stop the questions and see what was really true. Life is suffering, he said, and craving for things to last when they can't. My room the way it was, perfect, before the flood. My father before the accident at the Pompey, my mother now.

The future even if one day it has to end.

Rhonda squeezed up closer to Jack. Rhonda had her arms around Jack's neck and Jack's glasses were pushed up on his face. The two of them rolled, as if they were one person, off the scratchy blanket and onto the dry, dusty grass.

I picked up the waxed paper bag that held the rest of my sandwich. Grabbed my knapsack and stood up.

The Buddha said we have to work to be free of craving, to follow a path that will lead to what he called enlightenment, a path that leads to peace.

There was a half circle of truck tire stuck in the dirt across from the bald man's wooden spool, the tire ridges bumpy where I sat. I stuffed the rest of my sandwich in my mouth. Lettuce and soggy bread stuck to my back teeth.

I was so close I could stretch out my arm and touch him.

I stared at the cross-legged man.

Stared at his smooth pink lips and the hairs in his nose and his smooth bald head—different than my mother's with her thin patchy hair. Stared at the fingers on his upside-down hands, and the veins thick as ropes in his feet, resting toes up on his knees. Stared at him while I chewed and sweated and all the things I'd been thinking about all morning and even the night before a noisy chorus in my head, and all he did was not move, all he did was breathe, his naked chest going up and down, the sweat beading up and dripping down his forehead and into his closed eyes. Stared at him so long holding my own breath until all I could hear was a pounding around my ears, a rush of water, and Reverend Allabaugh's words— *And by the sweat of your face will you eat bread until you return to the ground, for out of it you were taken. For you are dust, and to dust you shall return.*

My mouth was so dry from chewing my sandwich I thought I would choke.

A wind came up, swirling the mud-dust and the cinders on the playground paths into a cloud in the air. Dust got in my eyes, but the wind felt good. Dust blew into the cross-legged man's eyes, too, but he didn't open his eyes or lift a hand to wipe the dust out. Even when a fly buzzed in front of his face and landed on his nose, when any other person would have swatted the fly, cursed when he missed killing it, the cross-legged, hairy man sat with his eyes shut, his chin lifted up to the sky, breathing in and out.

The Lord is my shepherd; I shall not want . . .

I willed this Henry to open his eyes.

I wanted to talk to him. About what I'd read in the Buddha book, ask him so many things.

Like where his shirt was and why he shaved his head. And how could he sit with his legs crossed for so long and not have his knees cramp or his feet go pins and needles and fall asleep.

Ask him if he could explain the parts in Amy's mother's book that said life is suffering, nothing is permanent, you can't control anything in this crazy unfair life.

Not mine accidents. Not floods. Certainly not death.

He leadeth me beside the still waters. He restoreth my soul . . .

I counted to twenty, whispering each number slow as I could. Then counted to twenty again.

I willed him to open his eyes.

He never once did.

I stood up and turned around, away from Henry and the table, ready to head across the grass, back to the dust in the church, back to moldy piles of choir robes and collection envelopes and Sunday school Bible lesson books.

Tightened the knot of the bandanna on my head, smoothed the legs of my fatigues. Lifted my knapsack from where it sat in the dirt and slung a strap over the crook of one arm.

Yeah, though I walk through the valley of the shadow of death, I will fear no evil . . .

I felt something, a foot, an almost-touch on the small of my back.

"Irene." His voice like he'd known me all my life.

I turned around. Henry's legs were now uncrossed, dangling over the edge of the table, his hands on the edge of the table, too. His eyes open. His eyes a brown so dark they were black as coal, black as my father's, black as night.

"There are beings whose eyes are only a little covered with dust," Henry said. "They will understand the truth."

Henry reached for my hand. His hand was cool as his fingers touched my palm, his pulse steady and calm.

"My mother is dying," I said.

NANCY FLYNN

"Dust to Dust" is my first work of fiction for young adults. It is based on my experiences during Hurricane Agnes, which led to the disastrous flooding of my hometown—and the entire Wyoming Valley region of Northeastern Pennsylvania—by the Susquehanna River in June 1972.

Like my character Irene, I worked on a flood cleanup crew the summer before my high school senior year. A close friend's mother was diagnosed with breast cancer not long after the flood and that friend didn't get to go to college with the rest of us in 1973. I met and worked with many VISTA volunteers who'd come to the area to help us get back on our feet. And my college friends were among the first practitioners of vipassana (insight) meditation in the United States; the character Henry is based on a composite of them.

Spirituality and religion have always been part of my life. I was raised in a churchgoing family and church-focused community. Every week my family attended the First Christian Church on Main Street in Plymouth, Pennsylvania, the former anthracite coal-mining town where I grew up; in fact, my maternal grandparents and my parents met at this church. I went to Sunday school, sang in the choir, and was baptized by immersion at the age of eleven. My first friends were church friends; the first boy I kissed was at Christian summer camp.

Living through a natural disaster at the age of sixteen had a profound and lasting effect on the rest of my life. With Hurricane Agnes, my childhood came to an abrupt end. Barbie dolls and Beatles albums and my scrapbooks of President Kennedy's assassination and Apollo 11 landing on the moon: anything I forgot to carry to the miraculously untouched second floor of our house was suddenly gone. During my admissions interview at Oberlin College that fall, I talked about what I'd learned from living through the flood—big life lessons that it usually takes many more years of living to get like the importance of family and community; the way people come together and help one another during a crisis; how love and generosity are what matters, not material things. Looking back, I can see that I was a fledgling Buddhist in my outlook and I didn't even know it yet!

Another deep faith I hold is in the healing, soul-nourishing power of art. My fiction focuses on the ways in which ordinary people find faith and hope and wisdom in spite of adversity and how acts of compassion and kindness win in the end.

In August 1998, I moved with my husband and our cats from Ithaca, New York, to the foothills of the Coast Range near Corvallis, Oregon, where, after sixteen years as a writer, editor, and publisher in the world of university information technology, I am now able to pursue my writing full-time.

THE MOTH OF GOD

BY JENNIFER ARMSTRONG

It was the year 1809. In the Belgian town of Spa, near the German border, there lived a modest and unremarkable family named Cuvier. By tradition, the members of the Cuvier family were attendants at the baths. It was in their nature to be attendants. They waited and served. The eldest son of this family, Benedictus, had this year reached the age when he worked at the baths, too.

From all over Belgium and Germany, from Holland and France, came the wealthy and the once wealthy to take the healing waters of Spa. Benedictus was one of the many small and insignificant people whose work it was to help the crippled, the palsied, the blind, and the faint of heart into the water. Trembling hands gripped his arm. The odors of minerals, of bodies, of mildew, were everywhere around Benedictus. The crimson bathing dresses, which were provided to the patients, ballooned around each body as it lowered into the water, and filled Benedictus's vision like drops of blood spreading through a pool.

On a Friday in June, Benedictus went to work as usual. The

voices of the sick and pained echoed in the vaulted ceiling. All sound was magnified, and the movement of one arm through the water on the far side of the pool was audible to Benedictus as he entered. *Drips, plinks, tinks, clurps*—all the water sounds purled and burbled, and upon these floated the sounds of people who took the water.

"Attendant," an old woman said the moment she spotted Benedictus. "Aide me. My limbs are weak."

"Madame." With bowed head, the strong, young Benedictus bent to her and lifted her, and carried her into the water, his bare toes testing the slick marble steps. The people who were used to paying for what they wanted were timid and dismayed in the face of their illness. The woman in his arms, a banker's wife, kept her eyes turned away from his. Benedictus knew his own strength made her hate him.

As he lowered her into the water, Benedictus saw a marquis with stuttering hands nearby. Not far from him he saw a once-famous beauty, whose youthful portrait hung in the chateau of an aristocrat, but who was now afflicted with a disease of the skin, which caused her to cry out whenever she was touched. He saw a young man wasted by the consumption, in spite of being the son of a powerful merchant who owned many wharves and warehouses in Antwerp. Toward Benedictus, some of these people behaved with a strange humility that struggled against their hauteur.

"Aide me," the marquis commanded, and then as Benedictus moved near, the man lowered his voice with a confiding leer. "Dr. Liebling has prescribed a purgative for me, and Monsieur Dr. de la Turenne has advised me against eating cheeses. Their reputations are sound, are they not? They have cured many people?"

"I believe——" Benedictus began, choosing his words with care and with equal care keeping his eyes lowered from the aristocrat's veiny face, for he dared not give his opinions forcefully; he was only a servant. "I believe that these doctors are as good as any here at Spa."

The marquis raised his hand to Benedictus's shoulder, and drops sprinkled from his withered fingertips like a blessing of holy water. Many of the wealthy patients informed Benedictus of their doctors' advice, wondering if he concurred, for he was young and in robust health, and it was the opinion of many who came there that a boy who was constantly in the waters of Spa must naturally have received many benefits from it, must naturally have a constitution well protected from the onslaughts of illness and accident. They wished to be like him: youthful, sound of limb, of strong heart, and with good digestion. Like him physically, but of course, not in station. Better to be ill.

And so, hale Benedictus heard their fears, and helped their bodies into the echoing, puckling baths, where each drop of vapor rising into the air carried the sound of a sigh or a moan and the scent of pain. This was his daily program. School had ended for him at a young age.

The marquis was about to confide further in Benedictus, when a young woman resting upon a submerged bench nearby began to weep. Benedictus hurried, as much as one striding through water can hurry, to her side.

"Do you need assistance?" he said.

Nodding, still weeping, she reached her arms around his neck and hung on him as he carried her toward the stairs. Benedictus tried to move as smoothly as a fish glides through dark depths, but she cried out in pain, startling him. He struggled not to drop her as he lost his balance for a moment on the slick marble steps. His elbow cracked against the stone railing, almost causing him to cry out himself. But he did not cry out, and he did not drop her. A female attendant came to assist the young woman, and ushered her away. Benedictus stood cupping his throbbing elbow with one hand, while water streamed from him and ran down the steps.

Then the banker's wife called to him, and he turned back to the water.

On Sunday morning Benedictus left the Cuvier home in the quarter of the city where most bath servants lived, and threaded his way through the damp streets to the Church of Saint Anne where he was a member of the choir. He was a tenor. His voice was good, but he did not put himself forward. The choirmaster had once said of him, "Benedictus I rely upon as I rely upon a strong mule. He does the work and can carry a load, but he is nothing that inspires me to brag. He can take a solo from time to time, although not on a Sunday of an important mass."

Inasmuch as this was a Sunday when there was not an important mass, Benedictus was scheduled to sing the Ave Verum. He arrived at the Church of Saint Anne in some consternation, because his elbow still gave him much pain, and he worried that it would interfere with his singing. He feared it would disturb his concentration from the passage of music he must sing.

The church was filled with the usual congregation. Aside from the residents of Spa who attended this church, each Sunday there was another contingent of visitors. They arrived for the mass on crutches, in bath chairs, coughing, or in a medicinal daze. Benedictus followed the mass with only half an ear, cradling his bruised elbow and wincing. The choirmaster, noticing Benedictus's distraction, attempted to signal the tenor by means of a lifted eyebrow, a low wave by the navel. The preluding note of the organ sounded, and at once, Benedictus stood to sing.

His voice, when he did sing, was different. The members of the choir sitting by him turned with undisguised surprise. Benedictus could hear it himself, how his voice was—stronger, clearer, sweeter. Every note was true and as pure as gold, as though the light streaming through the brilliant-colored windows of Saint Anne sang with her voice. Benedictus was astonished, and actually looked at the saint in the window as if expecting to see her singing.

Father Josquin paused in his ministrations and tipped his head to one side, the better to hear Benedictus. In the pews, the coughing was stilled, and women with crooked backs sat up straighter. Among the assembly, men with pains in the chest were released from the fearful grip. Each note chimed a sympathetic tremor in the breastbone of each one who listened. The marquis sighed; the banker's wife felt her stiff shoulders soften. And the members of the choir felt for the first time the greatness of what they did.

It was over much sooner than anyone wished. Benedictus himself felt a strange flush of embarrassment and pride. He had never sung so well in the Church of Saint Anne. He could not remember *anyone* singing so well there. And now the modest Benedictus found himself the object of quizzical attention. Eyes followed him as he returned to his seat, and Father Josquin was compelled to clear his throat several times to call attention back to himself and the sacraments. "The waters have finally done you some good, Cuvier," the tenor to his right said in a harsh whisper.

"I only . . . I just . . ." Benedictus caught the priest's stern gaze and submerged himself in confusion.

The continuing surprise and comment was unwelcome to Benedictus after the service, for he wanted only to go home with his family and eat their Sunday mutton pie, and perhaps drink some wine to dull the pain in his elbow. For the next few days, his fellow choir members hailed him when they met on the streets. They urged him to sing again, sing right there on the sidewalk in front of the hatmaker's shop and the apothecary, but he shyly refused. His mother basked in the reflected glow of their golden-voiced son. Oh yes, she told their neighbors. I always knew he would be a credit to us and to the church.

By the following Sunday, Benedictus had made a complete recovery from his bruised elbow. The choirmaster asked him to take the Ave Verum again, and when Benedictus sang, all heads inclined toward him, awaiting the heavenly voice of Saint Anne.

It was not there. The tenor sang in his former voice—the voice of which no choirmaster could brag. Disappointment and then contempt showed in the eyes of his fellow choristers, and his family ceased preening and gloating. It had been a freakish thing after all. The voice of Saint Anne had sung through Benedictus one day, but had gone on to seek a finer instrument elsewhere. It came as no surprise to *him* that he had been found unworthy to keep such a divine gift. No surprise but rather a great relief.

Later, Benedictus marveled at the strangeness of it all. He stood at the window of his room with a cup of coffee in one hand and sang a short air in an experimental way. His voice was a workaday voice.

"Saint Anne must have made a mistake last week," he scolded himself. Then he blushed, fearing the saint might have heard his blasphemy.

And then a sudden shriek from his mother, who stood below his window scolding a peddler, caused him to jerk and cringe, as though indeed Saint Anne had caught him. The hot coffee from his cup leaped onto his wrist and hand, scalding him.

"Ah!" Benedictus dropped his cup. He put his hand to his mouth.

"What are *you* yelling about?" his mother called up to him. "You sound like a skewered cat."

He pulled back from the window. "Nothing, Maman," he whispered.

He closed his eyes and leaned his head against the window frame. "Oh, what a weary world," he sighed. All day long, every day, he must minister to the frail and petulant bathers, must listen to them complaining of their pains. And now he himself was plagued by pain, and he could not sing as he wished, and really—it was such a weary world. Why should Saint Anne give him a gift only to take it away? Was it fair? Was it kind? Was this how God toyed with His children?

Rebellion stirred in his humble heart. He would try again. Tucking his burned hand under his other elbow, Benedictus sang the Kyrie, Lord, Have Mercy. And this time his voice was the voice of Saint Anne, again as true and angelic as it had been last Sunday. He sang through the Kyrie, standing by the window, enchanted by his own singing. When he was finished, he happened to notice his maman and the peddler below his window, gaping up at him with expressions of wonder on their faces.

"My son! Hear how he sings!" Mme. Cuvier exclaimed with outthrust hand.

Benedictus drew back from the window again. How was it that he had sung divinely one moment, but not the next? Could it have been the sacred text that produced divine singing? In a low voice he sang a bawdy tavern song—the one about the buck-toothed wench and the one-eyed margrave— and knew that this was just as inspired as it had been in the Kyrie. And hadn't he sung in his ordinary voice in church only that morning, while singing an Agnus Dei? His scalded hand throbbed as he pressed it to his forehead in concentration.

But now Benedictus recalled that on the previous occasion, he had been suffering from a bruised elbow. Now he was suffering from the pain of a water burn. He had much to think about for the rest of the day.

During the following week, Benedictus was again at his job in the baths. "Attendant," the bathers would address him. "I am in much discomfort." Or "Attendant, my constitution is destroyed by years of debauchery." And he saw their wasted limbs, heard their coughs and wheezes, saw their tremors and their grimaces of pain and the grainy film of regret and self-disgust upon their eyes.

And now, when these bathers asked for his opinion, he advised, "Madame"—or of course it might be "Sir"— "May I suggest you give comfort to your soul as well? Will you not go to the Church of Saint Anne this Sunday for healing of another kind?" His skin prickled with fear and excitement as he made these recommendations, as it had when, as a boy, he success-fully stole a handful of sweets from the shop of M. Bardet.

On Sunday he was again in the choir, and in his pocket was a switch of nettles. His heart quaked as he considered what he might do, and he looked out upon the congregation shuffling to their seats. From the corner of his eye, he glimpsed the leer-ing face of a gargoyle mocking him from atop a column. His cheeks paled.

For the first time, he wondered if it was a power of a differ-ent hue that had bestowed this gift, made him believe he had been divinely chosen. Almost he decided not to go through with his experiment, but in a moment when his fellow choris-ters all turned their eyes to the choirmaster, Benedictus pulled out the nettles and dragged them across the tender skin on the inside of his arm. The stings and welts drew tears to his eyes. The plants fell from his fingers, and he crushed them beneath his feet. His arm burned with the fire of God.

The choirmaster raised his hand. The sopranos began their measures, and the altos joined them, and then the baritones added their notes. Benedictus and the other tenors then entered the music. But within only a few bars, the voices around him melted into silence as Benedictus sang with the voice of an angel.

Once again the sick and the lame in the pews felt balm and benison washing their pains away. Their wounds and afflictions ceased to hurt them. Their eyes became clear, and their breaths deeper and freer. When Benedictus at last finished, one great sigh arose from the people in the church, like the voice of the west wind blowing through the nave. Wonder and pride surged through him, and he wiped tears of pain and delight from his own eyes.

This Sunday marked a turning point for Benedictus in the choir at the Church of Saint Anne. Each Sunday, more and more worshipers thronged the church as word spread of the healing powers to be found there. Even the young woman who could not bear to be touched, and whose cry had caused Benedictus's first injury, had been seen shaking the hand of a viscountess. The fame of Benedictus's divine singing reached even beyond Spa, to people in towns and cities farther and farther away—Brussels, even, and Aachen. For a few weeks, at least, Father Josquin was delighted by the increased attendance at his church. He boasted to his bishop that, at last, the exhausted and debauched nobility who came to Spa to recover from their unchaste lives were returning to God.

And yet Father Josquin suspected that they came not for the sacraments, but to listen to Benedictus. And he chafed at the repute his tenor was gaining for healing the sick and bringing the lame to their feet. Nevertheless, he noticed with some alarm that Benedictus, whose voice every Sunday was more divine than ever, looked pale and tired—not at all the robust fellow he once was.

What the priest was not to know, however, was the pain the tenor suffered each week. At first, Benedictus had had to inflict only small injuries upon himself, small stings or cuts, pinpricks or bruises. But as the weeks stretched on, Benedictus found he must suffer greater and greater pains in order to sustain his miraculous voice. He was now covered with bruises and welts, cuts that he would not allow to heal. His stomach coiled and twisted from the bitter herbs he choked down. He limped with blisters on his heels from wearing tight boots with no hose. He hardly slept. His nights were torment, for it was then that evil doubts assailed him.

"Is it you, God?" he would whimper, his eyes burning. And then he would hunch the blanket around himself, for fear of hearing the answer.

Naturally, Benedictus did not tell his family what pains he suffered to produce his voice. His maman hovered over him anxiously, urging him to rest, eat some good soup. He sent her away.

He gave up his job, naturally. Benedictus could hardly afford to risk renewing his health by constant immersion in the healing waters of Spa. And yet even as he shunned their medicinal benefits, he doubted that they conferred half as much good to the bathers as did his own singing. For indeed, all the people who had trembled in the baths for months were now standing tall in the Church of Saint Anne. As a young man whose family had always lived in attendance on others, the novelty of such power was a heady drink. The more he mortified his body with pain, the greater he knew his power to be. "This must be God's power, if this is the effect," he muttered in the alleys on his way to church. "I am healing them. I, Benedictus Cuvier, am healing them. I am doing what the waters cannot do, what the church cannot do without me." He dared not stop. And yet he was terrified.

Then came the Sunday when a woman in the congregation, just before Father Josquin was to deliver the sacraments, called out in a passionate voice. "Let the tenor sing!" And a murmur of agreement rose into the vault of the church and echoed there: "Let him sing!" the walls of the church commanded. "Let him sing!"

This was of course insupportable for the priest, and for the bishop of Liege, who was in the church that Sunday. After the mass, they called Benedictus to the vestry to rebuke him.

"It is unseemly for a member of the choir to put himself forward and disrupt the holy sacraments, and make himself a figure of note, and to seek and accept that adulation which is due only to God," the bishop said.

"But I heal them," Benedictus croaked, looking with bloodshot, fevered eyes from priest to bishop. "My voice heals them. I believe it is a miracle."

"This is preposterous, heretical—"

"Outrageous, blasphemous," the bishop shouted over the priest. "That you should stand here in the Church of Saint Anne and take credit for the work of God is not to be tolerated, supported, or allowed to endure!"

"I forbid you to sing in this church again," Father Josquin

said, and then added with disdain wrinkling his nose, "besides, you are only an attendant at the baths. There is nothing miraculous about an attendant at the baths."

Benedictus felt the sting of these words as mere pinpricks compared to the wounds he had inflicted on himself. His hand shook as he held it up. "Allow me to prove it to you," he began, but Father Josquin flew into a rage, spitting foam from his white lips.

At that, the bishop of Liege took the priest aside and spoke so quietly that Benedictus, weaving a bit from side to side where he stood, could not hear him. A monotonous chorus rattled through his head: Is it you, God? Is it you?

When the clerics returned to him, they were both smiling, smiling as do those who hold the clue to the enemy's defeat.

"One week from now we will see how miraculous your voice is," the bishop said to Benedictus. And so they allowed him to go. He staggered toward his home, limping and dizzy, shaking his head, vainly trying to rid himself of the persistent buzzing in his ears. When he reached his room, he climbed into his bed, drawing the covers around his aching shoulders. He tried to think. Although many things lately had become unclear—such as remembering what year he had been born, how to carve a whistle from a twig, the name of his maman's friend the upholsterer's wife, such tasks and information that he had learned in his short life—one thing was clear to him: The priest and the bishop had agreed upon some scheme to discredit him, a test—a temptation? Therefore he must be prepared to meet a challenge next Sunday. What that challenge might be he could not contemplate. His head hurt him too much, and a spasm darting through his bones made him close his eyes and weep.

He returned to the Church of Saint Anne the following Sunday armed with a small knife, which he concealed in his sleeve. The choirmaster seemed to be in the confidence of Father Josquin, for he gave Benedictus a wry smile, and then turned away to hide a laugh.

Benedictus squinted his eyes to see through the fog that covered them. There was the goggle-eyed gargoyle, grinning into the choirstalls and making Benedictus shudder. "Is it you, God?" he whispered, turning his weak eyes away.

The church was filled with the sick and the hurt. The squeaking of bath-chair wheels rolling down the aisles was like the squealing of rats. The vaulted ceiling echoed with coughs and wheezes like the halls of a sanitarium. When every seat was filled, the doors by the chancel opened and the bishop of Liege entered, escorting an old man who leaned on a cane. This old man was led to the front pew and seated there with a blanket tucked around his legs.

Benedictus knew all these people had come to hear him sing, had come to be healed. His heart ached with pity for them, and for himself who had been afflicted with this gift. Although he could barely stand, he knew he must sing, he must grasp the burning sword of divine power in his hands. When the organ began the *praeludium,* Benedictus Cuvier stood. He was the only member of the choir now, all others being irrelevant. He gripped the railing of the choir stall in front of him for balance. He dimly spied his maman in the congregation. He began to sing.

His voice rose into the church, and the people in the pews seemed to follow it with their eyes. They looked up, and some raised their hands as if to catch the sound and swallow it. Benedictus closed his own eyes, steadying himself against the rail. He heard the clatter of canes falling to the stone floor. He heard the coughing grow still.

Yet when he opened his eyes and beheld the rapt looks of the congregation, he could see that the old man in the front pew was unmoved. This man sat scowling at the altar, oblivious to the stir around him. Even as Benedictus sang, he knew this was his test. The old man was deaf.

Benedictus glanced at Father Josquin and at the bishop and at the choirmaster. They smiled, each of them. Benedictus eased the knife out of his sleeve and into his hand, and without missing a note, pressed the point into his side.

At once, a woman in the congregation began to weep with joy as the voice of Benedictus penetrated her heart. In every corner of the church, people were staring in wonder at their own hands, feeling their limbs, drawing deep, soothing breaths, touching their own round and vivid cheeks and laughing tearful laughs. Still the old man in the front pew was unmoved, unhearing.

Benedictus pushed the knife in deeper. His voice caught and then steadied, and it seemed to the congregation that his voice came from all directions at once, and filled them as water fills a glass. People turned to their neighbors with shining eyes, free for the first time since they could remember of all pain, all sickness, all weakness and despair.

Is it you, God? ran the voice in Benedictus's head. *Is it you?*

The tenor's voice went on, and the old man in the front row suddenly sat upright, and looked around him and quavered, "Who is that singing? What is that music?"

The bishop of Liege jumped to his feet in murderous fury, but before he could take a step toward the tenor, Benedictus fell dead and his voice was stilled forever.

JENNIFER ARMSTRONG

The fictional scenario intrigues me. Benedictus is a humble young man mysteriously endowed with a divine gift. He's not really singing to heal anyone, but nor is he interested in his own glory. He's being burned alive by the power of God, which is more than a mortal can withstand, but at the same time, he is mesmerized by the power and unable to turn away from it. He is a moth to the flame.

Where does exceptional talent come from? Who deserves such a gift? What is the source of beauty? I know many people struggle with these questions. Some torment themselves— either because they have been blessed with talent, or because they haven't. This story is a rumination on the questions, not an answer, and certainly not my answer. My role as a writer is to explore these questions in a fictitious context, to give shape to them through character and scene. If I have anything definitive to say about this story it is that the world does not care what the source of the talent is, only that it be allowed to express itself and give us all joy. God knows we all need as much of that as we can get.

Jennifer Armstrong is the author of dozens of books for children and teens, including historical fiction, picture books, non-fiction, short stories, and speculative fiction. For details of her books please see her Web site at www.jennifer-armstrong.com. She lives in Saratoga Springs, New York, with her husband.

STAR VISION

BY SHONTO BEGAY

Dees'T'ii *(Vision Quest) ceremonies are done to visualize an illness and prescribe the proper healing ceremony. These arduous and eye-drying experiences are accompanied by beautiful chants or songs of medicine men, requiring deep concentration into the night sky, into fields of stars.*

I remember sitting that night upon a rise
two hundred yards north of our hogan.
My father and three older men seeking a vision among the
stars.
The low drone of the chant filtering into the clear night air.
Stars. Bright and layered.
It seems like we are drifting among them.
I sit off the west side,
gripping an arrowhead and a bag of corn pollen.
I am a guard for the elders
as they concentrate hard into the constellation.
I sit like I have sat some nights before,
silent and reverent.
I sit vigilant of anyone or anything that may disturb their
concentration.
Maybe a cold play of light,

a silent dark shadowy movement just off the edge.
I send my own prayers of courage into the indigo sky.
My thoughts to keep dark mysteries at bay.
My aunt's illness, heavy and pained,
keeps her tired and sad. Keeps her inside herself.
The medicine man,
with his vision seekers, tries to find a reason for this illness
and thus a possible remedy.
The moaning of this group chant rising now and then.
It continues.
I feel tired and uncomfortable sitting among the yuccas and
snakeweeds.
Occasional clearing of the throat,
occasional break in the chant punctuating the night.
This should be a good night for visions.
The sky clear of clouds. The sky wild with stars.
These old men have done this many times before,
captured and held visions in the stars.

In time I grow weary,
I wish the ceremony would end so I can sleep.
I have a sheep-herding job tomorrow.
Wiggling uncomfortably,
to reposition my tingling legs,
I let the arrowhead slip out of my hand momentarily,
I retrieve it quickly.
Aware of my job again,
I look up into the twinkling heaven and see shooting stars
bursting about.

But it is strange.
I glance up again and stare into a void of darkness,
a field of sky where no stars shine.
Like something huge had blocked my view,
the empty area at once grows lighter.
Stars upon this area dance and dart
like fireflies.

Upon this lighter area,
I begin to see colors and motions,
clearing like smoke parting.
A focusing.
I see and capture my first vision.
An old man I know riding a bay horse
moving into my frame from the north.
He wears a pink shirt.
Tufts of his white hair wave around his flowered headband.
He looks about nervously
as he dismounts in a sagebrush-covered area
dotted sparsely by young pinion pine.
He steps gently onto an anthill,
looks about again and kneels down.
He digs a hole and slips a small bundle of something into the
anthill.
Covering it quickly,
I see his lips move in a silent curse prayer.
He mounts his horse and rides out of the star field.

The night sky reclaims this vision space,

and I sit there puzzled as to what just happened.
The silent sentinels of sagebrush and yuccas
sit rooted in the dark.
Skeletal branches of bare junipers reach for the heavens.
Owls hoot far off in the night.

The elders eventually fall silent
and the vision quest ends.
We file back to the healing hogan silently,
picking our way through dark splotches of snakeweeds.
Inside the hogan,
strong brown faces lit by kerosene lamp,
voices low and reverent,
the elders determined to lay claim to a complete picture.
There was a vision of a hoofprint,
another of an anthill.
Another felt a threat from the north.
Collective and incomplete,
the image is fragmented and elusive.
Fragrance of burned sage and mountain tobacco
hangs and clings to the cribbed hogan walls.

I know I possess the whole picture.
A wave of fright and excitement washes over me.
I volunteer news of my sky vision and am quickly brushed
aside,
reprimanded for negligence of duty as a guard.
It is not my job to seek a vision.
I am young and not yet tested.

A stern voice even suggests that I be blamed for this incomplete vision.
Finally, exhaustion wins over.
The hogan falls silent for the night.

The morning finds the men encircling mutton stew and tortillas,
sipping hot coffee,
still trying to fit pieces of their visions together.
The illness of my aunt and this diagnostic vision quest
cannot be left disjointed.
Only through a complete and clear vision
can the cause of her illness be determined,
thus a proper ceremony prescribed.
Tired and sleepy, I try again to share my vision.
The image replays itself in my dreams.
I have to convince the old men.
They finally humor me and allow me to tell my story.
The sheep-herding job is given to my younger sister,
who gives me a hard cold look.

We drive to the site I saw my drama unfold the night before.
The groaning old truck rides the waves of sand dunes and slick rocks
out onto the sage-covered valley north of us.
We pile out, and with a little prayer and pollen-placing event,
my father digs into the mound of anthill.
He removes a bundle of cloth holding my aunt's hair.

The object of illness.
The dark bundle dangles from his outstretched arms like a
dead bird,
lifeless in resignation to eternity.
The real vision of an evil deed pierces me in the heart,
young and innocent heart.
The old man of my vision is a relative.
A clan uncle just up the valley toward the north.
The elders apply appropriate ceremony.
With the placing of corn pollen
they render the bundle harmless.

The old sorcerer grows weak in his practice
and eventually grows destitute and suffers for his evil.
My aunt recovers once again into her strong self.
I am called out whenever stargazing ceremonies happen.
At first, I thrive in this newfound ability and adulation.
I see it as a way to avoid hard and boring chores.
I am blessed with this vision.
I am special and am treated as such.
My older brothers are suspicious, as usual.
They taunt my gift
and say I may even be in alliance with the witches.
They are young,
envious, and tired.
In time I grow to see this as a chore,
not unlike hoeing weeds and hauling water and firewood.

I agonize at the expectation

as another strange truck pulls up to our hogan
in a cloud of dust.
Another vision seeker.
I often wish I were elsewhere in the middle of a vision
quest,
not missing community dances,
the girlfriends, and potential adventures.
I make up excuses to avoid stargazing.
I see it as an obstacle to my growing up.

In time I move on.
Remove myself from this picture.
Some say my vision has transferred itself onto my canvas.
I say, it was just my turn.

Shonto Begay

Shonto Begay, born in a hogan on a reservation in Arizona, was
the fifth of sixteen children. Their father was a Navaho medicine man, their mother a weaver of rugs.

He attended federal boarding schools on the Navajo reservation and later received a fine arts degree from the Institute of
American Indian Arts in Santa Fe, New Mexico. He has been a
professional artist since 1983, showing his work in galleries and
museums throughout the United States He was asked to con-
tribute to this anthology after the editor saw his *Navajo: Visions
and Voices Across the Mesa,* a book of poetry and artwork that
shows his special, highly spiritual relationship with his people
and his homeland.

Early in his youth, Shonto learned to see the world around

him and savor its beauty—the red mesas, pinion, and juniper. He has said, "My world was the circular line of the horizon. This was the place that harbored ancient gods and animal beings that were so alive in the stories of my people. The teachings of my elders made it very clear that this land is sacred and we belong to it; it does not belong to us. I learned that Nature was more than just what I saw—that she is life and therefore gives and maintains life. She commands respect."

"Star Vision" is a true story.

ELVIS LIVES

BY JOHN SLAYTON

Our Elvis. Who art in Elvis.
Hallowed be thy Elvis.
Give us this Elvis our daily Elvis.
Forgive us our Elvises
as we forgive those who Elvis against us.
Lead us not into Elvis,
but deliver us from Elvis.
For Elvis is the Elvis,
and the Elvis and the Elvis, forever.
Amen.

"That is nucking futs," Curtis said, sitting behind the wheel of his Dodge Dart. A strap of torn headliner hung from the ceiling of the car. It waved in the breeze, snapping like a blunt whip. "A dream? I still can't believe that's why we're going to Graceland? Because Elvis told you to in a dream."

"It seemed so damn real, like I could touch it," I said, sounding tired. We had left from Tampa early that morning and had been driving all day, and, about every fifty miles, I had to explain to Curtis why I wanted to go to Graceland. My arm rested on the open window of the passenger door.

"Elvis said there would be something there for me."

"Like what, Jack?" Curtis asked. He had a big round face with a cluster of three freckles below his right eye. His thick dark hair bushed out from his head.

"I don't know." I looked down at the seat and pulled at a loose thread hanging from one of the seams that was coming apart. "Something he said I needed."

Curtis looked at me. "Come on. That might be all that's holding the car together."

Curtis's dad bought the car for him six months before he died. Curtis went kind of nuts back then. I never understood that, because his dad treated him like crap. Curtis used to say that suicide was never the answer, but sometimes it was the solution. I thought he was kidding until he actually tried it. They put him in this mental place for a couple months. He dropped school for the rest of the year, maybe for life. Curtis and I hadn't talked about what happened. All I knew for sure was that an ambulance pulled up to his house with its rollers on and carried him out. Curtis never volunteered the information, and I avoided the subject like the plague. But I had to admit I was curious about it.

Since Curtis got out of the mental place, his mom watched him like a hawk. Curtis had to tell her that we were camping out over the long Memorial Day weekend to get away, and he let me know that if we got caught his butt was meat. My mom went away with her boyfriend for the weekend, so I didn't have to worry too much.

"Where is this something going to be?" Curtis asked, turning his head to face me.

"Keep your eyes on the road." Curtis faced front. "I don't know. His grave?"

"What exactly is it that we're looking for?" Curtis asked.

With a pause between each word, I said, "I don't know." I looked out the open window at the side of the road rushing past in a blur.

"Okay, but for someone telling you to drive all the way to Graceland, he didn't explain much."

Elvis had been dead three years, and since his death I had become fascinated with him. I loved him. I guess it was love. Whatever it was, I got a charge out of him. I had a poster of him in my room, of the young Elvis before he got fat and started wearing all those rhinestones and capes. He was wearing a loose yellow shirt and held a microphone. He wasn't singing or anything. He just stared ahead. He looked so intense. That was the thing about Elvis: his eyes. Even in that poster, those eyes seemed like they were still looking, looking into the future or through you and into the core of your heart.

I guess that's why I started having the Elvis dreams. They were always strange dreams that stuck with me, haunted me: Elvis floating down out of the sky dressed as my fairy godmother or Elvis as the pope leading a long procession. Finally, last week, Elvis and John Wayne rode up to me on horses, and Elvis told me to go to Graceland. It seemed right. Some things you can't explain.

We decided to find a place to rack out for the night, someplace that was free. We barely had enough money for gas and an occasional stop at the Golden Arches. Curtis got off the interstate, and we headed across the countryside. I saw a hand-made sign along the side of the road that read: COME ALONG HOUND DOG TO THE SATURDAY REVIVAL. 3:00 P.M. AT HAMILTON PARK. A few miles later we came across another sign: DON'T BE CRUEL! COME TO THE REVIVAL. Then another, IT'S NOW OR NEVER. TURN HERE.

"We can sleep at that park," Curtis said, turning on his blinker as we approached the entrance. "Maybe we'll catch Elvis."

The road into the park sloped upward and flattened at a large parking lot. Some people headed to their cars. A few had books, I guess Bibles, under their arms. We parked and went to an empty pavilion set back beneath some pine trees. We sat up on one of the tables underneath the pavilion and watched the people through the trees.

A guy, with long sideburns and slick black hair pushed up in a pompadour, stood under the main pavilion tearing posters and streamers off a long table. He balled them up and shoved them into a garbage can at the edge of the pavilion. He went back to the table and placed items that were spread across the table into a large trunk-style suitcase.

"That guy does look like Elvis," Curtis said, dipping his head toward him.

"Maybe it is," I said half seriously. He did look like Elvis from the distance.

After Elvis died, he kept coming back like Christ. Every week, when Curtis was in that mental place, I snuck the *National Enquirer* into his room, and I read Curtis stories from it about Elvis. They cheered Curtis up. There were stories about Elvis working at a car wash in Albuquerque or flopping Whoppers in Pittsburgh, or about the emergence of an Elvis love child or of Elvis being abducted by aliens and coming back with a revolutionary new diet. The articles always showed a picture of him, while he was on stage with his head bent down into his up-turned collar, his face contorted and covered with sweat. Next to that was a picture of the supposed mother holding the supposed baby in her arms or one of the supposed Elvis flopping Whoppers or of Elvis, holding a sample recipe from his new diet, with his arm around a bunch of aliens. It was a riot!

When Elvis finished, he closed the case, latched it shut and hefted it off the table. He leaned against the weight of the case as he carried it toward a blue pickup truck in the parking lot. Spotting us, he turned and headed our way.

As he got closer, his resemblance to Elvis faded. His hair was the way Elvis kept it, with long sideburns. But he had a beak nose, and his face was pockmarked like he used to have acne real bad. His boots huffed as he walked. They looked about two sizes too large for his feet.

"How are you fellows today?" he asked, grunting with effort as he hefted his case onto the table opposite Curtis and me.

"What do you have there?" I asked, leaning forward to get a look.

He turned the case, which scraped against the wood table, and opened it. Inside the case were key rings, statues, decals, and bumper stickers with Jesus or one of the disciples on them. "I sell religious articles, as you can see."

I stepped up to the case and looked through it. There was a

John the Baptist head key ring. There was a glass globe with a figure of Christ nailed to the cross inside. I picked it up, shook it, and watched the snowflakes fall around Jesus. I held it out for Curtis to see.

"What a bunch of crap," Curtis said, shaking his head.

I pulled the globe back away from Curtis and replaced it in the case.

Elvis looked at Curtis. "It's all in how you look at it, I guess. I had one lady who bought one of those Jesus key rings. She had liver cancer and as she lay in her bed dying, she had that key ring on her nightstand." Elvis rested his foot on the picnic bench and leaned on his knee. The shiny brown leather boot with an intricate carving like a huge peacock feather, came to just below his knee. "Her husband said that she would take it off the nightstand, look at it for hours some days, and smile. Somehow that little key ring cut through all her suffering and gave her hope."

"Those boots are cool," I said, bending over to take a closer look.

Curtis glanced at me, got off the picnic table, and stretched his body as he yawned.

"Those belonged to Daddy. He was a preacher. He went from town to town, preaching 'the Word.' When Daddy was alive that was another time. Back then, if someone broke down on the road, someone would stop and help them. But now, they just drive by. People should help one another when they have the chance."

"Why?" Curtis asked. He bent down to the ground and picked up a large handful of pine needles.

"Because we are all brothers," Elvis said, placing his hand flat on the table for balance.

"Maybe in Podunk, Arkansas that's true. Did you stop to think that your brother may try to gut you with a can opener? Anymore, it's every man for himself." Curtis climbed back up on the bench of the picnic table and sat down on the table.

"Then why not steal and cheat and lie? Why not just see how much you can get away with?"

"One good reason: jail." Curtis leaned forward, resting his elbows on his knees, and sorted through the pine needles, tossing them away one by one.

A small ivory statue in the case caught my eye. At first, I thought it was Jesus. The figure wore long robes like Jesus, but sideburns were painted unevenly on his face, and the top of his hair was styled in a pompadour. Jesus held a cross in front of his mouth like a microphone. Electric blue dots covered the eyes, and his mouth was shaped into a snarl.

"That's a statue of Elvis Christ," I said.

Elvis nodded. "That's one of my best sellers. I spend a lot of time in the Memphis area."

I took it out of the case. I held the statue of Elvis Christ in my hand. I felt the statue staring at me, burning a hole right through me.

"So there is no real reason for behaving morally other than society punishing you if you don't. Anyone can do anything as long as they are absolutely sure that they can get away with it? Is that it?" Elvis asked Curtis.

Curtis nodded thoughtfully.

Elvis went on. "How you behave, how you regard your

fellow man, determines the sum value of your soul."

"And what does that mean when you're six feet under?" Curtis asked, smiling.

"Your soul will achieve its final reward, if you also put your faith in the Lord Jesus."

"Do you really believe that?" Curtis asked.

"I have to hang my hat on something."

"What do you think, Jack?" Curtis asked.

I took my eyes away from the statue and shifted them back and forth between Curtis and Elvis. "I'd like to hope that he is right," I said, gripping the ivory statue.

"Do you think that he is right?" Curtis asked.

"I don't know," I said.

Curtis shook his head and looked away. "I'd rather take my odds with the *Publishers Clearing House Sweepstakes,*" Curtis said. He placed the tip of a pine needle in his mouth. "Let me ask you a question, Elvis. If there was a baby in a burning building, would you run in and save it at the risk of your own life?"

"Yes, I would."

"What if you knew prior to going in that you wouldn't make it back out but that you would save the baby?"

"How would he know that?" I asked.

"I don't know," Curtis said, straightening. "Just say that he would."

"I would save the baby," Elvis said, folding his arms across his chest.

Curtis laughed. "That's something that's real easy to say," Curtis said, tossing one of his pine needle spears in Elvis's direction. "But, if the situation ever happened, that baby would burn up, and you would stand there and moan about how cruel life is."

"You're right in one respect. I don't know what action I would take until I was in that situation, but I know what I would want to do, and I know that I would have to live with my actions after whatever I chose to do."

Curtis considered this for a moment, then shook his head. "It's all bullshit," he said. He tossed the rest of the pine needles and looked away.

"So, are you going to take the statue?" Elvis asked me.

I started to hand it back to him. "We don't have much money."

Elvis put his hand up to stop me. "Call that a gift." Elvis said, smiling.

"Thanks!"

Elvis winked as he closed his suitcase and dragged it off the table. He went to the sky blue pickup truck in the parking lot. Elvis opened the door and slid his case across the seat. The truck rumbled to life, and he drove away.

That night, I dreamed about Elvis. Elvis played ping-pong against a large cloud hovering above the opposite end of the table. A light emanated from the cloud and seemed to pulsate. Elvis wore a heavy sequined jumpsuit and a pair of sunglasses. I floated in the air above the table watching the ball click against the table back and forth between the two players. The cloud of light hit the ball, which nicked the edge of the table and fell to the floor.

"Your point, God," Elvis said, gathering the ball. "That's

10,548,932 to 0." Elvis moved his paddle toward the ball to serve.

"You've never scored?" I asked.

Elvis stopped his paddle before hitting the ball and looked up at me. "Don't you think God knows where I'm going to hit the ball?"

I shrugged my shoulders. "Elvis, why am I going to Graceland?"

"Why? Did Noah ask why when God told him to build the ark?"

"Yes."

"Well, did God tell him why?"

"I believe that he did."

"Well, you're not Noah. Are you?"

The cloud darkened and a low rumbling emitted from it.

"Be patient. I'll serve in a minute," Elvis said to the cloud, then to me, "I need to warn you, Jack. Watch out for Elvis."

"But aren't you Elvis?"

"Don't ask stupid questions. Pay attention to what I tell you."

"Then I shouldn't go to Graceland?"

Elvis thumped his paddle flat onto the table. "Did I tell you not to go to Graceland? You're starting to piss me off. Don't make me come up there and put my foot up your ass. Of course you need to go to Graceland. But watch out for Elvis."

"Okay," I said, rolling my eyes.

"Don't patronize me, son. Don't give up on Graceland. No matter what. Don't lose hope. I'll have something for you there. Look for my pride and joy." Elvis picked up his paddle and served the ball, which clumped into the net. "Your point again, God."

I drove most of the next day. Before we started, I placed the statue of Elvis on the dash just above a large cut that had grown in the late May heat and become a source of dried yellow flecks of foam that dotted the dashboard and bigger soft chunks that lay on the plastic surface and rolled down onto the car seat and the floor. A couple of times the statue tumbled off the dash into Curtis's lap. He looked at me as he put the statue back, each time thumping it down a little more heavily.

Early in the afternoon, we saw two vehicles pulled off the outside lane of the road. The first was a small white car with its flashers on and the hood up; the other, an old sky blue Ford pickup, was stopped about twenty yards ahead of the first car.

"Oh, my gosh," I said. "It's that salesman, Elvis."

Elvis stood in front of the white car. He wiped sweat off the back of his neck with his handkerchief. A large woman with a tent of a dress stood beside him.

"Let's blow on by. We're already running late," Curtis said.

I slowed and edged our car off onto the shoulder of the road. Curtis exhaled disgustedly. I got out of the car and went to Elvis and the lady. Curtis lagged behind me.

"Do you need any help?" I called ahead.

"Hello," he said, recognizing us. "Her engine overheated."

Two kids, around the ages of seven and ten, wrestled with each other on the grassy median, which sloped steeply like a trough between the north- and south-bound traffic. Curtis stopped a few feet away and folded his arms across his chest.

"I hooked the hose up," Elvis said, tromping around the front of his car. I could hear his boots breath out air with every step. "We need to get some water into the radiator."

I turned to Curtis. "Do we have any water in the car?"

Curtis tilted his head and looked at me like I was from outer space.

I heard a kid yelp. I turned to see the younger boy had fallen in the middle of the outside lane. A van headed toward him. Elvis jumped out into the lane, grabbed the boy, and threw him to the side. The van slammed on its brakes. The little boy sprawled across the median grass. Elvis tried to dive out of the way of the van skidding toward him, but his foot pulled up in his boot, which bent back underneath his foot, causing him to stumble. I'll never forget the sound, like a wet towel thrown hard against a cement wall. Elvis slid past me across the median grass and down the slope on his back like a bobsledder. He came to a rest at the bottom. His socks were half off and drooped limply over the top of his feet. I ran down the median and knelt beside him.

"Is the boy all right?" Elvis asked. He lay there unmoving.

I looked over and saw the mother holding the boy in her arms. "He's okay." Elvis reached up and clutched my shirt. I could see the pain in his face. "Hang on. We'll get you some help," I said. He released my shirt and closed his eyes. I felt a pulse on the side of his neck. I looked up at Curtis shifting back and forth on his feet uneasily.

A man walked up beside Curtis. "Is he okay?" the man asked.

I knelt on the grass, dazed. "Elvis got hit by a van," I said dumbly.

"I've got a CB. I'll call for help." The man went back to his car.

Curtis hopped down the bank and stood next to me. "We need to get out of here. Once the cops get here, they'll want to check out our story. They'll call my mom."

"But . . . but . . . he's hurt. He may be dying," I said, staring off.

"If I get caught out here, they'll put me back in that mental place," Curtis said. He grabbed me by the shirt and pulled me to my feet. "I know they will. I can't take that."

"We can't just leave him," I said, shaking my head.

"We don't even know him. There're other people here. They can take care of him," Curtis said. "Come on!" Curtis headed up the bank toward the car.

I stood up slowly with my head down and followed Curtis. When I got into the car, Curtis started it and put it in drive. I slumped in the seat and looked down at Elvis lying lifeless on the grass below. As we pulled out onto the interstate, I saw Elvis's boots standing in the middle of the passing lane, heels together and toes pointed slightly out, as if they had been set there, side by side facing the oncoming traffic.

We drove away. The statue sat on the dashboard above the yellow gash, pursed like a sideways eye, leaking dried yellow flakes of foam. The electric blue eyes of the statue burned ahead. With its arms raised, it perched above the gash spreading up in the heat like the final unfolding of a decaying flower.

We drove the rest of the way in almost complete silence. Late that night we arrived at Graceland. Curtis pulled a flashlight out of the glove compartment and shoved it in his pocket. We left the car about a half mile away and hopped the fieldstone fence onto the grounds. A light rain cleaned the air of the muggy heat. The full moon stood high above the misty air that coated it like a sheer drapery. We ran to the back corner of the house. Raindrops glistened off the leaves of the bushes next to the house; the leaves twitched as random drops of rain glanced off them. There were no lights on inside. The place looked deserted. I saw a circular brick structure behind the house. "That's the Meditation Gardens," I said. "That's where he's buried."

Several lamps dimly lit stained-glass windows set into the brick wall surrounding the garden. In the center one large fountain and five smaller fountains shot up from a round pool. Lights under the surface illuminated the spouting water that clapped back down.

Curtis and I stepped down the short stairs. The rain had seeped through my jeans and shirt, and I could feel it cold against my skin. We stood at the foot of Elvis's gravestone in front of the brick wall and the half circle of white columns. The eternal flame, encased in glass, wavered at the head of Elvis's grave. Three small statues of angels sat below the flame, their heads bent to the side looking down on the large stone slab.

"What are we looking for?" Curtis asked.

"He told me to look for his pride and joy," I said.

Curtis crinkled his nose. "It's a pretty good bet that's not his grave," Curtis said.

"I know, but I wanted to see his grave. And I have no idea what his pride and joy could be."

Curtis nodded. He offered me a cigarette, which I took; Curtis followed with a light. We watched the rain pelt off Elvis's gravestone.

"Do you think he's dead?" Curtis asked.

"I don't know," I said, not sure who he was talking about.

"Why did he give himself up for that kid," Curtis said, taking a drag.

"Like he said, he would've had a hard time looking himself in the mirror if he didn't try to save him." I looked at the ember of my cigarette. "We shouldn't have left."

Curtis was silent for a minute. "He thought he had time to save both himself and the kid when he went out there," Curtis said. "But he didn't. He screwed up."

"After it happened, the first thing he did was ask about that kid."

"Then he was a fool. My old man used to say that there isn't anyone in this world that's ever going to do anything for you but you."

"Do you believe that?"

"I don't know." Curtis stared at the ground. "Dad was always on me about something. When I washed the car, he always found some spot that I had missed or maybe the chrome wasn't quite shiny enough, but there was always something. I could never please him. No matter what I did." Curtis took a drag, sucking the smoke deep into his lungs. "It's hard when someone you look up to treats you like an asshole."

"He was your father."

Curtis nodded. "I still feel he's watching everything I do,

looking down at me, judging me. Sometimes, I can't stand it."

"Is that why you . . ." I stopped myself before completing the entire question.

Curtis squinted his eyes and nodded. "But you know, in the ambulance. That night. After I did it," he said. "You'd think that I would've been freaking out, but I lay there in the ambulance and felt free of everything."

"Why did you do it?"

"I don't know," he said. There was a long silence. Finally, Curtis said, "I'm hopeless."

"Would you try it again?" I said, looking at Curtis, trying to peer inside of him.

"Not like that," he said, shaking his head. Curtis crushed his cigarette against one of the statues next to the gravestone. The butt bent over and snapped at the filter like a broken finger. "Pride and joy, huh. Maybe he was talking about his car."

"That must be it," I said, straightening. I tossed my cigarette into the fountain.

We found a long carport between the house and a small building with a short white fence in front of it. The dark shapes of three cars rested on the floor of the carport. Curtis turned on the flashlight and shone it around. A latticework of white beams covered the ceiling making a pattern of uneven boxes. In the middle of the carport was Elvis's 1973 Stutz Blackhawk. A lot of people associate a pink Cadillac with Elvis. The truth is he bought that car for his mother. The Blackhawk was the car he drove.

The Blackhawk gleamed in the pale light of the carport. I went to the driver-side door and tried the handle. Curtis went around to the other side of the car. I was surprised when the door released. I pulled it open. The car was rich with the smell of the bright red leather that covered the interior. As I slid into the car, my wet pants burped across the seat. Curtis lifted the handle on the passenger's side. It was locked. I reached over and unlocked it. I closed the door and put my hands on the red steering wheel.

"Do you have any idea what we're looking for?" Curtis asked, getting into the car.

"No," I said.

I tried to open the glove compartment, which was locked, and felt the floor under the seat, but I couldn't find so much as a bottle cap on the floor. Curtis felt around underneath his seat as well. I reached over into the backseat and searched the floor and shoved my hand into the gap between the back and bottom of the seat. I didn't find anything. I slumped back into the driver's seat.

"Why don't we check the trunk?" Curtis asked. He got out of the car, closing the door behind him. "See if you can find a latch to open it."

I felt around underneath the dash for a latch or button. As I sat there, I felt Elvis watching me sitting in his car. I heard Elvis's voice from my dreams: "Something just for you, Jack." It was then that I caught a whiff of something that cut through the smell of leather like a knife. It was only for an instant, but it was distinct and pronounced and smelled like a fart. I thought maybe it could've been a fart. Elvis had probably farted in this car a whole bunch of times. That's something you never really think about, but you know that it's probably true. Actually, I thought that maybe he had farted in the car that last day he drove it and that fart had stayed in the car the whole time. Just for me.

I started cracking up, just about rolling on the seat, and, every time I moved, my pants burped, making me laugh harder.

"What's so damn funny?" Curtis asked, looking at me through the back window.

"I smelled one of Elvis's farts," I said.

"That's nice. See if you can get this trunk open."

"Don't you get it," I said. "That's it. That's what we came for."

"Huh," Curtis said. "You're kidding, right?"

"No, that's it. I know it."

"That's the whole pilgrimage right there. A fart? What's the point?"

"Maybe there isn't one. Maybe it doesn't have to make sense."

"But you believe the dreams and all that. That Elvis was sending you a message from the beyond."

"Yes."

"Why?"

"What else can I hang my hat on?"

We got back to Tampa late the next night. Nobody ever really knew that we were gone. A couple of weeks later, I saw a headline on the cover of the *National Enquirer* next to a picture of Elizabeth Taylor eating a chicken wing: ELVIS SERIOUSLY INJURED ON INTERSTATE WHILE SAVING LIFE OF YOUTH. It was a large article in the center of the magazine with several pictures. There was one of Elvis lying on the grass. Another picture showed that woman and her two kids standing there with dumb expressions on their faces. The article was a bunch of crap, mostly, except for talking about how Elvis saved that kid. It went on to say that Elvis had spent the last three years driving across the southeast selling religious articles in a sky blue pickup truck and that he would be released from the hospital sometime the following week.

Curtis cracked up when I showed him the article. I clipped the article out and tacked it up in my room next to the window. When Mom came in the next morning to wake me, she looked at the clipping, then looked at me like I was nucking futs. She never noticed the small statue of Elvis Christ, next to it on the windowsill, with its arms raised in the air, and its thin shadow stretching across the floor in the early morning light.

JOHN SLAYTON

John Slayton is a previously unpublished author and a graduate of the creative writing program at Florida International University. "Elvis Lives" is an excerpt from his current novel in progress *Running to Graceland*. He was moved to write it because Elvis was an idol who helped him steer his way through the trials and tribulations of adolescence and because faith and hope are qualities of the human heart that are most admirable.

The story "Elvis Lives" is set in May of 1980. To set the story in a historical perspective: Elvis Presley died August 16, 1977. He drove his Stutz Blackhawk a few hours before his death for a visit to the dentist. Originally buried at Forest Hill Cemetery in Memphis, Elvis's remains were moved to the Meditation Gardens at Graceland on October 2, 1977, with the remains of his mother, Gladys. His father, Vernon, lived at Graceland until his death on June 29, 1979. He was buried alongside Elvis. Graceland was opened to the general public on June 7, 1982. Over 600,000 people visit Graceland annually.

THE TIN MAN

BY LISA ROWE FRAUSTINO

Francesca "Cheese" Merel had an idea, a delicious idea, an idea she could barely wait to share with the others. As always when she left her room, though, she paused to read the list she'd taped on the door New Year's Day, resolving to live each minute to the fullest.

> *The Tao Te Cheese*
> 1. *Keep it simple.*
> 2. *Know your own heart.*
> 3. *Hold to your heart the wisdom of pizza.*
> 4. *Short or tall, big or small, Doc Franklin fits them all.*
> 5. *Patience. Timing. Perseverance. Accept it.*
> 6. *Don't let shit get to you.*
> 7. *Bend but don't break.*
> 8. *This isn't a crisis. It just is.*
> 9. *Feeling sorry for yourself doesn't change anything.*
> 10. *Death finds no place in those who are filled with life.*
>
> *P.S. There's no place like home.*

She'd written the list to stop feeling sorry for herself while the other patients were out in the rec room drinking fake champagne with family and friends. So the little ones had the flu and needed Mom to stay home with them because Dad had to work New Year's. So her grandparents had run out of frequent-flyer miles. So her friends all lived too far from the hospital to take a day out of their busy party schedules. So she'd been stuck in The Land of Oz for over two months already, waiting for a heart transplant. At least her family had been here for Christmas, and Thanksgiving, and her friends had shown up at her surprise seventeenth birthday party. At least she'd never been through cardiac arrest or strokes or money trouble like most of the others on the ward. She had it good.

With a sigh she ran her finger over the word *home*, then turned to push her IV pole along the faded yellow brick road that the first Tin Man had painted down the hallway years ago. Nobody even knew his real name anymore.

"Who feels lucky!" she called. Laughter trickled out doorways, and she added, "Last one there's the dumb scarecrow!"

It was time for their daily poker game. Along with the cards, she would deal out her proposal.

In the moment that the ref's hand releases the basketball, time seems to freeze, and with it Harmony Ali's racing heart. This is it, the day her fate will be determined, the last game of the state tournament her senior year, scouts in the audience, all eyes in the stadium riveted on her and her opponent, both crouched to jump ball. The other center has a good three inches of height over her, but Harmony knows she can win the tap. It's all in the timing.

"Zenith!" Her father's voice rings clear through the crowd's babble, as always, reminding her to tap the ball at the height of her jump.

Now.

She pushes off, power rippling the brown skin of her thighs, and she soars, her wrist arcing gracefully, fingers rising above the straining reach of her opponent, just barely, but enough to tap the ball. The game has begun.

"Pizza? You're gonna order pizza? Tonight!" Amar shook his head admiringly, wrinkles deepening around his eyes and mouth as he grinned. "That's why you're The Big Cheese and I'm just the tofu."

They all laughed. Amar was small and vegetarian, while Francesca was big for a girl, or at least she was supposed to be. The virus eating away at her heart had turned her into six feet of nothing but colorless skin and big bones. They'd started out calling her The Big Cheese as a joke, butchering her name to get a rise out of her— "Kees me, Fran-cheese-ka—" and she'd taken it over like a queen, saying, "Oui, the Grand Fromage, that's me."

"The audacity!" said Jacob, rubbing his middle-aged barrel belly in anticipation. "I like it! I'm in." Cheese had known he would be, with a type A personality guiding his work and play. Against Doc Franklin's orders he reported to work on the sly each day via the modem of his laptop computer. Now he threw a blue poker chip on the pile. "Hit me." Cheese dealt him the six of spades. Jacob winced at his other cards.

"I don't know about this pizza thing," said Peter. "What about our poles? And the nurses? And the rules? It's too complicated."

Cheese had expected that, too. Peter was . . . Peter. You had to spend energy uplifting him so he wouldn't drag you down. "Yo! *Tao Te Cheese* Numero Uno: Keep it simple. We call Three Guys Pies, set up a distraction for the nurses, unplug the poles from the monitors, get our asses on the elevator, punch G for ground floor, and when you get there, Peter, the pizza will be waiting for you all hot and ready to run down your chin."

"It's the grease that does that," said Amar dreamily.

"Isn't there someplace better than Three Rats?" said the Tin Man. His real name was Carlos, but for now he bore the name of honor given to the patient who had been in The Land of Oz (aka the transplant ward) waiting the longest for a heart. "They don't deliver beer."

"That's right!" said Jacob. "You can't have pizza without brews!"

"Hey, we aren't ordering any beer!" said Cheese. "This isn't a fraternity party!"

Peter was shaking his head. "You people aren't taking this seriously. I like pizza as much as the next guy, but it's so risky. If we got caught—"

"Aw, what can they do to us?" said Cheese. "Take away our salt substitute?"

Even Peter had to smile at that before he said, "The rules have reasons, you know. How will you feel if you're down in the lobby eating yourself sick when your heart comes, huh? How will you feel if something goes wrong when your monitor's unplugged?"

He stared the Tin Man down. They were all living on borrowed time or they wouldn't be there, hitched up to life support until the miracle happened, but Carlos was tempting fate.

Five months on the ward and he still hadn't had the luck of the draw. Cheese found herself staring at the makeshift ax that conveyed the title of Tin Man, with its empty wrapping paper tube for a handle, its aluminum-foil-covered cardboard for a blade, stuck in a crack between the upper parts of Carlos's pole. Tears welled as she remembered the ceremony when he'd received it from the last guy to receive a heart, three long weeks ago.

The air, suddenly heavy, pressed them into one of those clouds of self-pity that fogged up the ward a dozen times a day. They all felt the mood trying to jump onto their backs and push them down, but nobody said a word. Naming it out loud would only tempt despair. It was an unspoken law, immutable as stone: Ya gotta have faith. Without it, you couldn't survive this place—the wait, the transplant, the recovery. Save the down talk, the spill talk, the fear, for the group therapy sessions, when Doc Franklin led the way. She was the Wizard, only for real—no magic tricks in this Oz. Doc knew where they'd been, knew where they were going, knew exactly how to guide them through, if they'd let her.

"Peter's right," Cheese said, nodding. One by one, she stared the men down, pulling them all in out of the fog. She had that way about her, Francesca did—a way of getting people back on track, even though she was just a kid. Maybe *because* she was a kid.

"The Great Pizza Caper may be risky to your health," she said. "I don't much look forward to the aftershocks of 1,503 milligrams of sodium myself, but hey, a girl's gotta live, even if it kills her. You guys want out, fine by me. Be yourself. No apologies."

Amar spun a poker chip into the pile. "I'm in. Plain, no pepperoni. Hit me." He got a king and groaned. "This game's over for me."

The Tin Man dramatically dropped two chips on the pile. "I'll match that and raise you one slice with pepperoni. No more cards, though. I don't trust my luck."

"Oh, crap," said Jacob. Carlos was a lousy bluffer, and his grin could only mean that he had blackjack.

All heads turned to Peter, staring tragically at his cards, oblivious that it was his turn.

"Hey, is this a card game or are you doing your income taxes?" Cheese said.

"It's one of those hands you can't win for losing," Peter said, putting down his cards. "I'm tired anyway. I'll pass." He slowly brushed his chips into the pocket of his robe, got up, and drag-footed off, pushing his IV pole, leaving silence in the wake of his scuffing slippers.

Harmony has just scored again. That makes thirty-three points. Hello, Duke University, here I come! As she sprints back to defend the basket, she steals a glance at the clock. Tied score, two minutes and ticking. "Underneath!" *her father screams.* "Hustle!" *The other team's power forward has driven to the basket again at breakneck speed. Harmony pushes, gets there, leaps, blocks the shot, but slaps more than ball.*

"No more fouls!"

I know, Dad. I know. One more and she's out of the game.

They line up for the foul shots. "Rebound! Box out! Two hands on the ball!"

I know, Dad, I know. Shut the hell up!

> > >

"Sure hope that heart gets here before we start to beep."

Everyone looked puzzle-faced at Carlos.

"Well! Our batteries will be running low," he said.

Freudian slip. He meant pizza, not heart. Cheese gazed at the IV bag dangling beneath the Tin Man's ax, *drip, drip, drip,* slow and steady. The IV poles were their shadows, their handcuffs, their guardian angels. Low battery was only one of many offenses that could set the beeper off and bring a nurse running. At the moment this would not be a good thing.

"Maybe we should have done this another time," Amar said nervously, glancing at the sheet of snow outside the window and then at his watch for the twentieth time in as many minutes. "When the sun's out instead of a blizzard."

"All right, Peter the Second," Cheese teased, and immediately wished she could have the words back, Amar looked so distraught. "I must admit I didn't think of the weather," she added apologetically. "At least not as regards pizza delivery." Even Amar smiled at the inside joke, and the others laughed out loud. They always watched the weather closely because bad driving conditions were good for transplant donations.

"Hey, look at the bright side," Jacob called across the lobby. "Maybe there's been an accident!"

The strangers in the waiting area all turned their heads to stare at him—again. He'd been attracting attention already by hovering near the doorway where the smokers congregated, inhaling deeply whenever the door opened.

"We're sorry to offend you, m'am," Cheese said quickly to a woman who looked particularly shocked. "It's transplant humor."

"Oh," the woman said with a sad smile.

"I just luv, luv, luv this fresh air," Jacob said. "I'd ask those orderlies and nurses to come in and blow smoke in my face, but I don't want anyone to get fired."

"Jacob, you idiot, you're going to kill yourself doing that," said Carlos. "Suicide by second-hand smoke."

"If I only had a brain," said Jacob, smiling. He used to smoke two packs a day.

"Fresh air . . . ," said Carlos wistfully, moving toward the door. "Anybody want to walk down to the corner store with me? I'm gonna go buy my wife some chocolates for Valentine's Day. Surprise her."

The other three pinned him to the wall with their eyes.

"Tin Man! You must be joking," said Jacob.

"No joke," said Carlos.

"You can't go out in that blizzard!" said Cheese, her voice stretching high. "Your pole wheels won't roll in the snow. And you didn't bring a coat." She was leaning over him now like a willow over a fawn, her hand on his arm, her eyes pleading.

Softly he said something that the others couldn't make out, but the pain in his voice was clear.

"Come on, sit down," Cheese said gently. Carlos allowed her to lead him to a chair, but he was looking over his shoulder out the window, down to the corner where red lights in the shape of hearts blinked for attention.

"Wanna get something off your chest, Carlos?" Cheese said.

Carlos shook his head, blinking back tears. "I can't work, can't be a father to my kid, can't even walk down the block to buy my wife a goddamn box of chocolates. All I can do is wait for someone else to die so I can live, and I don't know if I can even do that anymore."

Jacob took one last deep breath of smoke and came to sit at his friend's side. "Oh yes you can. You're the Tin Man."

"Jesus will help you, son, if you ask him into your heart." The woman across the way opened her purse, pulled out a tissue and a religious tract, and offered them both.

"Thank you," Carlos said, accepting the tissue, tossing the tract back in the woman's lap. "No offense, but Jesus and me go back a long ways."

Cheese leaned toward the woman and explained in a whisper, "He's Catholic. A devout one." Rosary by his bed, cross over his door, daily mass on TV.

The woman looked puzzled, then shrugged and set the tract on the table.

"Brace yourself," Amar said, tipping his head toward the receptionist who was approaching them with her hands on her hips.

"What *are* you people doing here?" She sounded stern, but it was obvious from the play in her eyes that she was amused.

"What does it look like we're doing?" said Jacob, grasping his IV pole like a spear. "This is the waiting area. We're waiting."

"Delivery from Three Guys Pies," a voice called from the doorway.

"All right!" hooted Jacob.

The receptionist looked at the snow-studded delivery boy, then back at the grinning patients with their slippers and poles, then shook her head in disbelief. "I hear there are four heart transplant patients missing, and the nurses are turning the place upside down looking. You smart alecks wouldn't happen to be them, now, would you?"

"Is there a law against patients waiting in the waiting area?" Jacob said as Cheese overtipped for the pizzas. She set the boxes out on the end table, leaned over the pepperoni one to take a deep sniff, and slowly pulled a piece out so the mozzarella formed a long string, which she took into her mouth with loving twists of the tongue before the first bite. "Mmmm," she said. "Life is good."

The others lost no time joining her, chewing and moaning.

"Hey, lady, want a slice of heaven?" Amar asked the receptionist.

The receptionist pretended to pull her hair out in exasperation, then pointed to the humming elevator. "God help you people. Look who's coming."

"Yikes," said Jacob.

"That's an understatement," said Amar. Cheese had never seen Doc Franklin's fair face so red or animated. Every fiber of the doctor's petite body exuded rage.

"We're in trouble now," Cheese said cheerfully. "But it's worth it. Right Tin Man?"

Grease dripped from his smile down his chin. "Right, kid. That's right." Then he gazed up sheepishly at the small woman looming large over them. "Hey, Wiz, whassup?"

Five seconds left, the crowd counting down; Harmony's team is behind by two and being pressed hard; she goes to mid-court to help out, catches the long pass, hears him yell "Shoot!" She swirls, sends the ball sailing hail-Mary style, and sinks the last shot, swish, *a three-*

pointer too gorgeous to be real as the horn blares, they've won the game by one point, oh such happiness, it's heaven, except why's the ump shining a flashlight in her eyes?

Suddenly it's not an ump coming at Harmony anymore, but a truck, horn and lights blazing, and in an instant she realizes she's been dreaming. She fouled out of the game with a minute remaining. They lost.

"Dad!" she screams. "The truck! Watch out!" He groans, blinks hard, face sweaty, hands trembling on the steering wheel.

The next day none of the pizza eaters felt like moving, they were so sluggish and achy from all the fluid they were retaining. Jacob, who struggled chronically with congestive heart failure, had to dig deep for every breath. Carlos, whose high blood pressure put him at risk for strokes, felt like he had a jackhammer in his head. In this submissive state, they were in no condition to argue when Doc Franklin confined them to their beds for constant monitoring of their life signs.

Cheese listened contritely to Doc's lecture about what fools they'd been to risk not only their own lives but the lives of others on the ward due to the unnecessary diversion of the staff's time and attention; in fact, they'd threatened the very life of the hospital's entire transplant program. What if something went wrong and the media found out?

Cheese wouldn't do it again.

She wouldn't have not done it.

It was a little after noon when Peter floated into Cheese's room like a lost ghost. "Have you heard the news?" he said.

She picked her way up out of a prickly sleep. "What? News?"

"The new guy's getting his heart."

"The new guy?"

"Lang. You know, the little turd with the crew cut?"

Cheese sat up, head pounding, trying to concentrate. In the next bed, Jane, the only other woman on the ward, was curled under her hospital sheet like a question mark, her face mottled in shadows cast by sharp cheekbones. Cheese envied her roommate's ability to escape into hours of deep sleep.

"Sorry, Peter, my brains are cotton. I've got one helluva pizza hangover."

"I can't believe you people actually put one foot in the grave for one moment of pleasure."

Live and let live, she thought, but only said, "What about the little turd?"

"He's getting a heart. They're prepping him now."

Silently she soaked that in, but inside she was screaming: *No fair! Lang's only been here a few days! Carlos is the Tin Man! Then me, then Jacob, then you, Peter, then Amar . . .*

As if reading her thoughts, Peter moaned, "How are we ever going to make it when they're giving out hearts to the new guys first, huh?"

Cheese held her spinning head, trying to keep her thoughts straight. "There has to be a good reason for this. There are rules."

"Yeah. Power rules. Betcha Lang's got pull. He's probably the CEO of the hospital."

"He's too short to be CEO," Cheese said. "You gotta look up to people in power."

Peter granted her a reluctant smile. With all the razzing she took for her height, she was allowed to make short jokes. "Then he's the governor's brother-in-law. Or something."

"Peter, you know as well as I do, the waiting list isn't like that," Cheese said, trying to convince herself, too. "It's all based on matching. Tissues, body type—it's got to be a perfect match or the body will reject the organ. If this guy's getting a heart ahead of everyone else, then he's the only match available in the region. Maybe he has a rare blood or tissue type. Right?"

Peter shrugged. Grudgingly. "Maybe."

"Plus Lang is awfully small," Cheese added. "Putting his heart in your chest would be like putting a motorcycle engine in a Mack truck."

"But Carlos isn't any Mack truck."

"He's no motorcycle, either, though. He's more like a Honda Civic. And don't forget, this heart probably isn't his type, anyway. Have faith."

Peter nodded, sighed defeatedly. "I guess I'd better let you finish sleeping off your night on the town." Watching his feet, he shuffled out the door.

Transplant days were usually times of soaring spirits, hugs, tears of hope and fear. Today, though, things were out of order. Instead of gathering around the departing patient for the ritual of passing on the homemade ax to the next Tin Man, the patients watched Lang's exit from the somber shadows of their rooms. As the gurney wheeled off to surgery, Cheese slowly walked to the wall calendar where she kept track of her days in the hospital. In the white space around yesterday's date she wrote Day 118 and drew a big smiley face. In today's space she wrote Day 119 and drew a frown. After a moment of thought she added a tongue sticking out. Then she got back in bed, curled up on her side facing the wall, and cried herself to sleep.

Harmony's father slumps against the car window; his hands slip away from the steering wheel. "Dad!" she screams again, this time in terror for his life. He must be having a heart attack. All that yelling from the bleachers . . . zenith, underneath, box out, rebound, two hands on the ball, put it back up—how she hated hearing him yell all her life, how she wishes she could hear it again.

Cheese threw the ace of spades on the table. Peter slowly flipped over the queen of hearts. The others couldn't sit still— they were groaning, slapping the table, cursing their luck, making jokes like always when that card turned up—but even hitting blackjack didn't move Peter's face. In the past week since Lang's transplant, Peter seemed to have aged ten years. His face, previously plump, had taken on a yellow tone, with newborn wrinkles sagging at the eyes and jowls.

"Hey, Peter, lighten up," said Carlos. "Tomorrow's Valentine's Day. It's fate: I'm going to get my heart. Hell, lucky day like that, you'll probably get yours, too."

Peter didn't even look at him. "If a heart comes tomorrow, it'll probably go to the atheist who got Lang's bed." His voice was thin, sounded as though it was coming out of the ceiling.

"Come off it, Peter. You know that's not true," said Amar.

"Lang just got the luck of the draw," Cheese added. "The same as you hitting blackjack just now. Luck of the draw."

"Well, if God leaves things like that up to luck, I don't know what I'm sticking around here for," Peter said. "What's the point of all this, anyway? Struggle to live long enough to get the transplant, struggle to survive the transplant, struggle against rejection of the heart afterward . . . Life's just one big struggle."

"So? What's new?" said Jacob. "God never said it was going to be easy."

"That's the reason he sent Jesus," said Carlos.

Amar nodded. "Struggle gets prime position in all the religions I know of. You just have to go with the flow, my friend."

"Hey, Jacob, you're a Jew!" announced Carlos, as if it was an epiphany.

"Yeah," said Jacob. "And Amar's Hindu, and you're Catholic, and Cheese is I don't know what. An Amazon woman. A Tao List Maker."

"I'm soul searching," she said. "I'll take wisdom wherever I can find it. The Bible, Dear Abby, bathroom walls. I found some real cool shit in the *Tao Te Ching*. I like that it's not all about worshiping some guy. It's about quieting down and getting in synch with the Source, the Eternal, the One. It's beyond words," she said. "Lub dub, lub dub." Excitement had brought a touch of color to her pale cheeks.

"Iy yi yi!" said Jacob. "You're beautiful. Kees me, Fran-cheese-ka!"

Carlos leaned forward, looking young in his earnestness. "How are you going to feel, Jake, if you get the heart of a Christian who invited Jesus into it?"

Jacob grinned. "Like a born-again Jew," he said.

Peter moved, barely, shaking his head no. "Lang didn't have to struggle like us."

Cheese hesitated, then said, "How do you know that?" and tossed Carlos a card. "Sure, he didn't have to lie around here pinned to a pole for four months like the rest of us, but we don't know what else has gone wrong in his life. The poor guy's probably an orphan who was molested by his baby-sitter and grew up to become an unemployed garbage collector whose three wives all left him for taller men."

She'd gotten everyone laughing except Peter, who leaned his head back on the couch with his eyes shut. They dealt him out of the next few hands. It wasn't until they smelled the dinner cart coming and cashed in their chips to leave that they realized he wasn't going to wake up. He was done with waiting.

That night Cheese took the calendar down and put it in her drawer.

Harmony reaches for the wheel, but it's too late. In the blinding headlights she sees eternity, braces her arms against the dash, curls her head into her chest, thanks Allah that she gave her mother a hug this morning instead of an argument, Iloveyoumommy. . . .

Valentine's Day came and went, hope rising throughout the day, especially at the noontime weather report of icy roads for miles around. Carlos's wife and kid visited and received their gift of chocolates Carlos had charmed a nurse out to buy, but the chocolate box was the only heart exchanged on the ward that day.

Two nights later Cheese jolted from a shallow sleep with a feeling that she'd missed something. Jane was sound asleep, as usual, her way of coping. She'd even slept through the awful noise after Peter passed. All that crying, and his wife screaming at the doctors as if they'd murdered him instead of doing their damnedest to save his life. Couldn't she see that the man had simply given up?

Cheese checked the clock. A whopping two minutes of shut-eye. Might as well get up and find out what's going on. Focus the energy. Legs over side. Sit. *A journey of a thousand miles begins with one step,* one of her favorites from the *Tao Te Ching.* Grasp the pole. Push right foot into slipper. Push left foot into slipper. Push slippers one foot at a time.

Halfway to the door she heard a hoot in the hall. Midnight hall hooting could mean only one thing. *Dear God, if it's not for Carlos this time, let it be for me. But let it be for Carlos.* For this event Jane would drag herself out of sleep, out of bed, into the life of the ward. Cheese wiggled her roommate's foot and shouted, "Jane! Come on, get up, we're off to see the Wizard!"

Outside of his room Carlos was dancing with his pole, spending a week's worth of energy, while bedraggled patients lumbered into the hall. At the sight of him Cheese squealed, "Yes, yes, thank you, God!" The nurses coaxed him back into his room to get prepped while the line formed for the ritual.

Passing Peter's old room, Cheese saw the new guy in his bed, another fiftysomething with a beer belly and a bald spot, looking out in bewilderment. She fought the urge to look away and poked her head in the doorway. "Come on," she said, "it's a celebration. The Tin Man's getting his heart." *Myturn-next.*

Cheese didn't bother to explain, just went to him and

dragged the new guy stumbling and laughing to the end of the line forming behind Carlos, who was now lying on a gurney trying to hide the parts where the johnny stopped. Cheese took her place first in the line, and they began the parade, singing their theme song as they shuffled down the faded yellow brick road. At the end of the hall they stopped at the double doors where the nurses and orderlies and doctors had gathered for the send-off. Carlos's wife was there, too, behind a camera.

He cleared his throat. "I guess this is it. Time to pass the ax." Silence fell over the group as Carlos gently pried the shabby cardboard ax from his IV pole. He held it in his hands, turning it, twisting out the dents in the cardboard tube handle, soothing out the crunched edges of the aluminum foil blade. When he looked up at Cheese, tears were streaming down his face. She was already crying. They all were. She accepted the ax like a delicate bouquet.

"Good-bye, Tin Man," he said.

"Good-bye, Dorothy," she said, and everyone laughed and cried as they wheeled him away.

. . . amen.

LISA ROWE FRAUSTINO

The call came at ten to one in the morning, February 2, 1997. "It's time," Mama said. "They've found a big fat O negative heart for Daddy." My father had been waiting 172 days in a Philadelphia hospital for a heart transplant. Speeding, I reached the hospital at 3:30 A.M. to find Daddy dancing, the peppiest he'd been in ten years at death's door. The prep crew came at 4:15 to shave his chest, and after a one-minute shower in special surgical soap, Daddy was on the table frantically trying to cover up where the johnny left off, surrounded by transplant patients grasping their IV poles and wishing him much luck and love. Six months of waiting and all of a sudden there was a big hurry.

We lost our desperate eye contact as the elevator doors closed at 4:30, fearing what we dared not say: that this might be the last time we ever saw one another.

The last time Daddy had been on that elevator was the day of "The Great Escape," when he led a ragtag group of seven from the twenty-first floor to the lobby. There, to the horror of their doting doctors and nurses, the transplant waitees breathed fresh air and ordered out for pizza. Yes, that part of "The Tin Man" was inspired by fact, as was the calendar Francesca kept. Daddy's stubborn love of life gave his ward mates hope and, along with his size, earned him the nickname of The Big Cheese, hence my choice of Francesca's name. The rest of the details—the characters themselves, the Oz theme, the Harmony sequence—I created entirely out of my imagination.

None of the characters in "The Tin Man" are based on actual people, yet they are all true in spirit. The ward is a great equalizer. Old or young, male or female, rich or poor, Hindu or Muslim or Jewish or Christian, it all comes down to one thing: the value of the heart and all the things it holds. Hope. Faith. Love. Life.

Understanding this oneness, Francesca writes a list inspired by the ancient Chinese *Tao Te Ching,* which translates as "The

Book of the Way and Its Power." The *Tao Te Cheese* is the way Francesca finds the strength or power to live in the face of uncertainty.

It was soon after my father's heart transplant that I began planning a young adult literature anthology that explored the theme of soul searching, through as many different religions as possible. If you like this anthology, perhaps you'd also enjoy the first I edited, *Dirty Laundry: Stories About Family Secrets,* and my novel *Ash,* which was named a Best Book for Young Adults. When I'm not writing I'm teaching at Wyoming Seminary or Hollins University. My three children and I split our time between Pennsylvania and Maine, where I grew up, and where The Big Cheese lives now with his great big new O negative heart beating lickety-split.